ELLE GRAY | K.S. GRAY

OLIVIA KNIGHT
FBI MYSTERY THRILLER

LOVE, LIES, AND
SUICIDE

Love, Lies, and Suicide
Copyright © 2022 by Elle Gray | K.S. Gray

All rights reserved. Without limiting the rights under copyright reserved above, no part of this publication may be reproduced, stored in or intro-duced into retrieval system, or transmitted, in any form, or by any means (electronic, mechanical, photocopying, recording, or otherwise) without the prior written permission of both the copyright owner and the above publisher of this book.

This is a work of fiction. Names, characters, places, brands, media, and in-cidents are either the products of the author's imagination or are used fic-titiously. The author acknowledges the trademarked status and trademark owners of various products referenced in this work of fiction, which have been used without permission. The publication/use of these trademarks is not authorized, associated with, or sponsored by the trademark owners.

PROLOGUE

THE SOUNDS OF THE COUPLE STRUGGLING AGAINST THEIR bindings pleased him. They whined, they whimpered, they wriggled helplessly. He grinned.

As he circled his captives slowly, his shoes sinking in the expensive cream carpet, he toyed with the gun in his hand. Not his usual weapon of choice, but this time was different.

This time he would send a message.

The vintage record player was still spinning in the background. He hummed along under his breath. "You Can't Always Get What You Want" by the Rolling Stones. He thought it was fitting. The couple wanted to be alive, and he wanted them dead.

So, who was going to get what they wanted?

The woman was sobbing uncontrollably, trying her best to free herself from her chair. He placed a comforting hand on her shoulder, his leather glove crinkling on her cashmere sweater.

"You two didn't give me a choice, did you? You brought this on yourselves," he said. The woman shook her head over and over, the frantic nature of it all making her blonde tresses shake over her shoulders in a raggedy, uneven rhythm.

It was a pity. She was beautiful, in a way—in the way that expensive plastic surgery and designer clothing can make someone look like every other model or influencer in the world. She was accustomed to luxury and wealth, status and privilege. And here she was now, her eyes wide in terror as he slowly, deliberately made a show of loading the magazine into the chamber and ramming it home with an eerie metallic click.

All the wealth in the world could never save her now.

"Don't worry," he murmured. "I won't make you suffer much longer."

She tried to scream, but the sound was muffled behind the gag he'd forced into her mouth. Besides, he mused, no one would hear her in a house of that size. The mansion was so big he'd almost worried he might never find the couple within it. But find them he had, and now he could finally teach them a lesson.

It was almost time. The song was sweeping up; Mick Jagger's voice became engulfed in the sounds of the gospel choir, the fanfare, the rising swell of the music. He had a flair for the dramatic, and he wanted to do this right. He wanted to know that his subjects were scared, that they knew what was about to happen to them. What they were about to do to each other.

He walked over to the man and grabbed his wrist, forcing the gun into his hand. Then he made him point it at his wife.

"No, please, no," the man garbled from behind his gag, trying to force his arm away. But his captor didn't need him to pull the trigger himself. He just needed it to look like he had.

As the gun went off, he reveled in the deep, booming reverberations of the gunshot, of the blood pouring from the wound in the woman's head, of her glassy eyes and vacant expression.

His other victim sobbed uncontrollably, but as he twisted the gun to press against his temple, he didn't struggle. The fight had gone out of him. And by the time he was dead, too, the man felt

LOVE, LIES, AND SUICIDE

oddly moved by the whole thing. In the end, they'd chosen to be together.

It hadn't been what they wanted, but maybe, just maybe, it was what they needed.

CHAPTER ONE

OLIVIA STARED OUT OF THE WINDOW AS THE PLANE began to descend into Seattle—a city that made her heart ache. It was a place Olivia didn't go to often, but the moment that Paxton Arrington had called, she knew she'd get on a plane and fly out.

To her, it would always be the place that her sister was killed—and she knew now, beyond a shadow of a doubt, that she *was* killed. Part of her felt shame that she'd ever doubted what had happened. That she'd ever allowed herself to believe it really was a tragic accident. She'd been so stunned and shocked by its suddenness, and then sent reeling by her mother's subsequent disappearance, that she'd allowed herself to retreat into isolation, numbly accepting the story at face value despite Paxton's insistence otherwise.

She'd wanted to simply keep that wound buried deep inside her, pushed down where no one could harm it, while he seemed so intent on constantly picking at it. They'd never spoken much, but when they had, he would always press his latest theory that the car crash that took Veronica's life was no accident. She always told him he was simply seeing ghosts in his desperation for answers.

But in the end, he was right. And now that she had to come to terms with the truth, it was like losing her sister all over again.

Olivia didn't get to talk about her sister all that much. She'd long since abandoned the idea of speaking to her family about Veronica, especially since her mom's disappearing act that had left Olivia broken and alone in her darkest time. The only person she really spoke to about her sister was Brock, and he'd never even met her.

But seeing Pax was often a painful affair. He'd loved Veronica with all of his heart, and Olivia knew that he was more devastated than anyone when he found out that she was gone forever. He'd risked his life to find the answers, to take down the man responsible for her death, and to complete her work. It was only because Paxton had sent her that email that Olivia set up the raid to rescue him in the first place. She shuddered to think what would have happened had she not read his missive as had been her first instinct. Paxton had been held in a chamber beneath Lomtin Laboratories and was incredibly lucky he'd survived his ordeal.

The company had been conducting horrific experimentation and trials on kidnapped human beings on a massive scale in that underground chamber. They'd engaged in the outright bribery of public officials and took advantage of the rampant corruption in the system to bring their flawed drugs to market. Veronica, steadfast as ever, had been hot on the tail of their CEO, Didi Sjoberg. She had been just about to expose him and ruin him when he ordered her death.

Now that it was over, Olivia wondered whether Paxton would be able to try and move on. She knew that there was no way things would get easier for either of them and they'd spend the rest of their lives missing Veronica. But if there was a chance that things could get even a little better, they had to take it.

LOVE, LIES, AND SUICIDE

After landing in Seattle, Olivia hailed a cab and went straight to Cascades Memorial Park in Laurelhurst. She'd offered to meet him there, knowing that it would be a good chance to visit her sister too. If she was only going to be in Seattle for a few hours, she didn't want to miss the chance to see her.

As the cab pulled up outside the misty graveyard, Olivia could see Pax standing before the tall mausoleum already, a lone figure in a lonely place. In his hand, he clutched a bundle of soft apricot and cream-colored roses. Veronica's favorites. In his long, black overcoat, he looked like he was attending a funeral, still in mourning all these years after her death. Olivia swallowed down the lump in her throat.

This was going to be hard.

Olivia pulled her coat tightly around her as she weaved through the graves to meet with Pax. He looked up as she approached, nodding to her curtly. Their relationship had always been civil but never much more than that. Much like Olivia's sister, Pax had a different approach to life than Olivia did, always diving into the deep end without thinking too hard. Olivia thought he was reckless, and he thought she was a bore, she assumed. It didn't help that she and Paxton were on opposite ends of the spectrum but shared similar lines of work.

When they'd first met, over a decade ago at this point, she'd been no fan of the arrogant, heir to a multi-billion-dollar media empire. Veronica was the first to change him, to convince him to find ways to give back to the community rather than simply coast on his family name and fortune. And he really did change, becoming a police officer with the Seattle PD and then leaving the force to become a private investigator shortly after Veronica died. He had become increasingly reckless and brash over the last few years.

He couldn't be more different from Olivia, who felt like she was barely coming out from the darkness after the twin tragedies of her sister's death and her mother's disappearance left her reeling.

But now that the worst was behind them, they'd both changed in some ways. It was like they were getting closer to meeting in the middle. Olivia's confidence was growing by the day, and Paxton was learning better how to act without throwing himself into the flames. It certainly made it easier for the pair of them to connect.

"It's good to see you. I'm glad you came," Paxton said as Olivia joined him at Veronica's grave. The structure was tall and ornate, delicately carved of marble in an identical representation to the one just over to their left. The Arrington family mausoleum and the new one constructed just for Veronica stood side by side. The stone door remained shut; it was as if Paxton had been waiting for Olivia to arrive before entering the mausoleum.

"Thanks," she said. Whether it was a thanks for calling her, for meeting her here, or for waiting for her, she didn't know. In a way, it was all of them at once.

Olivia reached into her bag to pull out a key. She rarely used it, but it kept a permanent place on her key ring. She took a deep breath and inserted it into the lock, gave it a twist, and swung the door open.

Before her, in the center of the room on a simple pedestal and in a beautiful marble sarcophagus, lay the remains of her sister.

Paxton silently followed behind her and ran his fingers along the walls, his eyes distant as if reminiscing about lost days.

Olivia looked over to him for a moment, then fished something out of her pocket and bent to put it on top of the sarcophagus. Paxton let out a short laugh of surprise.

"Most people just bring flowers. I've never seen anyone leave an Oreo cookie before."

Olivia smiled, though it was a little strained. "There's a first time for everything, right? I was thinking about Veronica after you called, and I remembered something she said when we were kids. She told me that she'd miss cookies in the afterlife and that she wanted to be buried with a life's supply."

Paxton dug his hands deep in his pockets and managed a smile. "That sounds like my girl."

The pair of them stood quietly for a few minutes, looking at the sarcophagus with tight throats and hammering hearts at the sarcophagus. He let out a long sigh.

"I guess I thought it was going to get easier somehow when we found the truth. When we caught the guy who took her from us. Like I'd have a weight lifted from my shoulders. And in a way, it does feel better. But there's still a..."

"A gaping hole in your chest?"

"So to speak," he admitted.

"Sounds familiar," Olivia said quietly. She'd been searching for a similar kind of closure, a way to end the chapter, but she'd been unsuccessful too. Instead, her grief entwined itself into her life even though she tried to find ways to move forward instead of being trapped in the past. But now, she knew better than to resist that. She knew better than to think that grief had an expiration date.

Paxton cleared his throat, and Olivia knew it was his way of clearing the emotion from his voice. From his deep pockets, he took something out.

"I found something yesterday and wanted you to have it. It was clearly a part of your past, and I think she'd want you to have it."

Olivia held out her palm and felt something light drop into it. It was a silver locket. She hadn't seen it since she was a kid, but she recognized it instantly. She knew exactly what was inside it, and that knowledge sent a pang through her chest.

"Did you open it?"

Paxton hesitated. "I did."

"The paper is still inside?"

He nodded. Olivia slid the locket into her pocket without another word. She didn't need to look inside to know what was there. When Veronica had been a child, she'd worn that locket every single day. Then, she used to carry it around in her purse when she grew older. Inside that locket was a piece of paper where she and Veronica had written down all of their hopes and dreams for the future.

Veronica had come up with every single detail, writing about the career she wanted, the names of the children she planned to have, the big, white wedding she wanted. Olivia had wished for a happy life and nothing more.

Life hadn't panned out the way they thought at all.

"I know you and Veronica didn't always see eye to eye," Paxton said after a moment. "But she kept that in her bedside table for a long time. I only looked in there recently and... well, when I saw it, I knew it belonged to you. It would have been selfish for me to keep this from you."

Olivia kept her eyes trained on the sarcophagus. "I know we didn't always get along, but that's just family, isn't it? You love one another through thick and thin. Even when you're apart."

Olivia felt him place a hand on her shoulder, and she allowed herself a single second to feel the pain of the loss she'd endured. Then she shrugged it off. She'd long since learned how to do that. Because living with loss meant learning how to keep it on the back burner.

"Shall we sit?" Pax asked, nodding toward a bench to one side of the mausoleum. Olivia nodded and followed him to the seat. Neither of them looked at one another, their eyes still on Veronica's grave.

"I never really thanked you. For what you did for me," he commented.

That finally got her to tear her eyes off her sister and regard him with a raised eyebrow.

"Yes, you did. You said it about a hundred times in the hospital. Did they have you that hopped up on painkillers?"

Paxton gave a rueful chuckle. "Maybe they did," he admitted. "But I'm serious. If you hadn't done what you did for me..."

He trailed off, but Olivia already knew where that sentence would end: *"... I'd be in here too."*

"You'd have done the same for me," she replied. "That's what family does."

"I'm starting to get that. But seriously, thank you."

"Don't sweat it. Besides, I don't think Veronica would ever forgive me if she thought I wasn't keeping an eye on you. After all, of the three of us, I think I'm the only sane one."

Pax's face twisted into a smile. "Oh, there's no doubt. But she would've killed me herself if she knew what I was up to. I know you think she was the wild card, always getting herself into crazy situations, but when it came to me... she was always telling me to stop putting myself in the firing line and to be a little more cautious." He shook his head affectionately. "But if the positions were switched, she would've hunted them to the ends of the earth. She probably would have put herself in even more danger than I did."

"Of course, she would have," Olivia said, closing her eyes. "That was Veronica. The world's biggest hypocrite."

Paxton chuckled. "You're lucky she's not here to hear you say that."

Silence fell between them. It felt so wrong, laughing and joking around when she was dead and buried only a few feet away. But at the same time, it felt like she was there with them, making them see a silver lining even in the darkest of clouds. Olivia heaved a sigh. For a long time after her death and her mother's disappearance, she'd felt guilty for snippets of happiness, for ever being able to raise a smile when so much had happened. It had taken a long time to realize that those moments were not forgetting the loss but celebrating the love she'd once shared with her family.

Sometimes, Olivia wondered if Paxton felt cheated. Both of them had been, in her own mind. They were the ones who were putting their lives on the line in their work. Veronica was a journalist, a job with its own risks, but Olivia never thought it would result in her death. To Olivia, it felt wrong living her life on the edge every single day and only having brushes with death.

It sometimes felt like they should be the ones in Veronica's place.

"You can't go down that road," Pax spoke up after a while. Olivia turned her head to him, wondering how he'd managed to read her mind. He smiled.

"I know what you're thinking. I can see it in your face, and trust me, I've been there a thousand times. I've thought it should have been me instead of her more times than I can count."

"Didn't realize I was so predictable," she muttered.

He tapped his temple. "You two were a lot more alike than you think."

That made her laugh again and Paxton continued.

"I spent months wondering whether I'd put her in danger. Whether my line of work had made her a target. But we're not the only ones who live our lives on the edge, Olivia. You know how Veronica was. She was relentless and was always poking her nose into dangerous places. She ruffled feathers for fun and was always looking for new ways to rock the boat. And she wasn't ever going to let anything get in the way of exposing the truth. Not even her death. Of the three of us, I think she was the dangerous, unpredictable one. But that wouldn't have mattered anyway because we loved her. Still love her. And if it had to happen, I don't think she would've wanted things any other way."

Olivia felt in her pocket for the locket Paxton had given her. If she closed her eyes, she could still see her sister's handwriting, her list of demands for life that she'd established before most kids had even formed a personality. Veronica had always been so headstrong, so determined, so sure of what she wanted. But where had it led her? She didn't get to do half of the things she wanted to. Sure, she'd found Paxton, fallen madly in love, and had the wedding of her dreams. Sure, she'd pursued the career she had always wanted. In many ways, all her wildest dreams had come true.

But if her dreams hadn't come true, she'd still be alive.

"Can you be honest with me, Pax?" she asked.

"Of course."

She turned to look him in the eye. "Was she happy? In the end?"

Paxton leaned back on the bench, staring at Veronica's sarcophagus. "If there's one thing I know about Veronica, it's that she was always happy. She always saw the good in everything and did whatever the hell she wanted. She chased every whim she ever had and was always running from one adventure to another. Even when she knew she was in danger. I think she loved the thrill of it all. But that was her."

Olivia felt the lump in her throat harden even more. She couldn't look at him; the sound of pain in his voice was evident enough. She knew how much he suffered every day without Veronica. Olivia was fully aware that anyone wild enough to commit themselves to her sister for life would never recover after losing her. She was enigmatic; she was fiery; she was unlike anyone else in the world. How do you recover from losing someone so special? Someone who is completely one of a kind?

"I'm so sorry," Olivia whispered. "I've always been so caught up in my own grief, thinking about how it made me feel... I never stopped to think about how much you lost. And I know it doesn't count for much now, all these years later, but if you need anything... I'm here for you."

"I mean, I would certainly hope so. You did save my life," he responded. "But you don't have to apologize. I never checked in on you often enough either. That's why I'm glad we could talk a little today. Maybe from here, things might start to get better. The case is solved. We're safer now than we were before. Maybe this is the closest we've gotten to closure. The closest we'll ever get."

Olivia hung her head. "Maybe. But if it is... then it still sucks."

"Tell me about it."

Olivia closed her eyes. If she could turn back time to when her sister was alive, maybe she'd do things differently. Maybe she'd try harder—try to see eye to eye with her. But what was done was done. Opportunities to make things better had passed her by so many times that she wouldn't even know where to start.

There was no turning back the clock. She could only focus on the here and now. She glanced at her brother-in-law, her final connection to the sister she'd known and loved. Maybe he was the key to surviving the pain. Maybe for Veronica to remain alive in their hearts, they had to build some bridges.

"I'm flying back later today. I can't stay. But, hey—Thanksgiving is coming up. Maybe we could spend the day together?" Olivia asked tentatively. She already knew that the holidays were going to be rough. She had no great desire to spend them with her parents, who had only made her feel angry and rejected over the last few years. Things were better than they had been before, but still, spending the day with her sister's husband seemed preferable. Pax smiled tightly at her.

"I think I'll be spending the day with my parents. But let's not be strangers. I want you to know you can call me anytime. Even though Veronica's gone, you're right. We're family, and I'm not going anywhere."

Olivia sucked in a deep breath. "You don't know how good that is to hear. I'm glad we did this, Pax."

"And, hey—if you ever need someone to save your life, maybe I can return the favor someday."

Olivia smiled back. "I'll keep that in mind."

CHAPTER TWO

THE FLIGHT BACK HOME WAS EVEN HARDER THAN THE flight to Seattle. After Olivia had said goodbye to Paxton, she felt a pang in her chest. It felt like saying goodbye to Veronica, somehow. So, as she flew back to DC, Olivia ordered herself a cold beer and toasted to her sister, wishing that life had turned out differently.

Olivia took deep breaths and tried to think about what waited for her at home. She had planned to meet Brock that evening at the diner back in Belle Grove, and she knew he would be more than willing to listen to her tales of the day. In fact, she'd received several messages from him throughout the day checking up on her.

She was grateful for the happiness slipping through the cracks of her saddened heart. She did have things in her life that made the pain worth it. A friend she could truly rely on was one of them. Brock had been the one person that had been able to pull her out of the dark rut she'd been stuck in. Not even her lifelong friends or her family could manage that. But since he'd arrived in Belle Grove, Brock had proved to her over and over again that he was exactly who she needed in her life.

Olivia felt like a weight had been lifted from her chest by the time she got off the plane. She stalked through the massive parking garage to her car and headed home as the sky outside was darkening. She was in a better mood now, and when she felt her phone buzzing, she didn't even check the caller ID before she picked up.

"Knight."

"Hello, dear."

There was a twist in Olivia's stomach. It was her mother. She felt her anxieties returning. As much as Olivia wanted to get her relationship with her mom back on track, she sometimes still had trouble forgetting that she abandoned her family in the middle of the night with no warning. Sure, undercover work was important, and Olivia knew the dangers of getting family involved, but she also knew that the years she'd spent wondering whether her mother was alive or dead were the worst of her life. Now, each time she spoke with her mom, she struggled to separate that experience from her feelings toward her.

"Hey, Mom. How are you?"

"I'm great, darling. How was your trip to see Pax?"

Olivia frowned. "You heard about that?"

"Yes, he told me himself. We keep in touch a bit."

Olivia chewed the inside of her cheek. Of course, they did. Just because Olivia couldn't forgive her mother, it didn't mean others couldn't. Still, it felt strange knowing that Paxton probably shared more with her mom than she did.

"Well, it was good to see him. He gave me that locket that Veronica used to carry around with her when we were kids."

"That man is so thoughtful. I know that you're very different, but it's easy to see why Veronica loved him so much."

Veronica's name always sliced pain through Olivia's heart, but even more so when it was her mom speaking. Olivia swallowed.

"Yeah. He's a good man. I think he and I are going to spend more time together if we can. It was good to reconnect."

"Of course, it was. He's family. And speaking of family, that's the reason I called. I know that the last few years have been… complicated. And I don't know if you already have plans for Thanksgiving. But if you don't, would you consider coming home? It's been so long."

Home. Olivia almost laughed at that. The place where she'd made roots as a child didn't feel like home, especially considering that they'd moved many times before settling there. And when she thought of that house, she thought of Veronica's memory haunting the walls, of the lies her mother told her for so many years, of her father's deliberate silence. As far as she was concerned, that place would never be home to her.

And the thought of spending Thanksgiving with her family was a complicated one. She had things to be thankful for, of course. Her mother had practically come back from the dead, after all, and good things had finally come her way since she moved to Belle Grove.

But she was also fully aware that spending Thanksgiving with her parents would be almost like forgiving them. And she wasn't ready for that. They'd hurt her with their lies and deception. How could she put that aside for the day and pretend that it wasn't a big deal?

"Olivia? You're very quiet."

Olivia rubbed at her temple, suddenly wishing she hadn't had the beer on the plane. It wasn't helping her with the fog in her head. She didn't know how to respond to her mom without doing more damage. She wanted to say no. She'd spend the holiday alone if she had to. But it felt too hard to say it outright. She swallowed.

"Can I think about it, Mom?"

"What is there to think about? It's Thanksgiving! It's a family day."

Olivia chewed the inside of her cheek again, tasting blood. Sometimes, it really felt like her mom was clueless. "I know that. But we haven't had a family Thanksgiving since before all of this, and that's been enough. I'm just trying to figure out with myself how I feel about it now that you're back."

There was a long silence on the other end of the line, and Olivia felt a stab of guilt that she quickly pushed aside. She didn't want to feel guilty for the fact that her mom had disappeared without a trace and made her spend years questioning if she was gone forever. That wasn't fair to Olivia.

Her mom drew a deep breath. "Okay. I guess I can understand that. But please consider us, okay? Your father hasn't seen you in so long. He misses you."

Whose fault is that? Olivia wanted to ask, but she bit her tongue. She hadn't seen much of him since her mother's disappearance, but she could guess why that was. He felt guilty about having to lie about her mom. Another reason to be angry that her mother put them both in impossible situations.

"You can even bring a guest if you'd like!" Jean babbled. "You could bring some of your friends, or maybe Brock? Do any of them have plans for the holidays?"

"I'll think about it," Olivia replied bluntly. The thought of dragging one of her friends to dinner with her crazy family was a bad one. Even Brock, who was pretty much able to handle any form of drama, would probably run a mile to blow off steam after spending the day with the Knight family.

Olivia heard her sigh quietly. "Alright, darling. Just let us know. I hope you have a great week!"

"Bye, Mom."

As Olivia ended the call, she let out such a deep sigh that it almost felt like she was deflating like a balloon. She wondered if there would ever come a day when her family affairs seemed easier. When she could pretend things were normal again. But Olivia knew that her family had never been typical. Her childhood had been built on her mother's lies and her father's constant moving from place to place. Her adulthood had been shaped by her sister's murder and her mother's disappearance. Even now, having gained some modicum of control of her day-to-day existence, she was still an FBI agent. She never knew what the cards would hold for her future or where she'd be sent on a case. Those things didn't add up to normality, and she'd accepted that a long time ago.

LOVE, LIES, AND SUICIDE

As Belle Grove slowly came back into view, Olivia felt herself relax a little. The small town had slowly begun to feel like home. After so many years living in the hustle and bustle of the city, it felt like a refuge from the craziness that her life always seemed to bring her.

And with home came Brock. Olivia drove directly to the diner without even bothering to go to her cabin on the edge of town. She didn't really care that a day of flying and flitting around had left her disheveled and less than fresh. She just wanted to get back to familiarity as soon as she could, to finally take a load off and relax. She knew that the moment she walked into that diner, a weight would be lifted from her chest. He'd tease her gently, order more food than he had any business eating, and then listen to her tales of the day. Sometimes, when things got hard for her, an evening at the diner with Brock made all of that melt away.

He was waiting for her in their usual booth with the cracked, red leather seats, nursing both a black coffee and a strawberry milkshake. He looked up as she entered and grinned at her, making her flailing heart slow. Brock was one of the most chaotic, yet grounded, people that she knew, and that unusual combination seemed to make him her perfect match. Perfect friends, perfect partners, and perfect confidants.

"Hey, there," Brock called out as Olivia opened the door and slid into the booth opposite him. "Thank God you're back. You wouldn't believe how wild this town gets without you here."

"Somehow I doubt that," Olivia countered with a smile. "Let me guess, Maggie had her hands full with three traffic tickets today, and you needed to jump in to cover the beat?"

"*Four* tickets, actually," he replied. "And I helped bring Julie Ware's dog home after it got out this morning."

Olivia chuckled quietly. "Sounds like an eventful day."

"Never a dull moment in Belle Grove."

They enjoyed a laugh together as the waitress approached. Olivia ordered a Reuben sandwich and—to Brock's utter shock—a cup of chamomile tea instead of her usual coffee.

"Who are you, and what have you done with Olivia?" he demanded. "Are you a spy? A clone? An evil robot from the future?"

"I promise, I'm me," she protested. "It's just been a really, really long day."

Brock pointed two fingers at his own eyes and then at Olivia's as if to signify he was watching her, a glint of merriment in them, but within a moment, he switched to his serious mode.

Olivia had always found it strange since she met Brock that he had a softer side to him. He had always seemed to her like the life of the party, the sort of guy who didn't have time for emotional pit stops. But often, he seemed more in touch with his feelings than she was with her own. He was the best listener she'd ever met, and he always knew when she needed him. It was comforting that he could tell before she'd even said anything that she needed to vent.

"How was it?" Brock asked her gently. "Seeing Paxton?"

Olivia took a deep breath. "It was good. It was, really. I mean, it was hard. It always is. I wouldn't even know him if it wasn't for my sister, so seeing him…"

"…reminds you of her. Of course."

Olivia shrugged after a moment. "But it was good. I feel like we've finally found some common ground. I'm glad I went, and I'm glad he reached out in the first place. I was beginning to think we'd burned the bridges that Veronica built for us when she was alive—that we'd broken those connections. But apparently not. And it looks like Pax isn't going anywhere, anyway. He even calls my mom up from time to time, apparently? I think she was hoping he'd go to her house for Thanksgiving. We haven't had Thanksgiving since… well, since Veronica died and Mom disappeared."

Brock let out a puff of air. "Man, your family really has a flair for the dramatic."

Olivia laughed. She'd learned to see the lighter side of things when she was with Brock. It made life easier, and it made things hurt less. "Sure. But every family has drama around the holidays, right? Isn't that a Thanksgiving tradition right up there with the turkey and cranberry sauce?"

Brock smiled, but he shrugged sadly. "I don't know, really. It's been a long time since I had a family Thanksgiving."

Olivia waited patiently for Brock to open up. She knew that while he was a good listener and advisor, he struggled to share his own problems. It was one of the ways they clashed, and one of the reasons they'd had a falling out for the first time a few weeks prior. But she could see him digging deep, preparing to tell her something. He took a deep breath.

"I didn't have a big family growing up. It was just my parents and me, really. I never met my grandparents; they died before I was born. And since my parents passed away, Thanksgiving hasn't really been something that I celebrate anyway," he admitted.

Olivia felt a twinge of pain for him. As much as her own family life was complicated, at least she had family left. She had come close to knowing how it felt being all alone in the world, but for Brock, that was his reality. It was no wonder he sought out his own family, composed of lost strays like himself.

He'd recently told her about Lily, a girl he'd rescued during a mission and had kept in touch with long after. And then, of course, there was Olivia. He'd moved to Belle Grove to be closer to her and spent every day since building their bond. Did that make her a part of his chosen family?

"If you had someone to celebrate it with, would you still want to be a part of the holidays?" Olivia asked Brock. His brow creased.

"Are you asking if I want to spend Thanksgiving with you?"

Olivia smiled. "Well, I have no clue what I'm going to do yet. Mom wants me to spend it with our family, but I have reservations for obvious reasons. I invited Pax, but he says he'll probably be with his parents. And then my other option was to spend it at home, drinking beer and counting my blessings."

Brock grinned. "Counting your blessings? That's very unlike you."

"Well, I have to have at least one day a year where I don't whine about my life, right?" Olivia said, poking fun at herself. Brock cracked up and shook his head at her.

"Jeez, Olivia. That's very self-aware."

"Well, I do try," Olivia smiled. "The point is… I'm kind of at a loss too. I guess maybe what I'm saying is, we could stick the holiday out together? My mom said I could bring a guest to Thanksgiving. Maybe then it would be less tense. Or we can host our first Belle Grove Thanksgiving. See if Sam and Emily could even come down. I don't need an answer yet. Just think about it, yeah?"

Brock smiled, taking a long sip of his milkshake. "I will. Thanks, Olivia. You know, I think it could be really nice. Maybe we can start some new traditions."

"Okay, but as much as I love this diner, we are not coming here for Thanksgiving. We already have the tradition of coming here way too much."

"Deal."

Half an hour later, as Brock was polishing off the rest of Olivia's meal, they sat in contended silence. The sandwich had made her feel a few pounds heavier, but it was balanced by how much lighter her heart felt. That was usually the aftereffect of spending time with Brock. She sipped her milkshake and tried to remember a time when she was so at ease, so naturally comfortable without having to worry about anything. She couldn't. She was about to say as much when the door to the diner opened and a familiar face walked in. Someone that Olivia hadn't seen in quite some time, but someone she'd recognize anywhere.

Her breath caught in her throat. It had been some time since she'd thought about the man in the doorway. Tom Booker had once been the most important person in her life, someone she'd planned a future with, but she never thought she'd see him again. Even if she was currently living in the town that he grew up in.

"Earth to Olivia?" Brock prodded, nudging her leg under the table. "Who are you staring at?"

Olivia was too stunned to speak. Tom looked different from the last time she'd seen him. There were creases by his dark eyes that hadn't been there before, probably the product of long days working as a doctor. He'd grown a beard that suited his face more than she cared to admit. He was stockier than he had been when she saw him last, and his presence in the room seemed to be bigger than it used to be. Olivia should know.

She was staring at her ex-fiancé, after all.

"Who *is* that? Don't tell me you've got some long-lost brother or something too. That would really be the icing on the cake."

Olivia glanced back at Brock in shock, realizing something that struck her as crazy. She'd never told him about Tom. She'd never told him much about her love life, really, mostly because it was nonexistent those days. But Tom had been her partner for a long time. They'd gotten so close to getting married, to committing to one another forever.

And she hadn't told Brock a thing about him.

"Olivia? Are you alright?" Brock asked. He looked concerned about her, like she was about to fall apart right in front of him. She grappled for words, unable to explain what was going through her head. She felt guilty that she'd never told Brock about such a big part of her life. But at the same time, she'd never expected it to matter.

When she and Tom had parted ways, there was no reason they'd ever get in touch again. And though Olivia knew when she moved to Belle Grove that Tom had a past there, he'd insisted throughout their relationship that he'd never return there. He was a big city kind of guy, and the small town had always suffocated him. That's what he'd told her.

So, what was he doing back in town?

"You're scaring me," Brock said, frowning at Olivia. "Do you need a glass of water or something?"

Before Olivia could respond, she felt her phone buzzing. It took a few moments for it to register—for her to realize that she needed to answer the call.

"Hold that thought," Olivia murmured, picking up the phone. It was Jonathan. For once, Olivia couldn't be gladder to hear from him.

She picked up the call and put her issues on hold.

"Agent Knight here."

CHAPTER THREE

"**K**NIGHT. ARE YOU BACK FROM YOUR LEAVE YET?" HE asked abruptly. He didn't even so much as greet her.

"Yes." She wasn't sure whether to call a single personal day "leave," but that was the way Jonathan operated: all business all the time.

"Good. I have your next assignment. They expect you and Tanner at the scene first thing in the morning down in Richmond."

"Perfect," Olivia replied, glancing sideways at Tom. He didn't seem to have spotted her and was ordering at the counter. "We'll be ready to go."

"Good. A couple has been found dead in their home, both with bullet wounds to the head. It looks like a murder-suicide, but after the police investigated, they found a few things that made them question the validity of that. The shot angles don't seem to line up with a murder-suicide, and there is possible evidence of a break-in. The police are still trying to make heads or tails of the whole thing because there's a lot of contrasting evidence on the site."

"We can take a look. Anything else you can tell us?"

"Yes. The couple in question is quite high-profile. The female vic, Arabella Clifford, was a well-known social influencer, so this is going to be something that the media might latch on to. Both she and her husband Andrew worked in finance, and all reports indicate a pretty high-end lifestyle. They had a multi-million-dollar mansion."

"Okay... so they're rich, semi-famous, and potentially influential. If this is a murder-suicide, what's the motive? Did something happen within their little bubble?"

"Not that we know of. As far as we know on the surface level, these two were high-fliers without a care in the world. Social media reports and financial activity in the last few weeks don't seem to line up at all with a motive for a murder-suicide. Obviously, the majority of the time it's the husband in cases like these, but we haven't seen anything in his records that would indicate any plans for this. They paid all their bills on time and even had just booked a vacation flight. People who kill themselves don't plan on going on vacation."

"That's not much of an indication of anything. He could have just been trying to throw off the trail," Olivia countered.

"Agreed. That's why we need you and Tanner on the scene—to see whether there's anything amiss. Dig deeper, see if you can find anything out about their lives before they died. But go about it quickly and quietly before there's a media circus about the whole thing."

"Sure thing. Send me the address; we'll get there first thing in the morning."

"Good. It might be nothing. The police are just interested to get a second opinion. You might be in and out of there."

"No problem at all. We're on it."

As the call ended, Olivia felt herself crashing back into the present. Brock was watching her with narrowed eyes, and Olivia was certain that he wasn't wondering what Jonathan had said. He wanted to know why she was being cagey. Why she was so concerned about the man who had entered the diner. But the last thing Olivia wanted to do was talk about it. In fact, she just wanted to get out of there before Tom could spot her. She didn't feel prepared to deal with him yet. She'd barely gotten over the shock of seeing him.

"What's going on?" Brock asked her firmly. She picked up her purse, preparing herself to make a hurried escape.

"We have a case in Richmond. We should really head out now."

Brock regarded her with a skeptical look. "It's only a couple hours, right? We can leave in the morning. It's already late."

"Well, we should go home then and get some rest for an early start," Olivia attempted, starting to gather her things quickly.

"Not until you tell me what's got you so freaked."

Olivia felt like a deer in the headlights. She glanced toward the counter where Tom was standing, chatting with one of the waitresses. Perhaps she was an old friend from when he lived there as a kid. Olivia didn't care either way. She just knew it would be a good opportunity to slip out unnoticed.

"I'm fine. I thought I knew that guy, that's all," Olivia said quietly. "Let's go."

Brock stayed where he was, scowling at her. "You're acting weird, Olivia. I've never seen you look so shocked. What's on your mind?"

And all of a sudden, it was too late for Olivia to run because as Brock continued to glare at her, Tom turned around and locked eyes with her. Olivia felt her heart skip a beat. There was no going back now. There was no denying that they knew one another. And if Tom was back in town, Olivia suspected there wasn't much chance of them avoiding one another forever.

It was time to face up to it.

Tom made the first move, approaching her table slowly. Almost tentatively. A slow smile was spreading over his face. That was a relief, at least, Olivia thought. After the way they ended things between them, she couldn't be sure that he'd be glad to see her.

"Looks like he knows you too," Brock noted, folding his arms. But Olivia didn't have time to respond because there he was. Standing in front of her was the one man who had ever captured Olivia's heart, even if fleetingly. Olivia knew better than to be flustered by a man. She was a seasoned FBI agent and a tough one at that. She'd faced trials and tribulations of all manners. And yet, standing in front of her ex-fiancé felt like one of the hardest things she'd ever done.

"Olivia Knight. I wasn't expecting to bump into you quite so soon," Tom started with a warm smile. Olivia swallowed and tried to smile back.

"Tom... you look well."

Tom smiled back, touching his beard a little self-consciously. "What do you think of the beard? My mom hates it."

"It suits you," Olivia said tightly. The whole conversation was enough to make her feel uncomfortable. It was much too familiar to talk with him like this, even after so much time apart. Tom cocked his head to the side.

"And it looks like Belle Grove suits you. You must be the mysterious FBI agent who moved to town a few months ago. Everyone's talking about you. I guess you're the most exciting thing to happen to Belle Grove in a long time." Tom turned to look at Brock. "And, of course, this must be your partner."

"We're not together," Olivia said sharply. A little too sharply. The corners of Tom's lips twitched.

"I meant your work partner."

Olivia blushed, feeling the embarrassment heating up her cheeks. "Oh. Well, my mother made assumptions about Brock when they met. I guess I thought that was what you meant."

Olivia glanced at Brock and noticed his stony face. Maybe she'd been a little too quick to dismiss him, but why did it matter to him? It wasn't like they'd ever explored a romantic possibility between them, and he'd shown no signs that he wanted to. So, did it matter if she was making it clear to Tom who they were to one another? The question was, why did she really care if Tom thought she was in a relationship anyway?

"I should have been clearer," Tom said, his voice even and pleasant. "Anyway, like I said. You've made quite the impression.

I got here yesterday, and you're all my grandmother could talk about. She was telling me all about the kidnapping case you worked on. Made you out to be quite the hero."

Olivia winced. How could she have forgotten that Tom still had family in Belle Grove? She hadn't come across Tom's grandmother while she'd been living there, but then again, she'd spent most of her time on cases or hanging out at the diner with Brock. They didn't exactly run in the same circles.

"You're staying with your grandmother?" Olivia asked conversationally, trying to steer the subject away from her. Tom nodded.

"Just until I find somewhere else in town. There's not exactly a ton of choices around here when it comes to housing."

Olivia's eyes widened. "You mean you're staying?"

Tom smiled. "I guess I may as well tell you. I'm opening my own practice here in Belle Grove."

"What happened to big city living?" Olivia frowned. Wasn't that the very thing that had driven them apart in the first place? The pair of them had always been so wrapped up in work that their differences began to drive them apart—namely, his desire to live in the city and her desire to escape it. It wasn't their only issue, but it was certainly one of them.

"Things change. People change," Tom shrugged, his smile still holding up. He showed no signs of being as uncomfortable as Olivia was in the conversation. "I guess I felt like coming home. And imagine my surprise when I found out that you moved here. To be honest, I was glad when I heard. I thought it would be nice to reconnect. It's been too long, Olivia."

Has it? Olivia thought. She'd never had any desire to reconnect with her exes before, and seeing Tom then felt more nerve-wracking than anything else. She didn't exactly feel glad to see him. But she had often wondered how he was. And now that she could see that he was perfectly fine, living a good life without her, she didn't know how that was supposed to make her feel.

"I guess it has," Olivia said with a tight smile. She didn't know how else to respond. It had been a long time since she'd had to deal with anything remotely related to romance, and her ex appearing suddenly out of nowhere was the last thing she needed. Especially when they were clearly going to be seeing more of one another.

"We should be leaving, right Olivia?" Brock prodded, standing up. His expression was still neutral, and Tom took a step back almost instinctively. Brock looked at her with a raised eyebrow. "You were saying how urgently we need to leave. To get ready for the case?"

Olivia felt oddly glad that Brock had brought it up, even if he was being a little rude. She felt like she had to leave and sort her feelings out before she saw Tom again. She'd been thrown off, and the case was the perfect excuse to leave her own reality for a while.

"Yeah, we do, actually. My boss just called with a new case for us," Olivia said apologetically, though the tension was already lifting from her chest. Tom nodded seriously.

"Of course. Sorry to hold you up. I just couldn't ignore seeing you over here. Well, it was nice to meet you, Brock. And I really hope I run into you again soon, Olivia. Hey, is your number the same? Maybe I could call you?"

"Yes, sure," Olivia said, a little flustered. She hadn't expected that. It made sense for them to exchange pleasantries if they were going to be living in such close proximity, but did it need to extend beyond that? Why would he want it to? Olivia didn't have time to analyze it. She had to get out of there before she said anything stupid and embarrassed herself.

"See you around," Tom said. Olivia gave him a fleeting smile as she and Brock left the diner. She felt her stomach twist. The past ten minutes had brought up so many feelings she thought she'd left in the past. With no warning at all, she was suddenly stacking up her personal issues, unsure of which she was going to solve first.

"So, um, should we take your car?" Olivia asked, trying to avoid the inevitable conversation she and Brock were about to have. She made for his passengers' side, but he stayed stock-still.

"I think we can leave in the morning."

"Oh."

"Who was that guy? You've never mentioned any Tom before."

"Haven't I?" Olivia asked, but she regretted it right away. She wasn't being honest with him or with herself. She'd buried

Tom so deep in her memories that she'd almost blocked him out herself. She'd had to after they'd split, just to protect herself. And now, she was being forced to face up to all of that. She was going to have to explain to Brock why she kept such a huge part of her past from him. And judging by his reaction in the diner, he wasn't going to be happy about it.

"He... we were together. We were... engaged," Olivia admitted. She said it so quietly that she wasn't sure he had even heard her.

But when she focused on Brock's face, she saw something that she wasn't expecting. Pain. And it slowly dawned on her that after all they'd been through, and all they'd shared, Brock thought he knew everything about her. He didn't trust many people and kept his circle small, just like she did. To find out that he didn't know her as well as he thought he did... she may as well have just punched him in the jaw.

"Engaged?" he asked. He was standing perfectly still, like the news had frozen him in place. "But you... you never once mentioned that you were engaged. Did you not... did you not think that was worth mentioning?"

Olivia said nothing, standing there in the parking lot at her own car, the distance between them feeling like an insurmountable chasm.

"We don't need to talk about this right now," she offered. "It's late."

"It is. Well, I'll see you in the morning, I guess. Good night."

"Good night."

The interaction felt so stiff, so formal, that it was like they'd taken several steps back, and Olivia didn't know where they stood anymore.

Olivia got into her car and headed to her cabin at the edge of the woods, silently kicking herself for how poorly she'd handled practically every aspect of that day.

What a day.

Suddenly, the prospect of a new case was exactly what she needed.

CHAPTER FOUR

OLIVIA WAS ALREADY AWAKE AND HAD HER BELONGINGS packed at the crack of dawn. She was sipping her coffee and reminiscing about pasts she'd forgotten when the familiar sound of Brock's truck rumbled into her driveway. She got up, double-checked all the locks on her door, and headed out to his car. Brock's trademark grin was absent, and it didn't take a federal investigator to know why.

"Morning," she said.

"Morning," he replied.

Without a further word, he started up the engine and pulled up the directions to the crime scene on his phone. Olivia tried to figure out what she should say, her chest tight.

"I would have mentioned it to you eventually…"

Brock kept his eyes on the road as he pulled out of the parking space. He didn't look angry, but he also didn't look like his usual jovial self. And that's when Olivia knew she'd made a mistake by leaving Brock in the dark. Whatever his reasons were for being offended that he wasn't told, Olivia knew he felt hurt. And now she had to try to find some way of fixing it while also figuring out what on earth was going on in her own head.

The ride to Richmond was almost silent, aside from Brock occasionally asking Olivia for details about the case they'd be working on. Olivia knew that she'd made a huge mistake not telling Brock about her past, but he was no stranger to keeping secrets from her, so why did it matter? Just because she was usually an open book when it came to him, it didn't mean she always had to be.

But she did feel guilty. In the back of her mind, she knew she hadn't mentioned it because she wasn't sure how he'd react. She and Brock had been in a sort of bubble since they met, spending nearly every hour of every day together. Outside influences usually came only from their cases. So, the thought of something personal meddling with their version of normalcy made Olivia feel uncomfortable. In her mind, some things were just better off remaining hidden.

But now she'd upset Brock. He hadn't said as much, but she could tell from his quietness, from the way his jaw tensed, from the way he kept his eyes directly on the road instead of glancing over at her to chat. Olivia knew that if the tables were turned, she'd be shocked if Brock told her that he had a secret ex-fiancée, but then again, there was plenty she didn't know about him. She slumped in her seat, feeling a little moody. Did she owe him an explanation, or was he being unfair to her?

It wasn't that she didn't want him to know about her life. Of course, she did. She'd told Brock more than she'd told some of her oldest friends. It felt easy with him, especially when they spent so much of their time together. But when it came to Tom, things were a little different. Olivia's heart hammered in her chest at the thought of him. He had been the one guy in her life who had even come close to her heart. She always kept it well-guarded, but she'd really thought at one time that he was "the one." She'd really imagined them getting married, maybe having a family someday, sharing everything in their lives.

And when all of that ended, it was the closest Olivia had ever come to heartbreak. At least, heartbreak of the romantic sort. It had been mutual, in a way. He was so wrapped up in his work, and she was constantly working unsociable hours for the Bureau. They just didn't have time for one another anymore. But that didn't mean it didn't hurt when they parted ways, when they returned their engagement rings, when they stored all of their good times in the past and left them there to gather dust. She'd hoped their business would remain unfinished, but clearly, the sight of him had dredged up something Olivia had never expected to feel again.

Olivia tried not to think about it. After all, they had a case to solve. She was hoping for something she could really sink her teeth into—something that would keep them both busy for a few weeks, at least. She mulled over the information that Jonathan had given to her. She'd never taken a murder-suicide before. Her mind began to whir, thinking of all of the possibilities the scene held. She was intrigued to look into something new. At least it would be a welcome distraction.

The sun was well on its way to its apex when they finally made it to Richmond. Olivia forced her doubts back into the shadows, preferring instead to welcome the sunshine. She felt bright and alert, ready to take on the case.

They passed through streets of expensive houses to get to the victims' residence, and Olivia's eyes scanned the streets. What could possibly cause a couple who seemingly had everything to commit a murder-suicide? What problems could these people possibly have when living the lives of lavish multi-millionaires?

Olivia wasn't so naïve as to believe that money can buy happiness, of course. But she also knew it had a funny way of getting rid of problems. Now, behind the closed doors of a house more expensive than what Olivia would make in a lifetime, someone had decided to do something unthinkable, something horrible. What problems did this couple face that made them turn to something so grisly?

It was Olivia's job to find out.

The directions for the house took Olivia and Brock away from the rows of expensive houses and down a windy road surrounded by trees. Olivia was sure that the house they'd find at the end of the road was going to be even grander than the ones they'd passed.

And she was right. Because as they emerged from the trees, it was like entering a private paradise. The boxy, modernist house in front of them was made almost entirely of glass and white brick. The huge windows at the front of the house served to show off the luxury interior, even though the metal gate at the front of the property kept onlookers out. Besides, the house was so far away from anything else that it seemed like the couple only had visits from people who were invited.

And now, those huge windows revealed the horrific scene within. Olivia could see two expensive wooden chairs placed by the window. The couple was slumped in them, facing one another with their heads bowed, in front of a backdrop of blood splattered against the pristine white walls. Surrounding this scene were several officers in windbreakers taking pictures of the scene and gathering evidence.

"First impressions?" Olivia asked as Brock rolled down the window to input the gate code that Jonathan had sent them. Brock sniffed.

"Looks like rich people getting bored with their lives," Brock said. "Wouldn't be the first time."

"You think it's just a murder-suicide? Nothing more?"

"I guess we'll find out when we're inside."

Olivia fell silent. So, Brock didn't want to talk. That was fine. It would have to be. She knew him well enough to know that he was very difficult to coax out of a bad mood. She'd just have to wait for it to blow over. She sighed quietly to herself. She didn't like the silence between them. It not only made their friendship hard work but also their working relationship. It helped to go into a case as a team. Now, she felt like she was walking into it with an acquaintance, not a partner.

They parked behind the several police cars and vans in the driveway and approached the open door of the house. Two officers were inside talking quietly. One of them, a man with a thick, bushy mustache and a smooth head, nodded to them as they entered.

"Special Agent Olivia Knight, FBI," Olivia said, holding her hand out for him to shake. The officer took her hand with a firm grip. "This is Special Agent Brock Tanner."

The officer shook Brock's hand as well and ushered them in. "Cliff Wyatt, Richmond PD. I'm glad you came. I was the first on the scene, and I don't like the way this whole thing looks."

"What can you tell us?" Brock asked.

"Now, I'm no expert on murder-suicides, but something's fishy about this one. Come and see for yourself."

Olivia followed him up the stairs, trying not to stare at the beautiful house. It wasn't often she was surrounded by such expensive things. Having said that, the house was equally minimalist, sleek, and beautiful in its design and carefully placed ornaments. The white walls and marble countertops gleamed brightly against the darkness. Everything was polished to a sheen and dusted within an inch of its life. It was hard to even tell that anyone actually lived here. It looked like a place too perfect for the act that had occurred upstairs.

As Olivia entered the room where the crime had occurred, she couldn't help staring at the body of Arabella Clifford. She had been a beautiful woman when she was alive. Her blonde hair was arranged in perfect ringlets, but her blue eyes were vacant, staring ahead as her head slumped back onto the back of the chair she was tied to. She wore an expensive designer dress, almost as if she was about to go out for the evening, but there was blood pooled around the heels of her stilettos. She looked like she didn't belong there, and it made Olivia even more curious to find out what had happened there.

As she tore her gaze from Arabella, her eyes fell immediately on a pistol that lay on the ground beside the supposed killer. Andrew Clifford was also a handsome human being, but she could see signs of distress around him. His tie was knotted loose, and she could see dark circles where sweat had stained his armpits. Killing his wife had clearly been a stressful ordeal for him in the end.

Olivia noted the bullet wound in the side of his head and could immediately see how the scenario was supposed to have played out. The woman was tied to a chair opposite her husband. One shot had been made to her head, the killing shot. Then the man had finished himself off. Simple.

Or was it? Olivia approached the scene slowly and stood behind the dead man, staring at his wife. She bent a little, as though to see the scene through his eyes instead of an outsider's. And that's when she understood what was wrong.

Olivia turned to Wyatt. "The angle of the shot—if he was sitting down opposite her, then it's aimed from too high up. The blood splatter is on the floor. Almost as if the shot was done execution-style. That's what you're thinking, right?"

Wyatt nodded. "And not just that. Look here," he pointed. "There are fibers of the same type of rope used to tie up Arabella around the husband's wrist."

Olivia pulled on a pair of nitrile gloves that she'd been keeping in her pocket and moved toward the body of Andrew Clifford. She crouched down to squint closely at the body. Sure enough, there they were: red markings on his wrists and elbows as well as tiny fibers indicating he'd also been tied up.

"Were they both tied up?" Olivia frowned.

Wyatt nodded. "First thing I noticed when I walked in. But that's the thing: Did he untie himself, tie her down, and kill her? And here's another thing: we already did a swab of the scene. There's gunshot residue on Andrew's clothes, but none on his hands."

"So, he didn't fire the gun?" Brock asked.

"Well, it's on his clothes. So clearly the gunshot came from his direction. But what—did he wash his hands after killing his wife? It just doesn't make sense," said Wyatt.

Olivia circled around the two bodies, looking more intently. "This... this was premeditated, whatever happened. He, or someone else, had the foresight to tie her to the chair, to make sure that she couldn't get away. It wasn't a spur-of-the-moment thing. Maybe he sat down opposite to talk to her, but then he couldn't see a way out. Maybe he realized he'd taken it too far and then killed himself... But if he went to all this trouble to set up this dramatic scene, why tie himself up first? Why untie himself, get up and wash his hands, and then kill himself? And what's the motive, anyway?"

"It was romantic to him somehow," Brock offered, his eyes glued onto the scene. "Like a Romeo and Juliet scenario, but with guns instead of poison. He killed her but decided he couldn't be without her. He sat back down, put the gun to his head, and ended it so that he could be with her."

Olivia nodded, but it didn't feel right. The crime scene techs continued taking photos of the scene, and in the meantime, she took out her phone and typed in Arabella Clifford. She wanted to see the woman's life for herself through the eyes of the media. Not with a bullet through her brain.

She found her social media accounts and scrolled through them. Arabella had uploaded a photograph of her and Andrew only the day before. Both of them were smiling, impossibly white teeth gleaming just as bright as the rest of the house.

"If this is a murder-suicide, then we're still looking for a reason that he would do this. They look so… happy?" Olivia turned the phone around for Wyatt and Brock to see. Brock shook his head.

"They look happy for the internet's benefit. Social media is for a bunch of professional liars trying to make their lives look beautiful and shiny," he said. His eyes fell on Olivia. "You never really know what's going on in people's lives, right?"

Olivia completely ignored the dig. She wasn't in the mood for this unspoken fight she was having with Brock.

"Alright, so let's imagine instead that they had problems. Infidelity? Maybe she was seeing someone else on the sly. So, maybe he was toying with her. Walking around, making her feel intimidated. He stops, just by the chair he's set out. He decides he's had enough and shoots her. But he put that chair opposite her for a reason. If he was really so angry, wouldn't he want to sit directly opposite her, look her in the eyes as he ends her life?"

"Or maybe he'd rather stand. Tower over her as he kills her," Brock offered with a shrug. "He felt that she had humiliated him somehow, or made a slight to his masculinity. So, he proves to her once and for all that he has this power over her."

It was a disturbing, sick thought, but Olivia nodded. "That would be a motive," she noted glumly.

"It's the only one I can think of," Brock shrugged. "We'll have to dig in to their financials, of course, but something this intense, this personal… it's sick. This had to have been building for a long time."

Some part of Olivia felt grateful that even in the midst of an argument between them, she and Brock could still click when it really mattered: when solving a case.

"That still doesn't account for the rope-tying though."

Brock shrugged. "Maybe it was a sex thing."

"I guess," she acknowledged. "But if it was, would they be fully clothed like they were about to go out dancing? Would he be tied up, untie himself, stand up, kill her, go wash his hands, then sit back down and kill himself? That's a lot of steps—and it still doesn't account for the fact that if he shot himself in the head, he'd have residue on his hands."

"Sometimes gunshot residue doesn't end up on the hands if it's a point-blank shot," Brock noted. "He still could have pressed it to his own head." He turned to Wyatt. "Is there any evidence at all that anyone else was here?"

Wyatt nodded. "We have a report from the alarm system that there was an unauthorized entry to the house at around 9 p.m. last night. But that could just as well have been the homeowners themselves. And on the carpet, there are some signs of a struggle. But again, we have no way of knowing who or why."

Brock rubbed his chin and shared a look with Olivia. "Seems odd that someone going to all this trouble to stage a murder-suicide would forget something as simple as an alarm."

Olivia nodded. "How long after the unauthorized entry did you arrive?"

"Typically, the alarm company gives a two-minute grace period for the homeowner to deactivate the alarm using a code. That was done, but the event was still noted on the alarm log," Wyatt told her.

"So how did you know to come for the alarm check?" she asked.

"We didn't. It wasn't until we got reports of gunshots that we came. The alarm company only calls the police department when that two-minute grace period is up without anyone inputting the code."

Brock nodded. "We'll have to follow up with those records."

"What about the gun?" Olivia asked. "Any fingerprints on it?"

Wyatt shook his head. "None, other than right at the grip where Andrew held it, but apparently may not have shot it."

"So, so far all we really have is a possible unauthorized entrance—with the alarm neutralized—an odd angle of a shot, some unusual rope tying, and a *lack* of GSR."

Wyatt took a breath. "I know it's not much, but I just don't think this makes a whole lot of sense. I'm sorry if you think I'm wasting your time—"

"No, we don't think that. I don't," Olivia said firmly. She stood behind Andrew once again. The more she stared at the wound in Arabella's head, the more it seemed like it was shot from above. Of course, the investigation would tell them more, but she could feel her heart racing, as it always did at the start of a new case. It was almost like her body was getting her ready for the sleepless nights, the constant ticking over in her brain, the endless speculation about it all. She turned to Wyatt.

"Brock's right. We're going to need more to go on. But forensics will help with that. I think you're onto something here. I'm going to take a look around, see if there's anything that we might have missed."

One of the crime scene techs came up behind Wyatt to ask something.

"If you'll excuse me, agents, I'd like to finish cataloging this evidence. Hopefully, soon we'll find something of use."

"Here's hoping," Olivia replied. Then he left her and Brock to it, heading back to talk with the others.

The room was eerily quiet, and it had little to do with the two bodies in the room. Olivia moved over to the window to scan the perimeter. There was so much wide-open space outside, so many places where someone could hide. So many places to run. She walked slowly past the big windows, hoping to see something out of the ordinary, but all she saw was Brock watching her in the reflection of the window.

"What are we doing here?" Brock grumbled. "This isn't of interest to us."

"Open your mind, Brock. We're here now. It's our job to try and uncover anything unusual. If we come up with nothing, then at least the police have answers. You can see why this would rattle them, right? Powerful couples seem so untouchable, especially couples like these two. None of this fits into the life they presented to the world. It's likely reminded them that anyone can die. Anyone can lose it and kill someone."

Brock didn't respond, and Olivia continued to walk around the room. She clocked a scuff on the carpet and made a mental note of it, wondering if someone else had been in there, muddying the carpets that Arabella and Andrew kept so otherwise meticulous. Though now, with blood staining the cream floors, it all seemed like it was for nothing. Olivia paused, looking into Andrew's vacant eyes.

"Why throw it all away?" she murmured. "If you have everything… why would you want to leave it all behind?"

Brock wandered off, half-heartedly checking the place out, but Olivia stayed where she was, surrounded by the silence of the place. Everything felt a little off, but she couldn't put her finger on why. She felt a sudden urge to throw herself headfirst into the case, to let it consume her every moment. It seemed preferable to her own life at that moment. She didn't want to think about her own issues for a while. She didn't want to fight with Brock or consider her Thanksgiving plans or get lost in her dark past. The scene in front of her was bleak, grisly, and disturbing—but at least it was a puzzle to be solved.

They stayed at the scene for several hours, going over evidence and coordinating with Wyatt. It was late when Brock and Olivia headed out of the house to find a motel. Brock muttered something about driving back to Belle Grove, but he didn't. He found them somewhere to stay, and they got ready for bed in silence, but Olivia was still thinking about the case. Tomorrow, maybe they'd know more.

Tomorrow, maybe they'd have something to sink their teeth into.

CHAPTER FIVE

It was just after five in the morning when Olivia began some solo investigating of her own. She'd managed a few hours of sleep, but the second she woke up needing a drink of water, she knew she wouldn't be able to drift off again. Still, she didn't mind. While Brock slept, she spent several hours getting lost in the online profiles of Arabella and Andrew.

It was Arabella's profile that interested her most. While Andrew posted very rarely, Arabella seemed to document every moment of her life on her profile, dragging Andrew into it as well. They really did seem to have a perfect life. Olivia found herself trawling through endless pictures of them on vacation, throwbacks to their lavish wedding, and plenty of advertisements and product endorsements. Each photograph had garnered thousands of likes and comments. It seemed that her following had only grown with each new post over the last few years. Olivia couldn't fathom how Arabella had managed to put together a profile that so many people were interested in, but as she checked the comment section on her photographs, she saw that it was already flooded with messages about her death. It was like the entire world was mourning her and her husband.

Olivia wondered how the nature of their deaths had been hidden from the press. The public statements by police were still vague on the cause of death. If people knew what had really happened, what would they say? Would they mourn the Cliffords with so many broken heart emojis and prayers for the lost ones? Would they dig deep into the couple's history like Internet sleuths, trying to solve the mystery before the authorities could?

The one thing that Olivia couldn't figure out was what Arabella and Andrew really did with their time. She looked through Arabella's profile at least ten times, trying to figure out how her social media life fit in with her supposed career, but she found very little about her work. Andrew's profile was much more reserved, too, so she couldn't glean much from his side of it. Olivia sat back, staring at her screen in confusion. How was it that someone who shared so much on social media could hide so much about her life?

She dug a little deeper, completing an online search of the supposed power couple. She couldn't find anything that said where they worked or who they worked for. There were plenty of short biographies that had been thrown together for both of them on fan sites, particularly Arabella, but they gave little information that couldn't be guessed at first glance of Arabella's page. The bios detailed her work with big fashion brands, praised her independent clothing line, and declared that she was an Aries, and yet, Olivia still couldn't figure out who she really was.

By the time Brock stirred, Olivia was beginning to feel a little irritated at her own lack of progress. She had been hoping to build up an image of the victims—so sure that their public lives would at least point her in the direction of what she needed to know—but she felt less sure than she had before she began searching.

"What are you up to?" Brock asked sleepily, propping up a pillow behind his back. Olivia sighed.

"Trying to get a better idea of who the victims are."

"You mean *victim*. Singular. Andrew killed her, and then he killed himself. He's not exactly a victim, is he?"

"We don't know that," she pointed out. "If the police are treating this as a break-in, we should at least look at all the angles."

He grunted wordlessly. She wondered how long this rift between them would hold. She was already sick of it. Was it such a crime for her to keep her love life to herself? It wasn't like she knew anything about his. "Whatever the scenario is, this is the case we have for now. We should probably work it, right?"

Brock shrugged and headed into the bathroom. Olivia was sure that Brock was going to spend the entire morning being difficult, but when he returned ten minutes later, he pulled up a wooden chair to sit beside her bed.

"So, you haven't found anything useful yet?" he asked. Olivia chewed the inside of her cheek.

"Well, I'm beginning to wonder if the lack of information about them is actually telling us something in itself," Olivia mused out loud. "Let's say that Andrew really did shoot his wife. We still don't have a motive in mind. I've spent hours looking at Arabella's profile, and honestly, I don't know when the hell she'd have time to have an affair. She was constantly posting online, showing where she was twenty-four-seven, and she spent most of that time with Andrew. That makes me think that this can't possibly have been about an affair. There aren't enough hours in the day. And given her following, I imagine that if she was seeing someone else, it would've been leaked by someone by now."

"Well, what else is there? Is it possible he just couldn't stand her?" Brock asked dryly. "I mean, maybe this was some long-simmering resentment. Some argument, I don't know, about her big following on social media."

"You think he didn't appreciate being so visible?"

"Well, we've established that his profile was pretty minimal. Maybe he was completely uncomfortable with being in the spotlight. They fought about it over and over, maybe eventually the pressure got to him, and he snapped."

"Maybe. But isn't it a bit extreme? To kill his wife for wanting to share a few pictures of him online?"

"Well, there's no other motive I can think of. I don't know. You said it yourself: she was running around with a camera all day, like his own personal paparazzi. For a reserved guy like that, that's a tiring way to live. Imagine not being able to eat dinner without your partner posting about it. He probably got scared that she'd start live-streaming him in the bathroom."

Olivia almost smirked, though she felt a little guilty given the situation.

"Maybe you're right. It's just hard to imagine what problems this couple possibly had. They were well-loved online, they had more money than they'd ever need, and they seemed to be in a loving, committed relationship. So, what else would stand in their way?"

Brock considered her for a minute. "It's like I said yesterday... the way we perceive people online isn't necessarily how they are. It's a trick of the mind. We see what we're told to see. Done right, it's a clever form of manipulation. So, maybe their lives weren't so perfect after all."

Olivia nodded. She knew all too well the difference between someone's confident, happy public persona and their tumultuous inner life. But if he was right, they would need to find something tangible to back that up. Something not on social media. Clearly, they had a decent enough standard of living, given the house they owned.

"But is that part of the mirage too?" Olivia said out loud to herself. She thought back to the house and imagined how much it would cost to keep it running. The striking modernist paintings on the walls, the exotic trinkets and statues, the luxury furniture. There were things in that house worth a fortune, but that didn't mean they had cash on hand. What if they were having financial difficulties?

"You think this might have to do with money?" Brock asked, reading Olivia's mind. She chewed her lip.

"Maybe? Money was clearly a big deal to them both, especially to Arabella. How far would she go to make the world think that they were living a life of luxury? Maybe once we get ahold of their accounts, we'll find mountains of debt that they've been trying, but failing, to manage. Maybe she started spending Andrew's money, and that's why he killed her. Maybe he was angry with her for that. Then maybe he was sorry afterward, and that's why he killed himself. I don't know. It's going to be a lot of guesswork until we can get access to their accounts."

"I think you're onto something though. If he did it, then he had to have had a good reason. He must have felt like there was nothing else left to do."

"Exactly. And to be honest, I'm still having a hard time figuring out how they got so rich in the first place. Arabella's profiles have all sorts of collaborations with brands and clothing lines, but there's no trace of what Andrew really did. They both supposedly worked in 'finance,' but that could mean anything."

"Perhaps that's one thing they tried hard to keep private. Working for a big company, everything you do reflects on them. Maybe it was their way of distancing their social media presence from their work life."

"Sure, that would make sense," Olivia agreed. "But one thing keeps sticking in my mind. The fact that Arabella was almost constantly online. I've watched through a lot of the videos she made on a daily basis. She'd post, like, every five minutes with updates. So, if she's in finance… when did she find time to work? In all those videos, she was running around all over the place, grabbing coffee, meeting other influencers, talking about her brand collaborations… but I can't think of a single time she mentioned her finance career. Don't you think that's odd? She's got that whole girl boss vibe, and clearly that's the dream she was trying to sell on her social media, so where is the evidence of that part of her life? Where does that come into play?"

Brock seemed stumped by the question. He paused for a long time, trying to put together a coherent answer. "So, you're saying that maybe it's a front for something? That all of that stuff she posts on the internet is more like a distraction from her real life?"

"Maybe so. And people were buying it. She must have been making a fortune from all of her social media activity anyway. I mean, this could all be too much speculation. Maybe she left her finance career once she really took off on social media."

"But what about Andrew?" Brock asked. "We've barely considered him. He's the one that decided to shoot them both. Even if Arabella was leading some kind of fake life, what did that mean for him, if anything? Maybe he actually did have a high-flying job, enough to support them both while she was doing her own thing. So where does that fit in with a murder-suicide? It doesn't."

Olivia drew in a breath. "Well, maybe that's the thing. Maybe this doesn't make sense because it wasn't a murder-suicide."

Brock sighed. "We're back to this?"

"This is the reason we're here, Brock. We have to consider that this isn't as it first appears. Now, consider Arabella's public presence. She has thousands upon thousands of followers. Those people feel like they know her through keeping up with her life. Maybe some of them even become obsessive about her and her husband. Maybe in one of her videos, she let slip a detail that allowed someone to find their home, to scout it out, to find a way in."

Brock frowned. "I guess that could make sense with the unauthorized entry the police mentioned, but still, that security code was put in. It has to be someone who knows the house well enough to know that code. I don't know if it would have been some obsessed fan."

"Well, a lot of the videos are in her house. Someone with knowledge of those systems might have been able to hack into it somehow to disable the alarm."

"Even still, that puts us at a suspect pool of, as you said, thousands upon thousands of people," Brock countered. "I'd have no idea where to start."

"Me neither," Olivia admitted.

They spent the next few minutes clicking through their profiles and reading some of the comments on their posts.

"Looks like all the well-wishers are out today," Brock muttered. "I see what you mean though. Some of these videos are..."

Olivia nodded. "Yeah. It's easy to be bitter and jealous of someone who is living a life of luxury, especially if they don't seem like they deserve it. I mean, it's a little sickening watching her prance around all day every day, claiming to be a pillar of

LOVE, LIES, AND SUICIDE

society while she's promoting teeth whitener and eating at swanky restaurants every day. I can understand how someone like her might rub people up the wrong way. She seemed so convinced that she'd built the life she wanted and deserved all by herself."

She closed her eyes for a moment to set the scene and narrated it out for him. "Imagine you come home from a ten-hour shift with less money than she makes in an hour, let alone a day. You're bone-tired, and you've got a family to care for, chores to do, no time to switch off for the day before you rinse and repeat. You log onto social media for some escapism… and there's Arabella Clifford. She's talking about how she spent the day in a hair and makeup studio to prepare for some photoshoot. Hashtag girlboss, or something along those lines. Don't you think that's the kind of oblivious behavior that could make someone really angry?"

"Angry enough to kill?"

"Maybe," she shrugged. "Maybe they feel powerful for the first time in their life. They find where she lives, find a way into the house. They've gotten farther than anyone else has before. They took a gun with them for their own protection, for self-defense, but then they panic. They come face to face with Arabella, and she's screaming about calling the police. They force her into a chair while they think about how to handle it. Andrew is home as well, so they have to prevent him from calling the cops, and suddenly they realize they've crossed the point of no return. Both of them are tied up now. They can't just turn around and leave or go back to their regular life. Their only choice is to kill them both. They don't consider at the time how to make it look realistic. They act on impulse, but try to make it look like a murder-suicide before fleeing… only they left flaws in the scene. Leading to our involvement."

Brock puffed out air. "I don't know, Olivia. I think we're reaching with this one. Sorry."

Olivia sighed. "Well, I guess we'll find out, won't we? But we really shouldn't dismiss this so easily. If I'm right about the alignment of the shots and the rope fibers, then the killer may have made other mistakes. Ones that aren't so easy to cover up."

Her phone began to ring. It was Wyatt. With her heart skipping several beats, she picked up the call.

"Knight here."

"Good morning, Agent Knight. I'm sorry to call you so early, but we've already found something of significant interest. I thought you'd like to know about it right away."

Olivia sat up a little straighter and pressed the speakerphone button. "You're on speaker. We're listening."

"We compared the bullets found in both of the victims to the gun."

"*Both* the victims?" Olivia asked, raising her eyebrow ever so slightly at Brock. "You mean to say that you're discounting this as a murder-suicide?"

"I think we have to. Because the bullets found in both bodies were not fired from the gun on the scene."

CHAPTER SIX

THE WORDS PLAYED ON REPEAT IN HER MIND:
The bullets found in both bodies were not fired from the gun on the scene…

It changed everything, and even Brock couldn't deny it. It definitively meant that someone else had been on the scene. It meant that, more than likely, Andrew Clifford never actually fired a shot, which solved the GSR mystery. It meant that whoever had been in the mansion had, for some reason, decided to end the lives of two people, and then tried to pass it off as a murder-suicide.

But why? Sure, it had bought the killer some time to get away, but Olivia was certain that such a clumsy move wasn't made by a professional. So, who wanted the Cliffords dead? And why had they gone to so much trouble to get the job done?

Those thoughts ran through her head while they were on the way to interview the friends and family of the victims. There was still so much to figure out. Did the killer attack Arabella and then finish Andrew off? Or did Andrew kill himself afterward when he found his wife dead? Did Andrew sit opposite her in the chair so that they could be together in his final moments? Or had the killer set up this twisted scene for his own amusement?

The possibilities seemed endless. While the police continued to analyze the forensic evidence, Olivia was hoping that speaking to the family and friends of the victims might shed some light on the situation. Perhaps they might know of someone that wanted them dead.

"I can't believe someone went to all that trouble to make it look like a murder-suicide," Brock remarked, shaking his head as he put the car in park. "Well, looks like they botched it. Why would they switch the gun on the scene?"

Olivia chewed her lip. "They must have made some mistake. Maybe they forgot to wear gloves when handling the murder weapon and had to improvise. That's why the whole thing seems so disjointed. The tying up, the lack of GSR... it sounds like the killer didn't really know what they were doing."

"It seems especially clumsy though, doesn't it? What kind of person are we dealing with here?"

"Let's focus on getting the interviews out of the way," Olivia suggested. "Once we build an idea of who the Clifford family was, then maybe we'll understand more."

Olivia and Brock headed into the police station together. The station was relatively quiet, save for the sound of someone blowing their nose loudly. As Olivia and Brock turned a corner to greet their interviewees, they found an older woman crying noisily, dabbing under her eyes with a tissue. She'd taken the time to do her makeup that morning, despite the news she'd received, and she was attempting to blot her tears before they cut lines through her foundation. She was tall in her heeled boots, and she wore all black, the color of mourning. Olivia saw how similar she looked to Arabella, especially since her skin had been pulled tight to keep it from wrinkling. She seemed like she might be in her early forties, but logic dictated that she must be older, given that she had a grown-up daughter.

Had.

Olivia approached the woman, who glared at her, offended by her very presence. Olivia offered her a kind smile.

"I'm so sorry to hear about your daughter, Mrs. King," Olivia started gently. "We appreciate you coming in to speak with us."

"I don't know why you're wasting time speaking to me when there's a cold-blooded *murderer* out there," Josephine King snapped, dabbing under her eye once again. Olivia kept her face straight, not wanting to provoke further irritation from Josephine.

"Our job right now is to try and paint a picture of the lives of the victims. Whatever you can tell us might help in figuring out who did this. Whenever you're ready, we can get started."

Josephine snootily gave her a once-over, still clearly sour about being asked to interview, but after a moment, she nodded. Olivia opened the door to her left, allowing Josephine into the room.

Josephine sat down at the table in the room, and Olivia took a seat opposite, shortly joined after by Brock. Olivia set out her notebook on the table and clicked her pen, ready for action.

"Mrs. King, your daughter was clearly very well-loved. She had hundreds of thousands of online fans. I'm sure that it's difficult to imagine anyone wanting to hurt her, but we now have reason to believe that Andrew didn't kill her. So, we have to look for other potential suspects. Is there anything you can tell us about her life, anything at all, that could point us in the right direction?"

"Well, what is there to say? It's like you said. Everybody loved her," Josephine sniffed. "She was a really wonderful person."

Brock leaned forward a little. "What Agent Knight is trying to say is that popular women like Arabella tend to attract the wrong type of attention as well. Did she ever have issues with stalkers, for example? It's not uncommon for women of a ... *high profile* to become the objects of obsession. Did she ever mention anything like that to you?"

Josephine leaned back in her chair, her eyes a little misty. "Well, she did mention a few times when she'd been harassed in the street. Fans wanted a slice of her precious time. But that's the price of fame. She was always so grateful to them. She didn't need to waste her time talking to them, but she always did, posing for photographs, offering autographs. My daughter was a patient woman. I can't imagine a scenario where she ever upset anyone."

"Did she ever mention any fans in particular? Ones who were maybe more persistent than others?" Olivia asked. Josephine shook her head.

"Not that I can recall. But Arabella met a lot of people over the years. How could she possibly be expected to remember every single encounter?"

Olivia nodded, making a few notes. She personally couldn't understand why anyone would be obsessed with an influencer, but she also knew that the modern world of social media was a minefield. Arabella had more followers than some actual celebrities. Surely there must be one person among them who would be likely to take things too far when meeting their hero.

"Tell us more about Arabella," Olivia said gently. "What kind of a person was she? Did she have any enemies, anyone she rubbed the wrong way?"

Josephine stiffened up again. "What kind of a question is that?"

"I'm simply asking if there was anything she—"

"Are you implying that my daughter *did* something to deserve this?" Josephine snapped. "Are you blaming *her* for this?" Her eyes brimmed with angry tears.

"Not at all, ma'am. We're not saying that she did anything. We just would like to get a better idea of who she was from those closest to her," Brock cut in, easing the tension in Josephine's shoulders a little. Still, she cast an irritated glance in Olivia's direction, as though she was deliberately being difficult.

"I see. Well, my daughter devoted her life to being a good person. That's how I raised her, after all. I taught her to be kind and charitable. You will see from her social media that she often spent time volunteering, attending charity events, giving to the needy…"

Olivia frowned a little. She hadn't seen any evidence of the sort when she'd been trawling through Arabella's pages. She wondered what Josephine was trying to achieve by telling such a blatant lie. Was she truly that naive? Or was she trying to protect her family name and stop Arabella from being dragged through the mud?

"Could you give an example of the sort of organizations she worked with?" Olivia asked, hoping that she was wrong about Josephine being untruthful. Josephine sniffed, not meeting Olivia's eye.

"Oh, I don't know. That was her world, not mine. I can't remember now where she spent her time. Hell, I barely knew anything about her work. It wasn't something we ever talked about."

Olivia narrowed her eyes. So, Arabella supposedly had a high-flying career, a philanthropist lifestyle, and a huge following, but she never spoke to her mother about it? Something was off. Either Josephine wasn't close with her daughter, or Arabella had been keeping her in the dark about her life. The question was, why?

"We had more important things to discuss, I assure you. Some of us don't live to work, you know," Josephine continued defensively. She paused. "Although, it did sometimes feel like I was estranged from that part of her life. I could never truly understand it. And it did make me feel in the dark. But I suppose my baby girl had her reasons for keeping things from me. Don't all daughters have a life separate from their parents?"

Olivia thought of her own mother then. In her case, it felt like the other way around. She'd never felt the need to hide her own life from her mother. That was, before she disappeared. Her mother, on the other hand…

Olivia cleared her throat. "What about the rest of your family? Arabella came into a lot of money over recent years. Did any of your family ever reach out, asking for money? And if so, did any of them get rejected?"

Josephine scowled. "What do you take my family for? Scavengers?"

"Not at all," Olivia said through gritted teeth. It felt like every response she received from the woman was a targeted attack. It was getting tiring. "I simply wondered if anyone in the family had fallen on hard times and reached out for help?"

Josephine snorted. "Absolutely not. Our family has always done just fine. We don't need to go around begging for scraps. There is no one in our family who has any need for Arabella's money."

"And Andrew's family?" Brock asked. Josephine shook her head.

"That family is filthy rich. They've never wanted for anything in their lives."

Olivia made a few notes, feeling at a loss. It felt like they weren't getting anywhere. She wondered what Josephine was holding back. It felt like there was something she was keeping from them. Did she want them to find answers, or was she hoping that they wouldn't?

Olivia swallowed. She had a question she desperately wanted to ask, but Mrs. King certainly wasn't going to be happy about it. She cleared her throat, preparing herself for Josephine's response.

"Mrs. King… may I ask who stands to inherit Arabella's estate? She didn't have any children, after all. Where is all that money going to?"

She watched as Josephine's nostrils flared in anger. "You dare to imply that someone might want her dead for the inheritance?"

"I didn't say that," Olivia replied coolly. "I'm just doing my job."

"Well, I find your line of questioning to be very intrusive."

"Mrs. King, with all due respect, I have to be intrusive. I'm trying to catch a killer here. I'm not implying anything. I just want a straight answer."

"Well, here's your answer. It's going to *me*, alright? I stand to inherit everything. That was agreed between myself, Andrew, and Arabella long ago. It's written into their will. But I don't care about the money one bit. You know what I care about? My daughter."

Josephine's lip trembled a little as she stared Olivia in the eye. For the first time, the mask of haughty anger slipped, and she finally looked like a real person. A real woman, mourning the loss of her daughter. "I would give anything to have her back. All that money… and what for? Her life was worth much more than that, and someone decided to end it. Happy now?"

Olivia couldn't look Josephine in the eye. Sometimes, her job was impossible. She'd never intended to upset her, but she also wasn't any closer to the answers she needed. Now, it felt like Josephine would close off from her for good.

"I'm sorry, Mrs. King," Olivia replied gently. "But we do want the same thing, I promise you. I want to find the person who did this to your daughter. And if that means asking uncomfortable questions, then that's what I have to do."

Josephine finally looked Olivia in the eye. Her stony exterior seemed to have softened a little. She sighed.

"Look, I don't know who would want Arabella dead," Josephine offered. "But our family had nothing to gain from her being gone. In fact, she was the glue holding us all together. Things will never be the same without her," Josephine whispered. "Is that all? Can I go now?"

Brock and Olivia exchanged a look. After a moment, Olivia nodded. "Yes, you can go. Please take my number. If you think of anything that might be of use, please call us."

"Just find who did this," Josephine said stiffly as she left the room. Olivia leaned back in her chair as the door closed behind Josephine. She let out a long breath.

"Well, that was rough."

"You can say that again," Brock muttered, shaking his head. "Who else do we have to speak to today?"

"Andrew's parents are coming, and his sister. A few close friends as well, I believe. But if all of them are as difficult as she was, I'm not sure what we're going to get out of this." Olivia chewed the inside of her cheek. "She was so defensive. Why? Do you think she was hiding something?"

"I don't know. It did strike me as odd that she knew very little about her daughter's working life."

"Right? What kind of mother doesn't even know what their child does for work?" Olivia agreed. "No judgment, but it does seem a little strange. And it begs the question again: Why was Arabella's work such a mystery to everyone? There's no sign of who she works for. No posts online. No documents or records at the house. Not even her own family seems to have answers. There's something fishy there…"

"Maybe some of her friends and family will have more answers. If not, her finances should help us make sense of it. Her money came from somewhere, after all. It'll all come together once we've got our hands on her bank statements."

Olivia nodded, though she still felt like there was something strange going on. Arabella Clifford's life was a huge puzzle where none of the pieces fit with the others. She was desperate to get to the bottom of it all, but if people continued to be uncooperative, it would surely make their job much more difficult.

As they were waiting for their next interviewee, Olivia felt her phone vibrate in her pocket. Frowning, she took it out to check her messages. She rarely got messages from anyone other than her family and Brock, so she was definitely shocked when she saw the name that popped up on her screen.

Tom.

Her heart skipped a beat. She didn't even realize that she still had his number. Apparently, she'd never felt the need to delete him completely from her life. She scanned the text, feeling anxious.

Tom: *Hey, stranger. It was good to see you last night.*

She didn't even know how she was supposed to respond to that. She still hadn't decided if she was glad to have seen Tom or not. But when she glanced at Brock and caught him watching her, she slipped the phone back into her pocket. The last thing she wanted to do was create more tension with her partner when they were in the middle of a case. And besides, she wanted him to forgive her for not telling him about Tom in the first place. It seemed like a bad idea to be flaunting the whole thing in his face. Olivia stretched her arms out with a yawn.

"Alright. Let's get the next interviewee in."

CHAPTER SEVEN

It was later that afternoon when Olivia and Brock sat down to take a look through the Clifford family's finances. They were back at the motel with paper cups filled with cheap coffee and a desperation for information. Olivia sipped from her cup as she delved into the first page of Arabella's bank statements.

"Alright, let's see what we've got here."

She slowly scrolled through the pages, examining each and every transaction with care. The further along she got, the more she found herself raising her eyebrows. Brock scoffed from next to her as he examined Andrew's finances.

"Boy, did these guys know how to spend their money," he muttered. "Are you seeing this? Two grand on a designer handbag.

Fifteen hundred in crypto investment. Twenty thousand spent on new furniture in one transaction..."

"You should see what Arabella just spent on her new car," Olivia added with a shake of her head. "These people had more money than sense."

"My thoughts exactly. And I don't know if I'm missing something, but I see absolutely no evidence of charitable giving here. I mean, they don't seem like they donate to a single charity. And yet every person we talked to harped on about them being complete philanthropists. Is there something we're not seeing here?"

"I guess it's not that unusual. After someone dies, their friends and family always like to say what good people they were. Maybe it was just a reflex to say that they were charitable people, especially given how much money they had. Their social media posts certainly seemed to imply it."

"Or maybe Arabella and Andrew were just massive liars. I mean, maybe they preferred to tell the world that they were spending all of their money on charitable causes than to admit they were buying new Persian rugs every Thursday."

Olivia chuckled. "Honestly, I don't understand how rich people find new things to spend money on all the time. Look at this: last week, they bought over a hundred books. I guess they needed something to fill those empty shelves in their library."

"I wonder when was the last time either of them picked up a book," Brock rolled his eyes. "This is ridiculous. They haven't spent a day without excessive spending in months. But where is all this money coming from?"

Olivia switched her tactics, filtering through to Arabella's incomings instead of her outgoings. She scrolled through, chewing her lips.

"Hm. Interesting..."

"What is?"

"All of these payments. There are some coming from the brands that Arabella worked with. That makes sense, at least. Monthly sales, endorsement royalties, stuff like that. Payouts from their investment dividends. But the rest... they're not coming from big companies. They're just personal payments. This one is from someone called Daniel Prentiss, a thousand dollars. Then there's another from Mark Kowalski. Three thousand. The list goes on. But why would all of these people be sending her such large sums of money?"

"For her, that kind of money is just a drop in the ocean, though, surely?" Brock pointed out. "That doesn't seem like all that much to someone who already lives in a million-dollar mansion."

"That's what seems even stranger to me. Because to someone else, that kind of money is huge. Can you imagine just wiring that kind of money to someone casually? It's a lot. So, what reason would someone have to send that much to someone already swimming in cash?"

Brock shrugged. "It's a good point. But maybe it's one of those rich-people-kind-of-things. Like, hey, here's a thousand dollars, go treat yourself to something nice. You see it all the time with celebrities, right? They send each other extravagant things just for the hell of it. It looks good on their socials too. Maybe that's what this is about."

Olivia wasn't convinced. She clicked on the transaction from Mark Kowalski, hoping for some clarity. She raised her eyebrow when she saw the payment reference.

"Hey, Brock. You know how I said that I didn't think Arabella had time for an affair? Well, maybe I was wrong."

She turned the screen of her laptop for Brock to look at. He frowned as he stared at it.

"What am I looking at?"

"The payment reference. It says, *all my love.*"

"Maybe it's just some secret admirer of hers. It doesn't mean she was having an affair."

"What kind of secret admirer would have her bank details on hand?" Olivia pointed out. "That's the sort of information you give to someone on a more intimate level, right? It feels like something was going on there."

"Maybe you're right. What about the other transactions? Perhaps we can glean something from those too."

Olivia clicked through some of the other recent transactions. "Look at all of these. All of them from men, all of them with sappy payment references. *For my love,* this one says. Or *for my beautiful woman.* There's something very odd going on here. She's got all of these men sending her large sums of money, all of them declaring their love for her. How was she getting away with this without Andrew noticing? It's like she was on a mass dating spree, collecting men wherever she could find them."

"And getting them all to send her money," Brock murmured. "But why? She was rolling in cash. What was the point in her taking money from all these guys?"

"She's clearly materialistic. Maybe that's her love language: being showered in gifts and money," Olivia suggested. "But you're right, it does seem strange given that she already had it all."

Olivia continued to scroll through the transactions, frowning at the screen. "Then again, maybe this is the reason she has so much money in the first place. Look at these transactions. Most of them are coming from personal accounts. Aside from the brands she works for, these seem to be a significant source of income. What are we dealing with here? A sugar baby scenario, maybe?"

"You might be onto something there. She was a young, beautiful woman with the world in the palm of her hand. It's easy to see how men might be enticed by that. But don't sugar babies tend to receive regular transactions? These all look like one-off payments."

He was right. Each of the transactions from the men seemed to be singular. Olivia couldn't make sense of it. How did she have so many guys falling at her feet, willing to give her everything they had just to keep her attention? How was she finding the time to hook them and reel them in? And more impressively, how had she been keeping it a secret?

Olivia considered the victim more closely. She was a high-profile woman with a secret life that nobody knew about, possibly not even her husband. If she was having affairs with multiple men—and any one of them found out—what if they had the motive to murder? To kill her for her lies, to kill her husband for simply being with her?

Or what if it was still the husband? Now that they'd discovered this, Brock's initial theory that it truly was a murder-suicide seemed to be more likely. But she knew there was no coincidence to all of this.

"I think we need to know who all these men are," Olivia murmured, counting off all the men sending her such big sums of money. There were at least twenty of them that she could see right off the bat. How had she managed to find so many men to give her their hard-earned money? "We need to speak to each of them and figure out what their relationship actually was with her. Though by the looks of it, it's going to take us quite some time to speak with all of these people."

"Um, Olivia? There might be something else of interest here."

Brock turned his own screen toward Olivia, and she scanned it. She felt her heart thundering against her chest as she realized what she was looking at.

It seemed that Arabella wasn't the only one with admirers. Andrew's account was also filled with transactions from adoring fans, except his weren't big paychecks. He had dozens and dozens, all in smaller amounts—fifty dollars here, twenty-five there—but it seemed to add up quickly. But that wasn't all. In Andrew's accounts, there were more messages than just expressions of love. *Hope this helps*, read one. *Best of luck to you*, read another. *My condolences*, came a third.

"Look at this one," he pointed. "*Sending love and prayers for your wife*," he read out. "That doesn't make any sense. What are these people offering condolences for?"

Brock and Olivia met one another's eyes.

"What the hell is going on here?" Olivia whispered. "This can't be a coincidence."

"Agreed."

"And whatever it is, it looks as though they were in it together. Do you think maybe this is some kind of scam? Or maybe this was some kind of sexual thing for them both? A game they played with other people for money?"

"I can't say I've ever seen anything like it. All of these personal transactions, with adoring notes or messages of support… and they were both up to it, so it couldn't have been a secret between them. They were definitely up to something." Brock shook his head. "We need to check out their computers and see what we can find on there. But whatever it is, I think it might be the root of what got them both killed."

It took some time for Olivia and Brock to get the laptops and phones of Arabella and Andrew out of police evidence. But after jumping through some hoops and talking with Wyatt, they were finally cleared to take the devices away for investigation. As Wyatt escorted them through the evidence room, Olivia fell in step with him.

"Any more news on the guns?" Olivia asked him. She was intrigued to know why the killer would've killed the victims with one gun and then left another in their wake. He let out a long breath as though he was very tired.

"Analysis showed that the bullets shot through both victims were from a Taurus 9mm handgun. Cheap and cheerful, as I'm sure you know. The Glock we found next to the bodies apparently belonged to the Clifford family, and was, of course, covered in their prints. But we haven't found much evidence of anyone else on the scene yet. We'll keep searching, but forensics isn't coming up with much."

Olivia felt a little disappointed. She was hoping for more, but the investigation was only beginning. As Wyatt handed the devices to them—two laptop computers, two tablets, and two phones—she offered him a reassuring smile.

"We're hoping that we can get some interesting stuff off these. We think, given what we found on the bank statements, that we might be able to find some potential suspects from whatever's on here."

"Here's hoping. You know, the victim's families have been putting a hell of a lot of pressure on the department. They're trying to speed things along, find someone to pin the blame on. They're pressing hard to move this along," Wyatt told Olivia. She raised her eyebrow.

"Really? Let me guess. You spoke with Josephine King?"

Wyatt nodded. "She wants this all to be done with. The media are hungry for a solution to this. You know how it is. An insignificant—but wealthy—white woman killed in her home along with her handsome husband. It gives them something to eat up on a quiet news day. So, you can see how the family is desperate to tie this up."

"Of course," Olivia nodded, though she did find it interesting that Josephine was sticking her nose in once again. She wasn't sure what she made of the victim's mother. Was she really concerned, or was she hoping to find some benefit from the whole thing?

As Olivia and Brock returned to their motel, Olivia felt the anticipation building up inside her. After what they'd found out in the bank records, she couldn't wait to find out more about the Clifford family. Arabella and Andrew had seemed clean-cut when she'd first examined the case, but she was beginning to feel like there was much more to them than she'd first imagined. A deep dive into their devices would be interesting, to say the least.

She felt her phone buzz in her pocket again, but this time, she didn't reach to check it. She already knew who the text was from. Why was Tom trying to reach out to her again? Hadn't they made it clear to one another where they stood after their break-up? Just because they were going to be living in the same town, it didn't mean they had to interact. They didn't have to be friends or even acquaintances. Why would they want that now, after so much time apart? Why was he trying to reconnect when they'd already broken every connection they had?

Olivia tried not to think about him as they got back to the motel and set up all the devices on the table. He wasn't a priority right now. In fact, he wasn't a priority at all. He was her past, and she was trying her best to stay grounded in the present.

Olivia stole a glance at Brock, wondering what he'd think if he knew Tom was sending her messages. Then she wondered why she cared what Brock thought.

Olivia blinked hard and returned her attention to the screen in front of her. She couldn't afford to be distracted by something as trivial as her personal life—not when they had a juicy case to get stuck into. She began scrolling through the email account that Arabella had last had open. Olivia could already tell that it was going to take a long time to trawl through the emails, given the sheer amount of them. Business emails from the brands she represented, order confirmations from expensive online stores, endless spam that she hadn't bothered to sort through…

"You'd think that someone like Arabella would have an assistant to go through all of her junk mail, right?" Olivia mused.

Brock shrugged. "Not if she had something to hide on there. Emails from all of her secret lovers, perhaps?"

"Well, she's coming up clean so far. I'm a little surprised, to be honest. I imagined she might keep in contact with the guys via email instead of texts or something. It seems more private."

"I don't know. Why don't we see if we can get into her social media?"

A perusal of her social media didn't reveal much more than what they'd already discovered. There was nothing particularly of note in the drafts, no unusual photos or data on the devices. She'd already called up Sam in the DC office and asked him to put together a spreadsheet of all the accounts that followed her and see if he could find anything notable, but with so many out there, she wasn't holding her breath for any big revelations from that angle anytime soon.

Olivia clicked back to Arabella's email, and an idea popped into her brain. "What about her deleted emails?" she asked. "Maybe there's something there."

Brock made a face. "Who deletes an email in this day and age? Just mark it as read."

"Exactly. You'd only bother to delete it if you wanted to keep it hidden."

She clicked on the deleted email folder and felt a surge of adrenaline shoot through her.

"Check it out. She was on a dating website. Singles Match dot com."

Brock's ears pricked up in interest. "Okay, that's juicy. So, what do we think? Secret affair behind Andrew's back? Polyamory? Maybe they were both bored in their marriage and wanted to spice things up?"

"I suppose we're about to find out."

Olivia clicked through to the site that Arabella had been signed up to. Luckily, her login details had been saved to the site, and she was able to log in right away. Olivia felt her heart jolt as she was taken directly to the messaging service. The inbox was filled to the brim with unopened messages.

LOVE, LIES, AND SUICIDE

"Someone was popular," Olivia murmured, scrolling through the messages. She spotted several familiar names right off the bat. "Look who we've got here. Daniel Prentiss. Mark Kowalski. This is where she met them."

"The question is, then, why were they sending her large sums of money?"

Olivia clicked on the messages between Arabella and Daniel. Except in the messages, she wasn't Arabella. She was simply Belle, and her profile picture was almost unrecognizable as her. Almost. Olivia was sure she was the woman in the picture, though, despite her face being concealed behind her curls and the photo being in black and white. It was sultry and seductive, but she could've been anyone from the way it was taken. Olivia suspected there was a reason for that.

"I smell a catfish," Brock muttered. Olivia checked out the messages, her heart racing as she read the last few messages shared between her and Daniel.

Belle: *I can't thank you enough. I just had to get away. I don't even know where I'll go.*

Daniel: *You should come to me. Belle, please, come to me. I know you're scared, but I'll protect you.*

Belle: *I can't put you in danger. You've already done so much for me. No, I need to disappear. I need to get out of the country. But I wish there was another way.*

Daniel: *Will I ever hear from you again?*

Belle: *I promise I'll try to find you when it's safe. I love you, Daniel. Thank you for all you've done for me.*

Daniel: *I love you too, Belle. I'll wait for you.*

Olivia was beginning to put the pieces of the puzzle together. A secret dating account... hundreds of transactions from the men she spoke to online...

"She was scamming them," Olivia whispered. She scrolled further up the conversation. "Look here. She managed to convince Daniel that she was running away from her abusive partner. She said she needed money to get out of the country. And he fell for it."

"Looks like he wasn't the only one," Brock noted sadly. "She had a story for every single one of these men."

"There are so many here," Olivia said. "It's not just Belle. There was Clarissa, Danielle, Evelyn, Franchesca… it's like she had fresh photos and profiles set up designed to lure in different types of men."

"Well, it worked."

Olivia and Brock fell silent as they untangled Arabella's web of lies. In one message, she claimed to need money to stop her from losing her home. In another, she said she needed to pay for her daughter's medical bills. There was such a creative array of stories woven into each message thread that Olivia was almost impressed. And the worst part was that by the end of each message thread, every single man had parted with a significant amount of money.

Brock raised a finger. "That gives me an idea."

He called up Andrew's tablet and phone, and after a few minutes of typing and searching, turned the screens around to her.

"Boom," he crowed.

"What am I looking at exactly?" Olivia asked. "This is just a bunch of words and numbers."

"They're accounts and passwords. Look."

Now he took his own phone and typed in the very first username in the list he'd called up. Sure enough, an account came up. There was a whole persona there, complete with random posts and interactions with others—but also, very regularly, there were posts begging people to donate to a charity cause.

"*Help Me Afford My Medicine*," Olivia whispered. "What is this?"

"Look at this one." Brock pulled up a second account. It seemed very similar to the first, except this time the fundraiser was for funeral costs for a family member who'd been hit by a drunk driver.

"There are at least three or four dozen accounts on that list," Brock said gravely. "I'm sure every one of them has a sob story."

"And every single one of them pressures people to send money for their misfortunes."

"They set this up together. This is how they keep themselves rich and happy. I'll bet that neither of them ever worked in finance. They were simply con artists all along. And there are hundreds of messages here. This has been going on for some time. I wonder if someone finally got their revenge on Arabella and Andrew."

"It's entirely possible," Olivia muttered. "And one thing's for sure: if we're looking for scorned lovers or scammed marks, we have a whole bunch of them here. I don't think we've just got one suspect here. I think we've got hundreds."

CHAPTER EIGHT

It was around 9 p.m. when Olivia and Brock decided to call it a night and order takeout. The vast number of catfish accounts, fake fundraisers, and other messages was simply staggering. It took Brock all evening just to get all the information organized, while Olivia spent hours reading through the messages between Arabella and the various scam victims. She was beginning to realize that any one of the victims might have been capable of killing her and her husband. Not only was she scamming them out of thousands of dollars, but she was also humiliating them in the process.

Olivia tried to put herself in the shoes of the victims and picture how they would feel. She would feel angry. Betrayed. It would be horrifying to lose so much money for such a terrible reason. To have someone you trusted, you supposedly loved, turn out to simply be using you.

But would it be enough to make her kill someone?

Maybe she was lucky enough to know that she could move on from something like that, but so many others wouldn't be able to. What if that online romance was the one thing they had going in their life? What if they cleared out their account for someone who didn't turn out to be real? That would crush her, she knew that much. But for some people, that might be enough to make them turn to murder.

The question was, which of the victims would go that far?

"Stop thinking about it," Brock told Olivia. She blinked.

"What?"

"The case. You never switch off. That's why you never sleep, you know."

Olivia sighed with a short laugh. "I can't help myself. I get caught up in it. Don't you?"

"Of course, I do. I love the mystery of it all. But I like to live in the real world sometimes too. I want to be right here, right now."

"Does that have anything to do with the fact that you just ordered a nineteen-inch meat feast pizza?"

Brock grinned at her. "Only partially."

Olivia felt grateful that Brock seemed to be much less frosty with her now. It was like he had forgotten about the whole ordeal with Tom. Olivia was hoping that maybe the subject wouldn't even come up again, but she was sure that they'd circle back to it. After all, she'd completely neglected to tell him about a huge part of her life. In his shoes, she would probably feel just as curious about his past.

But Tom was exactly that: the past. Yes, she had cared for him deeply once. Yes, she would never quite shake him off entirely. After all, they'd been engaged once upon a time. But that didn't matter because he didn't have a place in her future.

Or did he? Had he come to Belle Grove knowing that she would be there? Did he have regrets about the way they'd left things? And if he did, was he hoping for a second chance to fix it all? And was she willing to give it to him?

Olivia sighed and pushed away the thoughts. There she was again, never quite managing to switch off. Maybe that was why she could never make something last. She was too busy getting caught up in her own head, deliberating over every little thing. It would cost her down the line—she was sure of it. When she forced herself back into the present, Brock was staring at her, a small smile playing on his lips.

"What?" she asked, turning away from the intense scrutiny of his gaze. She sometimes forgot that having a partner in her line of work meant he noticed every little thing about her. She had no doubt that Brock could read her like a book.

"Nothing. Just watching you drift off again," he shrugged. "Let me guess. You're thinking about the scam? How a victim would feel if the person they thought they loved turned out to be fake?"

Olivia swallowed. She couldn't exactly be honest with him this time around. She couldn't tell him that she was thinking about Tom.

"I guess it was on my mind," she said carefully. Brock flopped down on his twin bed, staring up at the ceiling with his hands behind his head.

"My therapist once told me that our line of work is dangerous. Not because we throw ourselves into the firing line every day, but because we become consumed by it," Brock said. He glanced over at Olivia. "I used to be more like you. I could never switch off. Not quite as intense and obsessed though. I don't think anyone can match you in that department—"

"Hey!"

"—but I was pretty into the work. I used to push myself to my limit because I felt like I had to. I taught myself to be almost robotic, to go through the motions and to keep feelings off the table where a case was involved. I told myself that the more my heart was in it, the more dangerous it became. So, I applied my mind instead until I was exhausting myself. I worked myself to the bone. And it felt good in so many ways. How could it not when I was solving cases left, right, and center?"

"Is that a trick question? Because I feel like it actually is."

It was intended to be a joke, but Brock didn't laugh. He shot Olivia a glance that told her he was actually being serious for once.

"I lived that way for a few years. And when I finally came up for air, I realized how much my life had changed without me noticing. I'd let myself drift away from the people I cared about. I had lost so much that I hadn't even realized I had."

Brock closed his eyes for a moment, and Olivia realized that he was doing his best to be open with her. It was something he'd steered clear of before. In fact, she usually had to press him to speak this way. But she got the feeling that he wanted something in return.

He wanted answers out of her.

"I just think you should be careful," Brock said quietly. "Because before you know it, years will pass you by, and you won't even realize it. You'll wonder where the time went. You'll wonder why you never did those things you wanted to, right in the back of your mind." Brock paused, his eyes softer as he looked at Olivia. "I just have one question. And I promise I won't push you any farther after that, okay?"

Olivia shifted onto her side, looking directly at Brock. "Okay..."

"I just want to know, is that why you and Tom split up? Because you were both so consumed by your work?"

Olivia almost smiled. Brock really did know her well. He knew the one thing that would come between her and something she wanted was her work. Because it was true. She was obsessed. She cared about her work more than almost anything in the world.

But he wasn't entirely correct either. Because she knew that if she found someone worth her time, someone worth her attention, she'd give up everything to be with that person. The one thing she'd never truly admitted to herself was that was the reason she'd been okay when she and Tom broke up. It had hurt, sure. She'd mourned that love for some time, definitely. But there was one good reason why it didn't break her completely.

Because he wasn't what she was looking for.

"Partly," Olivia admitted. "Work was a big factor. He cared a lot about his work, just like I did. We both found ourselves with little time. But... but I think if it was meant to work out between us, then we would have found more time for one another."

Brock nodded and smiled a little. Olivia didn't know if it was because he was glad she'd opened up or because he liked her answer, but he did seem more at ease.

"And you don't think that you'll go back there?" Brock asked. Olivia raised her eyebrow at him.

"I thought you only had one question?"

Brock didn't say anything, but Olivia could see in his eyes that the answer was important to him. She didn't know why it mattered so much to him, but she didn't want to hold back any more secrets from him. It made no sense when he was always the person she wanted to share everything with. She felt closer to Brock than anyone else in her life. Why shouldn't he know the truth?

"I never rule anything out. But what happened between me and Tom happened for a good reason. I cared for him a lot. Maybe I will always have some love in my heart for him. But I don't see a world where we will be together again," Olivia said as honestly as she could. It wasn't much, but it would have to do.

Brock nodded, seeming to understand exactly where she was coming from. But as her phone buzzed on the nightstand, both of their eyes were drawn to it. There he was again. Olivia hadn't even replied to Tom's messages, hadn't even read what he had to say, and yet the messages kept coming. Brock sat up straight, raising his eyebrows.

"Does he know that?" Brock asked, suddenly withdrawn again. He stood up. "I'm gonna go pick up some beer from the corner store."

He left before Olivia could say anything. She cursed under her breath. Just when she thought that she and Brock were getting back on track, he was set off again. Why did it matter so much to him? She could understand him being upset about her keeping secrets from him. That much made sense to her. But why did he care if Olivia went back to Tom, or if Tom was still interested in her?

Olivia sat with her thoughts for a moment. For once, she felt completely grounded in the present moment. The case had well and truly been shoved to the back of her mind. She allowed herself to properly think about Brock and what he might want. Was it possible that this hostility was coming from a place of jealousy? Was the sudden appearance of her ex-fiancé making him feel like he'd been shunted away?

Olivia's heart was racing. The possibility that he might actually care about her as more than a friend, always lurking around the back of her mind, suddenly burst to the forefront. Their relationship had been fast-tracked from the beginning. They spent every waking hour together, even when they weren't working a case. They'd slept over at one another's places countless times, and they'd shared enough motel rooms that she knew the sound of him sleeping as well as she knew her ex-fiancé's breathing in the night.

But he had never said anything to make her think he was interested. Unless she counted all of the teasing, which she never had before. She suddenly felt like the reality of their situation was thrown into sharp relief, the edges of it clear against her mind, illuminating truths that she hadn't wanted to admit.

Had she ever really believed that Brock moved to Belle Grove simply because he thought they worked well together? Who would move to a sleepy little rural town just because their coworker was there?

Surely some part of her had never been convinced of that. But what did that mean now that the revelation was right there for her to openly contemplate?

She put her head in her hands, feeling like the whole world was crashing down on her shoulders. How were they supposed to go on as normal now with such a big elephant in the room? Was she supposed to acknowledge what she thought she knew? Was she supposed to reassure Brock when she wasn't even sure that was what he wanted?

No. Whatever was going on his head—or hers, for that matter—now wasn't the time or the place. They had to remain professional, at least until the case was over. Then, maybe they could talk about it. Maybe they could both try to untangle the complicated feelings that they'd stored up since they met. Because now there was no going back. There was no pushing it under the rug and hoping it wouldn't resurface.

She stood up and began to pace the room. It was a complication, this thing with Brock. And a complication was the last thing she needed or wanted in her life. She had enough on her plate with her family issues and her obsession with work. She really couldn't afford the stress of this on top of everything else.

But she also knew that some things were worth the stress. Some risks were worth it. Wasn't this thing she'd found with Brock special? She'd always thought so. Even if it turned out to be nothing more than a friendship, it was an important one. And whatever it took to keep the peace with Brock, she was willing to do it. Even if that meant telling Tom to back off.

Out of curiosity, she grabbed her phone and checked out the messages. She scanned them quickly, her heart softening a little as she read them.

Tom: *Sorry to keep messaging you. I know you must be busy. It's just that seeing you the other day made me feel some kind of way. Maybe it's just me?*

Tom: *I should stop texting you. You probably don't want to know. It's been so long since we last spoke, and we made things pretty clear between us when we split. But is it just me that hasn't let it go?*

Tom: *Sorry. Last message. I miss you, Olivia. Maybe we can try the whole friends thing? Let me know. Okay. I'll shut up now.*

Olivia found herself smiling at the messages. That was the Tom she knew. So suave until it came to matters of the heart, in times when it actually mattered or meant something. He had always seemed cool as a cucumber to everyone on the outside, but Olivia knew him better than that.

And suddenly, it felt cruel to ignore him. They used to be so close. Even when it had become clear to them both that their relationship was surviving on life support, she still cared deeply for him. Would being friends be such a bad thing? Wasn't it possible for them to be civil with one another without it having to mean anything?

Olivia wavered, wondering how to respond. She knew she was playing with fire. If she spoke to Tom, it would only encourage him. And entertaining Tom would be like punching Brock straight in the face. But from her perspective, she cared about them both. Maybe she hadn't figured out what they both meant to her yet, but they still mattered. She didn't want to upset either of them, but she also had to think about herself.

Olivia sighed as she slid her phone back into her pocket without responding to the messages. She needed more time to sort her head out. She didn't like that she was leaving Tom hanging, but she also knew she needed Brock to be on good terms with her during their case. It was ironic to her that for once, her mind wasn't on a case, but she wished it was. This was why she didn't linger for too long in the real world. It was all too messy, too complicated.

Brock returned several minutes later with a six-pack and offered one to Olivia. She took it, wondering what she was going to say to him. Brock sat down opposite her on his own bed, watching her intently.

"Did you see what Tom wanted?" he asked as he popped open his bottle. Olivia drew in a deep breath. So, he was diving straight in the deep end. He'd never been one to pry before, but then again, she usually told him everything. This was new territory, and she was treading carefully through it.

"He wants to try being friends."

"And what did you say to that? You know that guys never want to be just friends when they say that, right? Especially not your ex. There's a reason he said 'try' to be friends... because he doesn't see you that way."

"Brock?"

"Mmm?"

"I'm an FBI agent. I'm smart enough to know a guy's intentions," Olivia said with a smile. Brock paused before laughing to himself.

"Okay, sorry. That was the mansplaining of the century, right?"

"Apology accepted. But in answer to your question... I don't know what I'm going to say to him yet. I'm giving it some time. We're living in the same town now, so I guess it would be nice if we could be on a friendly level with one another." She paused, then continued. "But that doesn't mean I'm running back into his arms, Brock. Right now, my life is complicated enough. I haven't even thought about romance in so long. It's not at the top of my priorities. But what you said before struck a chord with me. It really did."

"About being intense and obsessed?"

She rolled her eyes. "About being more present in my own life. I guess what I'm trying to say is, I want to open myself up to possibilities. Seize life with both hands. And maybe somewhere along the way, that'll mean that something happens with… someone."

The pause between them was so long that it made Olivia's heart stop temporarily. He was looking at her so intently that it made her stomach do a backflip. Now there was something she hadn't experienced in a long time.

But she wasn't going to let herself be swept up. She had to sort the fact from fiction in her mind, to figure out what she was feeling. When she looked at Brock, she felt so many different things, but they all blended into one. She'd never really given herself time to sit down with her own emotions or decide what they meant. Now, she had to make sure that she did. She couldn't allow anyone to get hurt just because she was too oblivious to see what was right before her eyes.

She had to know if this was something more.

But fortunately, she didn't have to decide right at that moment. A knock on the motel door broke the spell between her and Brock. He smiled at her.

"Saved by the bell," he murmured. Olivia exhaled a sigh of relief as he got up to pay the delivery boy. She was in the clear for now.

But eventually, she would have to face up to her own feelings.

CHAPTER NINE

OLIVIA KNEW IT WAS GOING TO BE ANOTHER LONG DAY by the time she'd read through her fifth message chain on Arabella's account. In fact, it had been a few long days holed up in the little motel, scouring the devices for clues and making exhaustive lists of the scam victims.

Brock took charge of Andrew's various social media scams while Olivia looked through the catfishing profiles that Arabella ran. It seemed that the scams Arabella was running were both clever and targeted. Not only had she used her sex appeal and confidence to draw in men, but she had chosen very specific people for her exploits.

"Another divorcee," Olivia murmured, making notes as she went along. She was reading through the message chain between

Arabella's pseudonym 'Gayle' and a man named Kenneth Sands, who had told her that he had been divorced for a year and that his ex-wife had remarried already. Olivia clicked on Kenneth's profile to try to get a clearer idea of the sort of men that Arabella targeted. As with the previous four scam victims, Olivia could see that he was middle-aged, average-looking, and clearly lonely. His biography claimed that he was looking for a 'long-term companion' and a 'second-chance romance.' Olivia sighed. She could see how easy it must have been for Arabella to worm her way into the lives of these men. They were desperate to be loved, broken from previous marriages, and enticed by her good looks.

"Arabella really knew what she was doing when she picked these guys out," Olivia told Brock. He nodded. "Most of them living alone. No kids, or if they have them, they've flown the nest. These people weren't looking for something casual, that's for sure."

Brock nodded. "I'm thinking if we do find a suspect here it will be from one of Arabella's marks. Andrew's were more general—he wasn't asking people to send thousands to their lover. He was preying on their charity. On the people who want to make a difference by donating a little bit here or there to a good cause. But almost by necessity, that means they couldn't have had much emotional connection to the story. Not like yours."

Olivia nodded. "They wanted to fall in love, and Arabella let them," she said. She felt angry on behalf of all of the victims, but she almost wanted to shake them. How had they been so blind to what was happening to them? She stared at the screen in front of her, the words blurring together. "These people were all desperate. They wanted this more than anything. I wonder… did any of them realize after their lover dropped off the face of the earth that they'd been scammed?"

"How could they not?" Brock asked, shaking his head. "I mean, they must have had time to sit down and truly think about it, right? Anyone with half a brain could put two and two together and see that they disappeared right after they got the money."

"That's what I thought at first. But Arabella played it smart. She always said she had a reason to go off-grid before she disappeared. When she said she was running from her abusive partner, she claimed she needed to go into hiding. When she said she was visiting her long-lost sister, she said she needed some time to reconnect with her. She was smart about this. Maybe some of them are oblivious even now."

"At least after this is over, we can try to help these people get their money back. Though I'm sure Josephine will have something to say about us dipping into her inheritance," Brock rolled his eyes. "Money does strange things to people."

"No doubt. Have you seen anything yet that makes you think that the victims might have a murderous streak in them?"

Brock shook his head. "Not really. I'm figuring that Andrew's side of things might be a dry well."

"What makes you say that?"

"I just don't know that Andrew's victims would have such an emotional flare-up. I mean, you've seen all those fundraisers on social media before, right?"

Olivia nodded. "I've donated to a few."

"Same here. And for all we know, maybe some of them were scams. But it was just twenty bucks, you know? Not a big deal in the grand scheme."

"That probably made it easier for those people to quickly donate," Olivia noted. "They wouldn't have had to develop the intense personal relationships that Arabella was cultivating."

"My thoughts exactly. Most of these people dropped their twenty bucks and went on with their lives. I can't imagine someone would hunt down and kill someone over twenty bucks, right?"

"I'm not ruling anything out at this point," replied Olivia.

"Well, I just can't find anything indicating any threat or realization that they were scammed after all. That doesn't mean much though. We don't know anything about the people on the other side of the screen."

Olivia sighed. "That's true. I never really thought of it that way. Everyone puts up a front online, don't they? It's like a separate persona in some ways. It makes some people more confident and others more withdrawn. I guess we can't presume anything about these people based on these messages."

She rubbed at her temple. "This is going to be tough. There must be hundreds of message chains here. How are we supposed to sort through them all and decide who might be capable of murder or not? It's not possible."

"We just need to keep looking. Find some online activity that'd help us narrow things down a bit."

"I thought that's what you were doing," Olivia replied.

"And I am," he chuckled, showing her the notebook he'd been scribbling in all morning with the various information, connections, and observations of the accounts. "But Rome wasn't built in a day."

Olivia groaned and pinched the bridge of her nose. "This is going to take forever."

Brock regarded her with a kind look. "Hey, why don't you go and grab us some coffee, take a quick break? You look like you could use it."

Olivia found herself smiling. Since their slightly uncomfortable conversation the night before, she'd been looking at him in a new light. He wasn't just Brock anymore—her goofy, witty, smart partner and friend. He was something so much more. He was a man that she craved time with. He was someone that she knew would always have her back, no matter what. And most of all, he was a guy that she could see herself falling for.

And he knew her so well. He knew even before she did when she needed to take a break. He knew that there was more coffee than blood running through her veins. And he knew exactly how to make her feel better when days got tough.

"Okay. I'll be back soon." She left the motel room and walked down the balcony to the rickety old coffee machine. After fishing some coins from her pocket and waiting for the coffee to trickle out of the machine, she felt her phone buzz in her pocket. Her heart froze, wondering if it was Tom again. He'd promised to stop messaging, but she knew that he was a persistent man. She took out her phone but found herself relieved when she realized it wasn't him.

Until she saw that it was her mother.

Mom: Hey, Olivia. It's only a week until Thanksgiving now. Have you decided what your plans are yet? We would love for you to spend the holiday with us. Mom.

Olivia sighed and shoved her phone back into her pocket. Somehow, she'd managed to push Thanksgiving to the back of her mind. She hadn't even realized how close they were to the holiday. Now she was being forced to face a decision she really didn't want to make. She knew she would disappoint her family if she didn't show up; but then again, they had disappointed her plenty of times without caring much. Maybe it was her turn to be a little selfish. Why should she force herself to spend the holidays with her family after everything they'd put her through?

Because this is your chance to make things right with them again, Olivia told herself. The truth set a heaviness into the pit of her stomach that made her feel nauseous. She knew that the bridges that had been burned between them couldn't be fixed in a day, but she also knew that they'd never be fixed if she didn't put in some effort. She'd spent so long wishing her mother would come home, wishing that things would fix themselves once again. Wouldn't she be crazy to keep putting that off?

Olivia didn't know what to think as she grabbed the cups and headed back to the room. Brock looked up from Andrew's tablet with a smile as she returned, but his face soon fell when he clocked Olivia's expression.

"Tom again?"

Olivia sighed, setting down the cups on the nightstand. "I almost wish it was."

"Family stuff?" he prodded. "They're dogging you about Thanksgiving again?"

Olivia nodded, sitting down on the edge of the bed. "I wish they would just give me some space. It's too much pressure too soon. I know that they want to see me, to fix things... but I don't feel like I'm ready yet. I don't know when I will be. I mean, am I crazy? She was gone for five whole years. Five years of my life! And now she just wants to act like it never happened. Like it's as easy as sitting down to eat some turkey and picking up right where we left off."

"You're not crazy, Olivia. You're right," Brock said gently. "In your shoes, I think anyone would feel the same. They shouldn't have put you in this position. It's not fair. You've already done enough for them by even considering that you might forgive them. You don't owe them your Thanksgiving."

Olivia nodded, but she knew it was more complicated than that. She'd learned long ago that when it came to family, she wouldn't always get what she wanted. She also knew that if she wanted this mess to be cleaned up, then she had to comply with some rules. Olivia groaned in frustration and lay back on her bed for a moment.

"I know everything you're saying is true, but I feel so guilty," she began. "Like it's my fault that things are going so badly in our family. Like it's my fault that we can't move on from this. And I know that logically that isn't true because most people in my position would've given up a long time ago. But it's still in my hands, you know? As usual, my parents are putting the ball in my court, but still expecting me to do exactly as they want. It just… well, it sucks."

"I know," Brock said quietly. He offered her a smile. "You know, we never talked more about a quiet Thanksgiving in Belle Grove. Just you and me."

Olivia's heart skipped a beat. The offer had seemed innocent when they'd first talked about it, but now, it felt emotionally charged. What would it mean for them both if they spent an intimate Thanksgiving together? Would it mean taking their relationship to a new level?

The thought rocked Olivia to her core. She wasn't ready for that. She was still coming to terms with everything she was feeling. She had too many emotions going on at once for her to make sense of any of them. But Brock's face looked so hopeful, and she knew he was hoping that she would say yes. He wanted to know that they were on the same page.

But the problem was, she wasn't sure they were yet. It was too soon for her to commit to it, and way too complicated. If they were together, it would change everything. Their work relationship, their friendship, their entire lives. Olivia wasn't sure she was ready for that kind of explosion in her life.

LOVE, LIES, AND SUICIDE

But now she was stuck between a rock and a hard place. Brock had seemed like the safe Thanksgiving option before. She knew she could rely on having a good day with him without any pressure. But now, that felt different too. It felt like accepting the offer had to mean something. Olivia took a deep breath, not sure how she was going to respond to him. She allowed words to spill out of her mouth.

"I don't know what I'm going to do yet," Olivia said carefully. "I have to consider going to my parents. You understand, right?"

Brock nodded. Olivia felt terrible, knowing that it seemed like she was blowing him off, but that wasn't the case at all. Deep down, she knew that she'd rather spend the day with him. It would be a happier day, at least. But she didn't want to rush into something with him and then later regret it. He was the best thing that had happened to her in a long time. If anything was going to jeopardize that, then she didn't want to be a part of it.

"Sorry," she said. "I just need to figure this out."

"Don't worry about it," Brock said. "Take all the time you need. But the offer isn't going anywhere, Olivia. It's like I said. Thanksgiving doesn't mean much to me these days. But I'd rather spend it with you than anyone else."

Olivia tried to push the emotion away as she sat back down in front of Arabella's laptop. Her entire "break" had left her feeling more stressed than before. But she told herself to get her head down and concentrate on the case. At least the problem in front of her was one that she could eventually solve. No messy emotions had to be involved. It was just her and her brain against the case.

The hours seemed to drag on. Olivia spent hours staring at the screen until her eyes ached. The more messages she read, the more she began to resent Arabella and Andrew Clifford. They were terrible people, that much was clear. They spent all of their time conning innocent people into giving up their money just so that they could live a life of luxury in a house they didn't deserve. How many lies had they told the world? No wonder Arabella never wanted to discuss work with her mother. Not when her seemingly imaginary job in finance was actually just one big scam.

It made Olivia sick to her stomach. She could only imagine how the victims themselves felt. But even as she read through endless messages, she couldn't imagine a single one of them seeking out revenge. The people who were talking to Arabella were lonely, broken, and depressed, but they all seemed like good people. They had to be on some level to be willing to give up their hard-earned money to a stranger. None of these men seemed capable of hunting Arabella down and ending her life.

And that was another thing that struck Olivia as odd. How would they even go about finding her in the first place? Under the guise of Belle, Arabella never gave away any true personal details. She never even showed her full face. In fact, her entire personality on Singles Match was a lie. So how was anyone ever supposed to track her down? A normal person with no resources likely wouldn't have the means to try to find her. And clearly, none of them had thought to get in contact with the police because Arabella and Andrew had gotten off scot-free…

Until someone ended their lives.

Olivia still couldn't make sense of it. Maybe they were wrong. Maybe all this time had been wasted and the killer wasn't one of their scam victims after all. If Arabella and Andrew were capable of something as cruel as preying on vulnerable people for money, then maybe they were capable of much worse too. And if that was the case, maybe they had people practically lining up to get a shot at them.

The more Olivia tried to make sense of it, the more her head felt like it was going to explode. There was too much going on in her mind at once. She was over thirty messages in and was still watching victims fall to Arabella's charms like flies. And still, none of them seemed like likely subjects.

Until she opened the next message chain.

Olivia held her breath as she read the final message on the chain. Her eyes had been drawn to it right away, and now, as she processed what it said, she felt a rush of excitement.

Had they found their killer?

"Brock… you need to take a look at this."

Brock was at her side in an instant, reading the message on the screen. His eyes widened.

"I know that you scammed me," Olivia read aloud. "You must think you're so slick, taking advantage of people who have already lost everything. I'm going to make you pay for this. I'm going to hunt you down. And when I find you, you're dead."

Silence followed as Brock and Olivia considered the message on the screen. Olivia took a shaky breath.

"This guy, whoever he is … he sent this message several weeks ago. Is it possible that he found her somehow?"

"Maybe so," Brock breathed. "And he seems like a pretty impulsive guy. The fact that he didn't try to delete these messages makes it seem like he's not thinking straight. Instead of going to the police, he took matters into his own hands. Who is this guy?"

"Let's take a look at his profile and see if we can track him down," Olivia said, quickly clicking the biography of the man. A picture of a handsome man in his mid-thirties showed up on the screen. He seemed different from the other victims, somehow a less likely victim.

"Sergio Romero. Here for a good time, not a long time," Brock read aloud, wrinkling his nose. "Echhh."

"Single man, no baggage, looking for a beautiful lady to spoil rotten," Olivia continued. The whole profile struck her as odd for reasons she couldn't explain. But it was the best lead they had, and she knew they needed to follow it up. She scanned the rest of his details. "He's local. Just outside of Richmond. No address, but I'm sure we can find that pretty easily. And look here," she pointed.

Brock's eyebrows both raised suddenly. "He's an installer at SleepSafe Alarms?"

"The same company that installed the Cliffords' alarms," she confirmed.

"If anyone could hack into the system, it'd be him," Brock said, straightening up and grabbing his jacket. He shot Olivia a smile, like the thrill of it all had gotten to him. "Let's go."

Olivia couldn't help smiling back, because what was better than working a case with him? What was better than chasing down leads with him at her side? She felt a thrill pass through her like a shockwave as they left the motel room behind and headed for Brock's car. She never felt better than when she was with him.

And she didn't want to leave his side any time soon.

CHAPTER TEN

THE DRIVE TO SERGIO ROMERO'S HOME FELT AS EXCITING as being in a high-speed chase. Olivia was ready to put a close on the case, to pin the murders on the man who'd promised to make Arabella pay for what she'd done. It seemed perfect. Like it just made total sense. But Olivia tried to remind herself not to rush ahead. She knew that even clean-cut cases often had curveballs that she wasn't expecting.

Still, Sergio seemed like the only likely candidate out of so many. He had literally threatened to kill her himself. He wanted her dead for what she'd done. Now, Olivia was going to get answers out of him. Did he really have blood on his hands, or was he all talk?

LOVE, LIES, AND SUICIDE

As they closed in on Sergio's address, Olivia began to feel antsy with anticipation. If they could pin him as their killer, their case would be done in almost record time. She would be glad to see the back of the case and of the Cliffords. Then, she could focus on helping the victims of the scams get their money back. At least then some justice would be done.

So long as they could get Sergio to confess.

"When we get there, let's press him gently," Brock said. "If the messages he sent are anything to go by, it seems like he's pretty volatile. We don't want to give him any reason to get violent."

"Definitely not," Olivia agreed. "We can ask him about his profile and see if he gives anything up. And then, if he doesn't play fair, we can squeeze more out of him. I really feel like this has got to be it, Brock. Those messages seem clear as day to me."

"I'm with you. But you know this job. It's best to expect the unexpected."

Olivia nodded, trying to calm her racing heart. The thought of coming face to face with a potential killer was always a daunting one, but she was ready for it. Nearly a week of searching, and this was the first solid lead they'd turned up. She could only hope this path would bear fruit.

It was late afternoon, and the sun was beginning to disappear. As they parked in Sergio's neighborhood, Olivia was struck by how normal the place seemed. She was used to killers of all backgrounds—killers from rough neighborhoods or those who lived in huge mansions—but the sleepy little neighborhood seemed perfectly normal. There wasn't much of interest around. The lawns were well-manicured, and the cars seemed in reasonably good shape. It could have been any middle-class neighborhood. Olivia knew more than most how sleepy little places like this could still harbor dark secrets, but everything seemed, well, normal.

Olivia secured her gun on her belt and covered it with her jacket as they got out of the car and walked up the driveway to Sergio's home. The flower gardens out front waited patiently, their stalks bare, for spring to return. The hedges were neatly kept and freshly pruned for winter. Even the bougainvillea seemed perfectly trimmed. Inside, there was a light on in the living room, and the sound of laughter came from inside. It sent a shiver down her spine, and she looked at Brock.

"Why does it feel like we've got the wrong house already?" Olivia whispered to him. Brock checked his phone.

"This is the right place," he insisted, stepping up to the front door and rapping his fist on it. "Let's not let our guard down."

Olivia nodded. He was right. Just because the whole thing seemed off, it didn't mean that it was. She heard footsteps inside the house and more laughter, but she tried not to allow that to distract her focus. They had good enough reason to believe Sergio was the guy they were looking for. She couldn't forget that.

But when the door opened, and the man stood before them with a toddler rested on his hip and a smile on his face, Olivia was a little taken aback. Sergio was even more handsome than in his dating photographs, and he had the kind of smile that made strangers want to smile back. He blinked at Olivia and Brock, looking a little taken aback himself.

"Oh. I'm sorry. I was expecting the pizza guy. I had a tip ready and everything," Sergio said lightly, waving a few bills in his hand. Then his eyes fell on Brock's outstretched badge, and he looked shocked. His face fell a little. "Um. What is going on?"

"Are you Sergio Romero?" asked Brock.

Sergio adjusted the toddler on his hip, his face creased in concern. "Yes, that's right. Can I help you with something?"

"I'm Special Agent Brock Tanner, this is my partner Special Agent Olivia Knight, with the FBI. We just want a few minutes of your time. We have some questions for you."

Sergio wavered for a moment, completely speechless. Olivia followed his darting eyes, wondering if he was about to break for it. But after a moment, he set the toddler in his arms down on her feet and kissed the top of her head.

"Go and tell Mommy that I've got guests," he said gently, watching his child run back off into the kitchen. Then he straightened up and ushered them inside.

"Um. Okay. Come in. Let's sit in the lounge. I don't want to disturb my family."

Olivia felt tense as she stepped inside Romero's home and he closed the door behind them. It was a nice place; nothing too opulent or showy, but definitely the house of a real family. All around the room were tall plants in beautifully decorated pots: fiddle-leaf figs, snake plants, fishtail palms, and crotons. More plants were hung up in macrame hangers or on shelves mounted on the walls. One corner was set aside with larger pots resting under a grow light, waiting for the right time to return out front in warmer weather. It was obvious that the Romeros took pride in their collection.

She kept her eyes focused on the man as he led the way into the lounge. Brock stood by the sofa, waiting to be invited to sit down. It amazed Olivia that he was being so polite when they were potentially in the presence of a killer.

"Make yourselves at home, please," Sergio said. "Can I make you some tea? Coffee?"

"No, thank you. We'd prefer to just get to the point," Brock said. Sergio sank slowly into his seat, wringing his hands together.

"Okay... I'm really not sure what's going on here. Perhaps you can help me out," he said.

Brock nodded. "Okay, Mr. Romero. What we would really like to ask you about is your dating profile."

Shock crossed Sergio's face so fast that he didn't have a chance to cover it up. He glanced over at the doorway in horror.

"What the hell are you talking about?" he asked. "Dating profile?"

"Your profile on Singles Match?" Olivia pressed.

"Are you crazy?" he hissed. "My wife is in the other room!"

"I suppose that's something you like to keep private then?" she asked innocently. Sergio couldn't hide the horror from his face. He looked so guilty at that moment that Olivia wondered if her initial impression of him had been wrong after all.

"Look, I don't know what you want here, but I've got a beautiful wife two rooms over. I love her with all of my heart. Why the hell would I have a dating profile?" Sergio asked. "If she hears you saying that, I'm going to be in for a world of pain. Please, what is this really about?"

Olivia scrutinized his face, looking for any signs that he was bluffing, but she didn't think he was. He looked genuinely frustrated and confused at what they were saying. And rather than being concerned for himself, he seemed more worried that his wife might think badly of him.

"Is this you?" Brock asked, turning his phone around to show Sergio's profile, pulled up on the site. Sergio stared at it, blinking in disbelief.

"I—um—"

"Well?"

"Well, yes. But, no. I mean, that picture is of me, but I did *not* make that profile, I swear." He scrolled through some of the information written on the profile. "Interest in boating? What the hell is this?" he asked. "I'm telling you, this is not me. I've never been on a boat in my life."

They had no way of proving or disproving that, of course, but it was something to consider.

"So that's not your profile from when you were single?" Olivia prodded.

"Sarah and I have been married for five years. We dated for three years before that. I've never once used an online dating service. We met at a bar. Yes, that's my name and my picture, but I have nothing to do with it."

"Well, someone did," Brock said. "We have reason to believe that you were messaging a woman named Belle. She asked you for a large sum of money, which you provided for her. And after she took your money and disappeared, you then threatened to track her down and end her life. Does that ring any bells for you?"

Sergio's mouth fell open. "What? Of course not!"

"Everything okay, honey?" came a voice from the other room.

"Everything's fine," he replied.

"What's taking the piz—" the woman's voice trailed off as she rounded the corner into the room, "—za so long?" she tacked on, confusion written all over her face.

Olivia turned to her. "Special Agents Knight and Tanner with the FBI," she explained. "Just asking some questions to your husband here."

She immediately took up a spot next to him and laced her fingers in his. It was an automatic gesture, the kind that only comes from years of repetition. "Has something happened?"

LOVE, LIES, AND SUICIDE

Brock cleared his throat. "We're just investigating the possibility that your husband has been"—Sergio shot him a look—"possibly the victim of fraud or identity theft."

Sarah looked over at Sergio and he nodded. "Apparently somebody has been using my name and pictures to set up fake profiles on dating sites," he explained. Sarah's mouth fell open in shock. "But I swear it wasn't me. You know it wasn't," he cut in before she could react.

Olivia was torn. She still had no way of knowing whether or not this man was a killer. They had no proof either way. Either he was a very good actor, or he was telling the truth. But she couldn't write off that first option.

"If you don't mind, I'd like to confirm the evidence so we can get on with our investigation," she started. "You—or the person posing as you—sent a transaction in the amount of thirty-five hundred dollars to a woman named Belle just a few weeks ago, on the twenty-ninth of October. And then that woman disappeared, leaving you high and dry. After this, you—or the person posing as you—sent the following messages on November sixth."

She nodded her head to Brock to read them out loud. He cleared his throat and started from the beginning.

"... I'm going to make you pay for this. I'm going to hunt you down. And when I find you, you're dead."

Sergio sat there in stunned silence as the words rang out in the room.

"I'm telling you, agents, that's not me," he stammered. "I can't—I can't imagine any situation I'd say anything like that."

"Well, you'd better hope not, because the woman on the receiving end of those messages has been found murdered," Olivia told him. She decided to keep the very last bit of information back, just in case—that he worked for the same company that provided their alarm system. For now, she would see how they reacted.

Sarah clapped her hands over her mouth in shock. Sergio's mouth opened and closed like a fish.

"Murdered?" he finally whispered. "Oh, God. And I'm the suspect..."

A mix of emotions played out on Sarah's face. She didn't seem sure who to believe: the FBI agents presenting her the evidence or her own husband's protests.

"Agents," she started, looking from them to her husband and back. "What can we do to prove it wasn't him?"

"To start, we'd like to see your financial records from that time frame."

Sarah gave her husband an intent look. He gulped and nodded, fully aware of the situation he'd found himself in. "Of course. Take whatever you need. I can provide bank records. ID. Emails. What do you need to prove that this wasn't me?"

He seemed firm, determined to provide the evidence of his innocence. But the evidence had been right there in front of them. Sergio's messages to Belle had promised violence. But now he was claiming that he wasn't even the one who sent the messages.

Were Arabella and Andrew the only catfishes in town? Or were they dealing with another?

"There's something else you should know, Mr. Romero," Olivia said. "The victim had a security system installed by your employer, SafeSleep Alarms. There's record of an unauthorized entry the night of the murder, but the call was canceled by the two-minute grace period. As of now, it seems you have both motive and opportunity."

Sergio's eyes went wide. "I—that couldn't have been me," he stammered. "The alarm reset code is set by the homeowner. It's company policy that the installers have to leave before they do, so we can't reset it."

"We'll be following up with your employer for that," Olivia told him.

"I swear, this is not me. I've never heard of this Belle person in my life. That's not my account."

"If this account isn't made by you, then who could it be?" Brock pressed. "Is there anyone who would be willing to frame you for something like this? Someone who would try to assume your identity?"

Sergio shrugged. "Look, I have no idea why someone would do this to me. I still don't really understand what's going on. But

I will comply in any way I can. If you need help figuring out who has been doing this, then I'm in."

He turned and looked his wife in the eyes. "I love you. I love our family. I would never let anything get in the way of that," he said insistently. A beat passed, and Sarah nodded. She believed him.

And despite all her cynicism, so did Olivia.

Brock leaned forward a little. "Alright, Sergio. We'll level with you. This whole thing pointed in your direction. If you're not behind this account, then it must be someone who knows enough about you to make up your profile. They knew where you lived. They had access to lots of pictures of you. Your work information is on the profile too. So how many people in your life know that kind of information?"

Sergio shrugged helplessly. "I don't know. We have people over from time to time. I don't exactly go broadcasting my work though? I have no idea who it could be."

"Could it be someone you know? Maybe a coworker with a grudge? Any enemies?"

Sergio pondered for a moment and shook his head. "I don't know. None of the guys I work with have any reason to do this. I think. I swear, I have no idea why anyone would do this."

Brock scratched his chin. "Alright. Here's what we're going to do. You're going to show us everything you can that proves this has nothing to do with you. Agent Knight will take a look at that with you. And in the meantime, I'll check on a few things on my end. Sound good?"

Sergio nodded fervently. "We'll completely cooperate."

Olivia already knew what Brock was up to: he wanted to separate Sergio from his wife just in case she'd been afraid to tell the truth while he was there. If he was capable of making threats like that, there was no telling what he'd do to his own wife in private. Admittedly, it seemed less and less likely, but it was something they had to follow up on.

Sergio stood up and motioned for Olivia to follow him while Brock turned to Sarah. Olivia followed him upstairs, still keeping up her guard. He seemed genuine, but she could never be too careful in her line of work. He took her to an office.

"You can look at whatever you want in here. I have nothing to hide," Sergio said as Olivia glanced around the room. He began to pull up his online banking sites as fast as he could, clearly hastened by the pressure on him. He was sweating through the back of his shirt even though the weather outside was freezing. They'd clearly set him on edge. Sergio puffed out air as he stood back from his computer.

"I've pulled up all of my bank records, plus my emails."

"Thanks."

Olivia scanned through his accounts, looking for evidence of anything suspicious, but she didn't see anything of interest. She pored through his phone and found no indication of anything there as well. She even tried searching for Arabella's bank details and for emails from the dating site, but she came up short. Sergio stood behind her the whole time, biting his nails and waiting, like he was somehow going to catch himself in a lie that he hadn't told.

"You see?" Sergio said insistently. "I'm not responsible for this."

"Okay. I believe you," Olivia said, though she wasn't sure of anything at that current moment. She was baffled by it all. "Let's see if my partner has made any progress."

She allowed Sergio to lead her back downstairs, and they almost bumped right into Brock as he was coming out of the living room. Olivia gave a subtle tilt of her head toward Sarah, but he replied with a shake of the head that was just as subtle.

It seemed that she was on her husband's side. She believed him. The question was, was she right? Had Sergio been framed? Or was Sarah, too, in on this crime?

"Mrs. Romero pointed something out on this profile," he announced. "The phone number listed isn't yours. Whoever it was using your account was using this number to communicate."

Olivia glanced at the number and whipped out her own phone to dial it up immediately. This would be the true test. If this number rang somewhere inside the house, it would prove that Sergio had a secret phone line he'd been hiding from his wife. But that still didn't feel right. He had been so cooperative—jumpy, of course—but if this phone number really was his, wouldn't he have let that panic spill over by now?

LOVE, LIES, AND SUICIDE

Each small space of silence between the rings felt like an eternity. Olivia clutched her phone white-knuckle tight, hoping someone—anyone—would pick up on the other line.

And then she heard a click and a nervous, gruff voice answer the phone.

"Hello?"

"Hello, is this Sergio Romero?" she asked.

Without another word, the line disconnected. Olivia tried again, but this time, it just went straight to voicemail. She tried three more times over the next few minutes but couldn't get through.

"Damn," she muttered.

Just when they'd gotten so close to finding definitive proof of something, anything, it was ripped out from underneath them.

"Guess we'll have to look up that number and see who it's registered to," Brock offered.

"Wait," said Sergio. "Can I see that number?"

Olivia turned her phone to him to show the number she'd been calling. He squinted at it for a moment and then started scrolling through his own contact list.

"I think—I think I recognize that number," he muttered. Everyone waited with bated breath; he finally pulled something up on his screen and turned the phone back to Olivia and Brock.

"I work with this guy. His name is Derek Clarke."

CHAPTER ELEVEN

DEREK CLARKE. THEY FINALLY HAD A NAME FOR THEIR suspect. The man who had placed all those threats, who had seemingly stolen Sergio's identity. Olivia and Brock shared a look, and without even needing to spare a word, they sprung into action. Brock immediately pulled out his phone and began a social media search while Olivia continued the question.

"Do you work with Derek directly?" Olivia asked.

Sergio shook his head. "Not all that much. I'm usually out in the field, and he works in the office."

"So, would he be able to disable the alarm system?" Brock asked.

LOVE, LIES, AND SUICIDE

"I think so," Sergio nodded. "In the office, they have the capability to reset the alarm password to the default if a customer forgets the code. There are different confirmations and security checks, of course, but I think he would have access to that."

"And do you know him well?" asked Olivia.

"Um, not really. He's not a friend or anything. He's kind of a loner at work, doesn't have much luck with the ladies… or with anyone, really. I get along well with most of the guys at work, but I always steer clear of Derek. He's always been a little weird."

"Weird how?" Brock pushed. Sergio shuddered.

"He's… intense. He always stares right into your eyes when he talks to you. And he's sort of aggressive. That's the only word I can think of to describe him. He gets angry easily. Runs his mouth. He's been in trouble a few times with the bosses. I don't even know why they keep him on. Something to do with a rehabilitation program, I think. I know he did time, but I have no idea what for."

Olivia stared at the man. He seemed to be telling them all the right answers: a man without much luck in romance and a history of aggression who impersonated a much more handsome man to catfish women online; a coworker with access to the security system that had been disabled; a man who'd already run afoul of the law before. It all seemed to be lining up perfectly—maybe a little too perfectly.

"It's got to be him, right?" Sergio asked, eager for answers. Olivia could tell that he was ready to close this chapter of his life, short as it had been. She couldn't blame him. Just minutes ago, he'd been ready to have pizza with his wife and kids, and now he was a primary murder suspect. But she couldn't just let him off the hook that easily.

"We need to be sure," Olivia said. She shared a long look with Brock. They could either keep following this rabbit hole, but the phone number pretty definitively proved that Sergio had not sent those messages. The lead to Derek wasn't airtight, but it was much better than what they had now.

Olivia handed Sergio her card. "Don't leave town for a bit," she said. "We may have further questions for you."

Sergio nodded.

"In the meantime, do you know where we can find Derek?"

It was close to midnight when they finally got Derek down to the police station. It was safe to say that he hadn't come quietly. From the moment Olivia and Brock showed up with the police, Derek put up a fight, claiming not to have done anything, claiming that he had nothing to hide. But by the look in his eyes, Olivia knew that was a lie. Derek was guilty of something, and he knew it. He knew that he had no way to fight them, so he'd chosen to throw a fist at an officer's face and take off on foot.

And now, he was sitting alone behind the two-way mirror, slumped in his chair. He looked miserable. Olivia and Brock watched him carefully, trying to figure him out.

"He's calmed down, at least," Brock commented, never taking his eyes off of Derek. "Do you think it's time we spoke to him?"

"I think so. The longer we leave it, the longer he has to get himself wound up again," Olivia nodded. She felt like she was about to enter a room with a live wire. She didn't want to do anything that was going to trigger his violent tendencies, even if he was handcuffed to the table. She drew in a deep breath, and Brock placed a hand on her shoulder, sending a shock through her.

Perhaps Derek wasn't the only live wire.

"Let's do this," Brock murmured, and as he moved away, Olivia truly felt the absence of his touch. She blinked several times, shaking her head into the present.

"Pull yourself together," she muttered for her ears only, and then she trailed Brock into the interrogation room.

Derek glared at them as they entered the room. Olivia and Brock sat down opposite him and waited several moments, watching him in return. He squirmed under their gaze.

"I don't know what the hell you want with me," he grumbled. "I ain't done nothin'."

"We all know that's not true," Brock said plainly. "Let's not tell any lies in here, Mr. Clarke. This is on the record."

Derek flared with anger, trying to bang his bound hands against the table. "You pigs never listen! I'm telling you, I ain't done nothin'!"

"Derek," Olivia began calmly. "We have enough evidence now to connect you to the impersonation of your coworker,

LOVE, LIES, AND **SUICIDE**

Sergio Romero. We know you set up a profile on Singles Match using his identity to speak to a woman who called herself Belle. She stole quite a bit of money from you, didn't she? And then you threatened her life."

"I didn't do anything to that con woman. Hell, someone got there first, clearly," Derek snapped. "You listen here. I'm telling the God-honest truth here. I was mad, yeah, and I said something I shouldn't have. And yeah, I tried to find her. I wanted revenge. I wanted my money."

"And you didn't think the police would be a better option than going on a manhunt?" Brock asked, raising his eyebrow. Derek scowled.

"You think the police care what a man like me has to say? I've done time. They don't care what the hell I've got to say."

"Well, we're listening," Olivia said gently. Derek wavered for a minute.

"For real?"

"Yes," she assured him. Derek leaned back in his chair again, the handcuffs around his wrists clanking.

"Alright then," he muttered. "She stole thirty-five hundred off of me. Did you know that? That kind of money is no joke for me. Hell, she would've cleaned out my account eventually, I reckon."

"So, you really cared about her?" she asked.

"I fell for her, and I fell for her con. I felt like a goddamn idiot. And when I realized what she'd done to me, I was angry. Wouldn't you be, huh? So yeah, I said something I didn't mean. And yeah, I did go looking for her, but not to hurt her. I don't know, maybe I would've been that way inclined when I finally saw her. But I just wanted to get my money back."

"And now she's dead. But you knew that already, didn't you?" Brock countered. Derek's entire face turned red once again.

"I didn't kill her!" Derek snarled. "She probably wound someone else up the wrong way, and they offed her for her trouble. It's like I said, I couldn't find her. She didn't give me much to go by. Fake name, fake location, fake pictures. Or at least, pictures that didn't give me enough to really go on. Hell, I just saw the rack on her, and that was enough to hook me."

Olivia shifted uncomfortably in her chair. Brock could see her discomfort, and he took over for a minute.

"So you never found her?"

"No! It wasn't until I heard the news about that rich lady and her husband that I even put it together. She seemed familiar to me, but I couldn't put my finger on why. And then I realized how similar she seemed to Belle. And her name. How could I have missed the name?"

Derek shook his head, sadness suddenly filling his expression. "I don't know… I must have been pretty dumb not to figure it out. That woman got rich off dummies like me. I just know it. And you know what the worst part is? Not that I lost the money. Not that she humiliated me. But… she was someone to talk to. I really cared about her. Damn it, I loved her. Or I thought I did."

"I'm sorry for your loss," Olivia said, but that didn't feel quite right. Was it a loss when it had never been real in the first place?

He sniffled. "I guess she did always seem too good to be true, but there was me thinking that maybe my luck finally changed. That maybe I was finally getting a break. Hell, I was wrong."

Olivia felt herself soften a little. She could completely understand why Arabella and Andrew had left a trail of broken hearts behind them. They were good at what they did. They didn't just con people out of their money. They stole their hearts too.

"I got used to the idea that I wasn't going to find her. After a while, the money stopped mattering too. There's always more money in the world. I've had less before. I know how to be without that. But she left a hole in my life. I didn't know what to do with myself. So, I decided to take a trip. Money ain't worth so much when you realize that it dies with you, and I knew I wasn't living, sitting at home moping over her. So, I did what any self-respecting man would do. I went all out and partied in Las Vegas for a week," Derek said.

His lips twitched into a smile. "And sure enough, by the end of that week, I was down a lot of dollars, but I wasn't thinking about my girl no more. But then I got home and reality hit. She was gone. And then I saw the news and put it all together. I saw the pictures she posted and knew it had to be her. And I thought about those messages I sent, and I knew I couldn't tell the police what I knew. I figured you'd all figure it out eventually."

"Got any proof of that?" Brock asked.

"Sure as hell," he nodded. "Look in my phone."

He tilted his head toward his pocket. Olivia reached over and pulled it out.

Sure enough, there was lots of evidence: ticket stubs for a flight to Vegas, withdrawals at casinos, hotel stays, and even selfies taken in front of the lighted fountains timestamped on the same night as the Cliffords' murders.

Olivia sighed. If Derek wasn't their killer, where would they look next? She guessed it was back to square one, back to checking out the other scam victims. She couldn't deny that it would be disappointing. The last twenty-four hours of investigation had been both thrilling and exhausting.

But she was ready to get back on it.

CHAPTER TWELVE

"**W**HY IS IT ALWAYS THE PEOPLE WE LEAST EXPECT? I mean, why couldn't the sketchiest guy on earth turn out to be our guy for once?"

Olivia chuckled. Brock wasn't wrong. It felt like every time they worked a case together, the person they were trying to catch was always so far off their radar that they seemed like the least possible subject. It was the morning after their interview with Derek Clarke, and they were back to trawling through the hundreds of messages on Andrew and Arabella's dating accounts. A deeper dive into their computers had also found other avenues for their scams: sugar baby websites, online forums, and even social media groups for luxury items. Olivia found even more of Arabella's messages to people via Rolex watch groups and

LOVE, LIES, AND SUICIDE

Lamborghini fan pages where she targeted rich, old men with plenty of money and no one to spend it on. She didn't think these men minded that they were being scammed because they made repeat payments into Arabella's account, but the newfound information broadened their search considerably. It seemed like their scam had spread so far and wide that they'd never uncover the entire extent of it all.

That might seem discouraging to some, but Olivia felt a renewed burst of confidence. They had plenty of leads for once, and she had no doubt that they'd find the person they wanted via the avenues they were exploring. People like Arabella and Andrew made a lot of enemies in their day-to-day lives, but no one was more likely to murder than someone who had already lost everything. The Clifford family not only drained their victims dry like blood-sucking vampires—they also expected to get away with it.

Someone else had clearly thought otherwise.

There was a lot to do, but Olivia was okay with that too. She didn't like to sit idly, twiddling her thumbs and waiting for something to happen. Her eyes were tired from staring at screens all day, and she was sick of seeing innocent people getting scammed, but she knew it would be worth it if she could solve the case and help the victims get their money back.

Brock sighed. "Derek really seemed like an obvious candidate, didn't he? Do you think we're overlooking a lot of these candidates just because they don't seem like they have violent tendencies? I mean, I'm reading messages here between Andrew and this woman, Violet Marsh. She stood out to me from the start because she's unlike most of his other victims. It seems to be a romance scam on the same level as Arabella's."

"That's unusual," Olivia frowned. "You don't really see many women falling for this sort of thing the way men do."

"Yeah, yeah, we think with a different head. I know. But it seems Andrew found a way anyway."

"Inspiring."

"Very," Brock nodded. "So, Violet Marsh. She's in her late fifties, and unlike a lot of the others, she wasn't divorced."

"She never got married?"

"She did. She was widowed. She got married in her thirties to the love of her life, but he died a few weeks after the wedding—just after she discovered that she was pregnant with their son."

Olivia felt a pang in her heart. "That's awful. How did her husband die?"

"Undiagnosed brain tumor, apparently. So, as you can imagine, this woman has been living with a broken heart for years. She told Andrew via the messages that she's only just opening her heart to love again after all this time."

"Wow. So, she's nothing like the other victims then. Do you think that's significant?"

"Who knows? There's just so much data here to sort through. It could take us years, and we still might never figure out which person did this. This isn't a two-man job, is it?"

Olivia sighed. "I don't know. But we don't have years. We need to get these people some justice—not just the scam victims, but the Cliffords. They may have been horrible people, but they still deserve justice."

"Look at you, being all principled and upholding your values."

"It's the worst," Olivia griped, drawing a grin from Brock. "But anyway, yes—maybe we should be taking a look at less likely candidates. Tell me more about Violet. She seems like a candidate of interest."

"So, she decided to get back on the dating scene just a few days before she started speaking to Andrew. I think he must have done some prior research on all of his victims before speaking to them because he knew exactly how to win her over. It was like he'd logged all of her interests. Mined information from her social media to create the perfect man for her—someone she could trust—someone she'd open up to and be interested in right away. She even put some of the information on her dating profile about her past marriage, so he must have seen her as a gold mine. She took the bait—hook, line, and sinker. Within a few days of talking, she was getting invested, telling Andrew that she hadn't been so happy in so long."

Olivia felt a flash of anger through her. She had long since decided that she couldn't stand Andrew or Arabella for what they did to people, but this particular case was so coldhearted that she almost didn't want to find the killer. Almost. She didn't believe anyone ever deserved to be killed, but the scam they had been running almost invited retaliation.

"How did he catch her?" Olivia whispered. Brock scanned back through the messages.

"He told her that his son was sick. He said he was struggling to pay for his medical bills and was working long hours. Well, you can imagine how that played with her heartstrings after what she went through. He didn't even ask her for the money. She said she wanted to do whatever she could to help out. She said her son had grown up, established himself—she didn't need to be sitting on piles of money anymore. She sent the money over almost right away. Ten thousand dollars."

Olivia was stunned to silence for a long moment. "Wow. That's a big deal," she finally attempted.

"Yeah. Violet was clearly very invested. Or deluded. I guess when you're falling for someone for the first time in over twenty years, it's easy to get ahead of yourself. I think she's a very lonely woman, maybe on the verge of breaking apart. And then after she sent the money, Andrew barely even pretended with her. He just disappeared on her. It's awful. There must be at least twenty or thirty messages here of her just talking into the void. Telling him she misses him, that she hopes his son is doing okay. She says she understands that he needs space, but she also wants him to respond. But he never did. And then there's just one final message."

"What does it say?" Olivia asked, though, in many ways, she didn't want to know. Brock sighed.

"It says, *I understand now. I know that none of this was real. I hope you got what you wanted.*"

Olivia puffed out air. "That's just… brutal. Some of these people that they scammed just acted like it didn't matter all that much to them, but this… you can just feel that pain in her message."

"And we know how pain can do horrible things to people," Brock pointed out. "If I'd put my heart on the line like that, only to be scammed? I think I'd be angry. How far could that feeling carry her?"

Olivia nodded. She knew what he was implying. He was implying that Violet might have been pushed to murder. Olivia's mind was whirling as she thought of what they should do next.

"We should try to speak to her," Olivia said. "If we can get her details, we can contact her, tell her that we're investigating a mass scam that happened on Singles Match. We don't have to even mention the murder. If we can get her on the phone, we might be able to gauge who she is, what she's capable of."

Brock nodded, taking out his phone. "She left her phone number on her profile. Let's try it. See what comes up."

Olivia moved to sit beside Brock on his bed where he put his phone on speaker. The phone rang for a long time, for so long that Olivia was sure that no one would pick up. But at the last minute, someone picked up. Static crackled on the other end of the line.

"...hello?"

Olivia and Brock exchanged a look. It was a man's voice. Brock cleared his throat, not allowing himself to be thrown off.

"Hello. This is Agent Brock Tanner with the FBI. I'm investigating a case involving an online scam involving theft and fraud, and I'm looking for Violet Marsh to discuss her experience. We believe she may have been targeted by a scammer who took a large sum of money from her."

The person on the other end of the line was silent. Brock frowned.

"Is she available for a quick chat? We won't take up much of her time."

There was a strangled breath on the other end of the phone. Brock's frown deepened.

"Is everything okay, sir?"

After a moment, there was a sniffle.

"Um... you're speaking to Violet's son. I'm sorry, but she can't come to the phone right now."

Olivia and Brock exchanged a look. Something very odd was going on. Why was her son answering the phone, sounding like he was crying?

"I understand why she might be hesitant to talk to us, but this is important. We are hoping we can help her out. Isn't that what she wants?"

LOVE, LIES, AND SUICIDE

"No. I don't think it matters to her," the man replied glumly.

"And why not?" Brock pressed, looking more bewildered the more he pushed the subject. The man let out a strangled noise again.

"Because she's gone. She killed herself a few months ago."

Olivia felt her entire body go cold. Even Brock, who was usually so calm and collected, couldn't hide the shock and the horror from his face. He scrambled for words.

"I—I'm sorry. What did you say?"

"She killed herself," the man repeated on the other end of the line. He was clearly crying now, his voice wobbling with every word he uttered. "She... she couldn't take it. She'd been lonely for so long. And then she told me she fell for someone online. I worried about her. She'd never done anything like that, but she fell hard. And then she stopped talking about the guy a few weeks later. I asked her what happened, and she didn't want to talk about it. It was only after she killed herself that I found out what had happened." The man sniffed, and Olivia realized she was holding her breath. Her heart was aching in her chest as he spoke.

"She didn't care about the money. I know that didn't mean a thing to her. It was the betrayal. That's what killed her. She had all that love to give, and someone threw it back in her face." There was a tinge of anger in the young man's voice, but it was overwhelmed by the pain he was clearly feeling.

"I'm so sorry for your loss," said Brock.

"Thank you," replied the man.

"If you don't mind, we'd—we'd like to help you get answers for your mother," he attempted. "We're trying to find out who's responsible for this."

It was a lie, but in this case, it would be better than telling him, *we know who did this, and we suspected your mother might have murdered him.*

"She left a note, telling me not to worry about it. She said she wanted to go back to my father. Maybe she's finally happy now. So, I'm sorry, whoever you are, but I don't think I can help you today."

"Sir, please, we want to help you—"

"I'm sorry, I can't—I don't know if there's anything you or anyone can do," the young man sniffed. "I came to her house to put her affairs in order. I'll be disconnecting this phone. Please don't contact me or my family again."

Before Brock could say anything further, the call ended. He let out a long, drawn-out breath, dropping the phone and running a hand through his hair.

"Well, I guess we can cross one suspect off our list," he murmured. "That poor woman…"

Olivia shook her head in disbelief. "It feels so wrong. They were living happy, carefree lives while driving people to suicide. It's disgusting."

Olivia felt her stomach churning. Her work put her in contact with the worst of the worst, but she wasn't used to the true villains being their victims. Olivia felt a little hopeless all of a sudden. Any one of the scam victims could have flipped and killed the horrible couple. But instead, they'd discovered that someone had turned the gun on themselves.

Olivia felt a warm hand covering her own. She looked up and saw Brock looking at her. There was pain in his eyes too. There was no denying it. Sometimes, their job struck them right through the heart. They were only human. How could they let something so awful just get brushed under the rug with all of the other terrible things they'd seen?

"We're going to get to the bottom of this. For Violet. For all of them," Brock murmured. Olivia nodded, her throat tight. There was a pain in her chest, but Brock's hand on hers felt good. It felt safe. She drew in a deep breath, forcing herself to pull her hand away from his. He was right. They needed to solve the case. And sitting around wasn't going to get anything done for them.

"We have to push on," Olivia murmured. Brock nodded.

"Yeah. Okay."

Olivia returned to her laptop and gave herself a moment to push through her tangle of emotions. Sometimes, people saw her emotions as a hindrance in her job. They thought they held her back, even clouded her judgment. But she knew that wasn't true. In fact, she knew that when her heart was truly in it, she was at her best. And right at that moment, she'd never been so determined to get things done.

And she was stronger than ever.

LOVE, LIES, AND SUICIDE

The day dragged on, and still, Olivia and Brock struggled to connect the dots. The sheer number of victims shocked Olivia to her core, and the only thing she could do to help was to keep going. While Brock was ordering them dinner, Olivia pushed on. She'd had an idea to cross-reference every victim with gun registration records, which was a feat in and of itself considering the victims came from a myriad of states. On top of this, it was entirely possible that the killer had obtained the gun illegally, given that they clearly weren't above breaking the rules, but she also knew it might help them narrow their search. The way things were going, they had to narrow the scope somehow, or they'd never get this case solved.

Olivia finally allowed herself to relax a little as she ate her dinner in front of the motel TV. She zoned out from the sitcom that was playing on the screen, thinking about Violet once again. She wondered how the son had felt, suddenly discovering that his mom had ended her life. The whole thing seemed so avoidable, so ludicrous when put in perspective. She couldn't imagine how hard it must have been for the son, knowing he'd warned his mother against being so reckless, but she'd ignored him anyway. Now, a life had been lost, and he would never get the opportunity to bring his mom back from the brink.

Olivia thought of her own family and felt a pang of guilt. She knew how it felt to lose someone suddenly, to have them slip through her fingers before she even had a chance to close her fist to catch them. Veronica's death had been so out of the blue that she hadn't had time to prepare. And while she was still reeling from that, her own mother had disappeared too. She had always told herself that if she had a chance to make things right, to have things go back to the way they used to be, then she'd take it.

And yet here she was, deliberating over whether to spend Thanksgiving with her parents—the only family she had left. Sure, they'd let her down, but didn't every family have issues? Maybe hers were bigger than most, but they were forgivable, right?

Olivia chewed her lip. Wasn't this her chance to give thanks for what she had left, even if the life she once knew had been destroyed? Like Violet's son, didn't she always wish she could borrow some extra time? At least she had the chance. He never would.

Olivia turned to look at Brock. He was engrossed in the TV, already halfway through his dinner while she'd barely touched hers. She swallowed. She wished she could spend the holiday alone with him. She wished that she could have the luxury of exploring the feelings he was bringing up inside her. But she had wished for a happy family for longer. Jean had promised to make things right. She just had to give her a chance.

"Brock?"

"Mm?"

Olivia took a deep breath. "I have to go home for Thanksgiving."

Brock tore his eyes away from the screen to look at Olivia. He didn't seem surprised.

"I know," he said gently. Olivia sighed.

"I'm sorry."

"I know that too."

"You could come with me. My mom said she's happy for me to bring a guest..."

Brock offered her a small smile. "Olivia, we both know you have enough to deal with on Thanksgiving. Don't worry about me. You need to use this time to reconnect with them. Make things right."

Olivia nodded. As usual, Brock was right. He knew exactly what to say when it came to her. He smiled at her again and turned back to the TV. Olivia tried to eat her dinner, but she felt nervous, knowing she was going home. It was the first time since the invite had been extended that it felt real to her. Now, she was really going to have to face the music.

"Happy holidays to me," she murmured.

CHAPTER THIRTEEN

Olivia tried hard to remember Thanksgiving as a child while she was heading over to her parent's house. Her family life had always been a little chaotic, long before her sister was killed in cold blood and her mom disappeared. Her father's military career had meant moving around a lot as a child, and now Olivia recalled that both her parents had missed the occasional Christmas or Thanksgiving celebration if her father was on deployment or her mother was away on one of her secretive trips.

But mostly, Olivia had good memories of Thanksgiving. She could remember indulging in all the same traditions that families across the country had but also a few special family traditions too. There was breaking the wishbone, taking a long walk after a hearty dinner, and sometimes watching football—things that were common among her friends too. Of course, they all went around and said what they were thankful for, and they all ate way too much pumpkin pie.

But the best parts of Thanksgiving were always the traditions that only her family did. Every year, they would visit the local soup kitchen to donate an afternoon of their time and a bunch of groceries. Olivia remembered fighting over a ladle with Veronica one year, both of them desperate to aid in feeding the homeless. She had been barely eight or nine. They ended up spilling hot soup down their fronts and crying, but the memory made Olivia smile.

And then there was the annual game of dominoes that Olivia's father always made them play. He was the only one who ever wanted to play, but everyone always humored him because it was the one thing he ever asked of them. While Olivia and Veronica played footsie under the kitchen table to entertain themselves, Olivia's father would play the game in his quiet, calm manner, smiling to himself like he'd never been happier.

And then there was the one tradition that Olivia always remembered the most. She remembered it feeling so special: helping her mother make the cranberry sauce for the turkey. Veronica's specialty was mashed potatoes. But Olivia and her mother would *always* make the cranberry sauce together. This was not a house where they'd simply plop a can onto a plate and watch it awkwardly slump into a pile still retaining the cylindrical shape. No, the Knights always preferred the real deal.

She recalled stirring sugar and orange juice in a pan, waiting for it to boil and for the sweet smell to hit her nose. If Olivia closed her eyes, she could smell it then, the smell of Thanksgiving.

And then came the cranberries. Always fresh, never frozen. Olivia remembered how her mom would slowly add them to the sugar concoction, allowing them to cascade in a purplish rain into the pan. Then they'd stir and stir until the sauce was thick and goopy and ready to serve.

It was such a simple thing. It never really took any skill to make. But doing that one thing with her mother always made Olivia feel special. It made her feel as though the day belonged to them. Back then, her mom had been everything to her. Her

LOVE, LIES, AND SUICIDE

best friend, her confidant. When she wasn't around, Olivia would almost crave her, wishing for her to come home so that the status quo could resume.

But then one day, she didn't come home.

Olivia was brought back to reality by the memory of her mom's disappearance. Now that she knew where she'd gone and why, all she could feel was the anger it brought up inside her. All that time, she'd thought she meant more to her mother. She thought she was too important to leave behind without a word. But now she knew differently.

Olivia rubbed her forehead as she drove. She couldn't go down that route again. She needed to be more forgiving if the day was going to go well. She had to remember that she was there to fix things, not reopen old wounds. Both of her parents were going to try so hard to pretend everything was fine, and she needed to do the same. Just for one day. It wouldn't be like the Thanksgivings of her past—those bright, happy memories that were buried so deep now. But it might be okay. It might be good if she gave it a chance.

She hadn't been to her parent's house in so long. In the five years that her mother had been gone, she'd only visited a handful of times. But she still remembered the way like the back of her hand. Driving through the town she had once called home, she felt the tug of nostalgia on her heartstrings. She hoped it would last long enough to get her through the day. She was going to need it.

But all too soon, she was closing in on the house. She didn't feel prepared, but she reminded herself that she was too strong to let this crack her. She'd survived so much worse than dinner with her parents.

She parked up a little way from the house. She didn't want the big welcome fanfare she knew was waiting for her when she arrived, so she hoped she could take them by surprise. Then again, she wouldn't be shocked if her mom was waiting in the window, hoping to watch her arrive. She could already tell that her parents were going to be trying much harder than was bearable. She took a deep breath of autumn air, letting the coldness fill her lungs up.

It was time.

She walked as slowly as she could up to the house, like she was scared that each step might cause the world to blow up beneath her feet. She watched the house, noting the ways it had changed and the ways it hadn't. It had been home to her once, but now, it felt like she was invading somehow. She didn't belong there anymore, but she had to try. This was the last chance to make things right.

The door opened before she could even knock, and Jean pulled her into an uncomfortably tight hug. Olivia hadn't planned on doing much hugging, but she allowed it, for the sake of the day going smoothly. When her mom pulled back, she clutched Olivia's face in her hands, her eyes a little misty.

"Welcome home, darling. Happy Thanksgiving."

"Happy Thanksgiving, Mom," Olivia replied stiffly. She didn't know how to talk to her anymore. It felt like an effort to force each word out of her mouth. She already felt exhausted.

Get it together, get it together, get it together…

"Well, don't just stand there, silly! Let's get you inside. Shoes off, please!"

Olivia kicked off her boots and unwound her scarf from around her neck. She closed her eyes and took in the smell of the turkey baking, the coldness that rested on her skin, and the hum of the oven in the kitchen. It took her back twenty years, and for a moment, she raised a smile.

But when she opened her eyes, the feeling dissipated. This wasn't the house where she'd stood on a stool to make cranberry sauce with her mom. Her mother wasn't the same woman she'd looked up to back then. Her father wasn't the man who smiled and played dominoes anymore.

And Veronica simply wasn't anything anymore except an empty chair at the table.

"Come on in," Jean told her, ushering her through the place as though she'd never been there before. Olivia's heart was racing in her chest. If it was uncomfortable this early on, how was it going to be when the three of them were all together?

The living room was warm and inviting with the log fire burning, but Olivia still felt a shiver running down her spine. Roger was sitting in an armchair, his face concealed by a newspaper.

Olivia couldn't even recall the last time she'd seen someone read a newspaper.

When her father let the paper fold away from his face, she saw him for the first time in too long. It shocked her how different he looked. His cheeks were gaunt, and his eyes seemed to have dulled in color. She hadn't expected him to be that way. He was the family's pillar of strength, the one who never cried, not even at Veronica's funeral. But here he was, an almost ghostly version of himself. Olivia wondered what had done it to him. Was it Veronica? Was it her mother who had disappeared into thin air?

Or was it the daughter who had pulled away from him?

"Olivia," he said, putting his paper to one side. His face didn't change one bit. He didn't smile, but he did stand and cross the room to hug her. "It's good to see you," he said, though it didn't sound true. Olivia felt deep guilt tunneling through her. She knew that her father had withdrawn into himself in recent years and that he kept himself busy with work. They had called occasionally, but even that had dropped off. Could she have done more? Could she have stopped him from becoming this version of himself?

"Isn't it wonderful? Having the family back together?" Jean asked. She said it as though she wasn't actually sure of the answer. Olivia breathed in her father for a moment. He always smelled like coffee to her, but this time it was faint, like he was fading away. He felt different too. More fragile. Smaller.

Maybe she wasn't the only broken one.

"Sit down, sit down," she fussed, plumping up a cushion. Olivia did as she was told, but she was still a little shell-shocked from seeing her father. She had been so focused on her mom for so long, on being angry at her or worried for her, that she'd almost forgotten about her dad. It was like she'd managed to forget that he was going through all of the same things as she was. Like she'd forgotten that he was in pain too.

But he had also lied to her. Maybe that was why he'd burrowed himself into work all these years. He didn't want to put himself through the dishonesty of it all. And within seconds, Olivia's feelings were flitting to anger again.

"The turkey is almost done," Olivia's mom announced. "I made cranberry sauce, Olivia. Your favorite."

Olivia felt an odd sinking feeling inside her. She didn't mention that she didn't even really like cranberry sauce. That was never what the whole cranberry sauce thing was about. She sat stiffly in her seat while Jean disappeared back into the kitchen. The room suddenly felt too hot, and Olivia pulled at the neck of her sweater. Olivia's dad cleared his throat and reached for the TV remote.

"Maybe the game is on now," he grumbled. Neither of them mentioned that he didn't care about football much. In fact, neither of them spoke again until Jean called them to the dinner table an hour later.

Olivia could feel the day sucking the energy out of her. She wished she could borrow some of her mom's enthusiasm. She watched her bustling around, adding dishes to the table. There was a mountain of food, considering there were only three of them. Olivia was going to make a remark about it but opted not to. She sat down and avoided eye contact with both her parents as she waited for them to get seated.

"Well, I'm starving!" Jean announced, grinning to herself. It was only then that Olivia caught her father's eye, and he managed a small smile for her. She could read his mind. He was thinking, just like she was, that it was almost like her mom had walked into the wrong house. Didn't she sense the tension? Didn't she realize that things weren't okay just because she'd managed to get them there?

Still, Olivia wanted to try harder. She got herself some food and asked her parents questions. Safe questions for her father about work and if he was considering retirement soon. Safe questions for her mother like asking her where she'd gotten all the food from. Work was definitely not a topic she wanted to broach with her.

"So... no Brock today, Olivia?" Jean asked. Olivia kept her face level.

"Meaning?"

"Well, I just thought the two of you were getting closer. I assumed you'd want him here today."

"He had other plans," Olivia lied smoothly. She didn't want to discuss what she and Brock were to one another, especially when she wasn't even sure herself yet. Besides, that would lead to having to explain that she didn't feel comfortable bringing him around her explosive family just yet.

"Oh, well that is a shame. I think your father would have liked to have met him."

"Or you would have liked to have been nosy about him. That's what you mean, right, Mom?"

Roger let out a low chuckle and Olivia found herself smiling properly for the first time all day. Jean joined in the laughter, even if the joke was at her expense.

"Oh, I just take an interest in your life. Is that so bad? I just want to know that my daughter is happy."

Olivia raised her eyebrow but held her tongue. She had a few things that she could say in response to that, but none of them were good. They were halfway through dinner, and she'd managed to keep the peace so far. That had to be considered progress.

"Well, you should know he's welcome here anytime. You both are," her mother said with a warm smile. Then she cleared her throat and glanced up at her husband. It was subtle, so Olivia almost missed it, but she'd been watching her parents like a hawk. Her mom was hiding something. She was about to tell her something that she'd been keeping back from her. Olivia straightened up in her chair, suddenly on guard.

"But what?" Olivia asked, folding her arms over her chest. "There's a but, right?"

Olivia's mom picked up her glass of water and took a sip. "Well, it's just that you're welcome to drop by whenever… but things at work are picking up for me again. So, I might not be around much."

Olivia narrowed her eyes. She knew, of course, that her mother wasn't about to quit her position in the FBI. That much was fine. But it was what she wasn't saying that bothered Olivia. What was it?

"Okay…"

"You see…" Jean cleared her throat. "I know we talked about my line of work and the dangers it poses… and I heard you. I really did. And I know that I promised you that I'd step back from the case I was working. But I shouldn't have done that."

There it was. Olivia shook her head, scoffing to herself. There was the punchline.

"You shouldn't have. Because you're going to break that promise, aren't you?"

Jean wavered. "Look, I know it's not what you want to hear…"

"No, you're right, it isn't. But I probably should have expected it, right? Because that's what you do now. Break promises to me."

"I don't think that's true, Olivia. I've told you why this case is so important. It's a big deal, and someone has to deal with it. This was my case all along. The one I risked my life for. The one I sacrificed everything for. And I'm the only one who can solve it. I just feel it in my bones, Olivia. You must know how it feels to be in my shoes?"

Olivia shook her head. She was done trying now. This was exactly why she'd had her guard up. She had clearly known on some level that she was about to be betrayed again. And this time, she wasn't standing for it. "I have no idea what it's like to be in your shoes, Mom. Because if I were you, I would have walked away without walking back."

"You can't say that. I know how committed you are to your job, Olivia. You've taken risks of your own, done things that put everything in jeopardy—"

"But not at the expense of my family. At the expense of no one but myself," Olivia said, quietly seething. "I told you what it was going to take for me to forgive what you did. You didn't listen to me. You never do."

"You're being childish, Olivia. Come on, let's talk this out properly. You should at least know the reasons why I want to do this."

Olivia stood up from the table. "No. No, Mom. The thing is, I don't care what those reasons are. Because when you made a promise to me this time, I was stupid enough to believe you would go through with it. I thought that after everything we've lost, you'd see sense and walk away. I thought that after the hell you put us through all these years, you'd think twice about doing that again. But I see what's important to you now, and it sure as hell isn't me."

LOVE, LIES, AND SUICIDE

"Don't speak to your mother that way," Roger growled. Olivia turned on him.

"Why not? Look at what she's done to us! To this family, to *you*! I barely recognize you, Dad! She keeps doing whatever she likes, putting her interests first… But what about us? Where does that leave us?"

"Lower your voice."

"No. I tried to play by your rules today. I really did. I tried to play nice with you both because I knew it was what you wanted. Even after the misery I went through, I wanted to make sure you were both happy. And now look at the mess this has made. Look at what it's costing us. No one wins. Congratulations."

"Please," Olivia's mom said gently. "I know you're upset, and I can't blame you. I know that maybe you would do things differently, but I—"

"Of course, I'd do things differently!" Olivia cried out. "We're clinging on for dear life here. Look around! You've destroyed this family. We were cracked on the surface after Veronica, and you decided to go ahead and blow the rest up. You're the only person here walking around unscathed. If you put yourself in my shoes, in Dad's shoes, for just one minute, you wouldn't be sitting there telling me how to feel. You wouldn't be going back to that project. You'd get out the superglue and try to fix us instead."

Olivia shook her head and shoved her chair back. "You know what I'm grateful for? The fact that I'm coming to my senses and walking out that door right now."

"Olivia, come back right now!"

But Olivia was done with the entire thing. She could have been spending a peaceful Thanksgiving in Belle Grove with Brock. Instead, she was fighting alone once again against her mother. When would it end? When would her mom realize what she was doing to her?

Olivia stormed out to her car. She'd forgotten her scarf, but she was too angry to go back for it. She never wanted to set foot in that house again. All she wanted was to go home, back to Belle Grove, where none of this could touch her. Back to a place that made sense.

Back to Brock.

She called his number as she was starting up her car. He answered within the first few rings.

"Happy Thanksgiving, Olivia," he said. She snorted.

"Is it?"

"Huh?"

"Dinner with my parents is a bust," Olivia muttered, starting up the engine. "Do you have plans?"

"I have a crate of beer. Does that count?"

Olivia smiled. There was home. She began to drive away.

"Mind if I join you?"

CHAPTER FOURTEEN

When Olivia woke up the day after Thanksgiving with a pounding headache and a nauseous stomach, she groaned as she tried to sit up. She was in Brock's bed, but she remembered the night before how he'd set her up in his bedroom before taking the couch for himself. She'd had one too many beers the night before—or a few too many.

She groaned again, the world spinning around her. She wasn't a big drinker most of the time, but her disastrous Thanksgiving dinner with her parents had made her want to drink from the moment she arrived at Brock's apartment.

"Great. Now I've poisoned myself. What a way to make myself feel better," Olivia griped to herself as she swung her legs out of bed and padded into the kitchen to get herself a glass of water.

As she left the bedroom, she found Brock lounging on the sofa with a book in his hand looking very smug and annoyingly unaffected by the beers he'd also been drinking. He grinned at Olivia as she entered the room.

"Well, good morning, party animal. How's the head?"

"Pounding," Olivia muttered as she headed over to the sink. "Why do you seem fine?"

"Ah, well, you know, everything in moderation. You ready to hit the Black Friday sales?"

"Get lost."

Brock cackled, and Olivia raised a smile as she fetched her glass of water. She had to admit, the worst Thanksgiving of her life had turned out to be not so bad after she arrived at Brock's place. He definitely made her feel better. He didn't push her to talk about what had happened that day at all, and she didn't try to tell him. They kicked back on the couch and watched a movie until Olivia was too tipsy to concentrate. Then, they chatted for a few hours, watching the crate of beers turn into a pile of empty cans. By the time Brock put her to bed, she was drunk enough to forget about the day she'd had, but not so drunk as to forget how good Brock had made her feel.

She felt herself blushing at the thought. Once again, she felt like she wanted to put her feelings on hold for a while. They were getting a little too close to comfort. Sure, she was still technically off duty, and the case could wait one more day in that regard, but with everything going on with her family, she wanted to put Brock at a distance for just a little longer.

"Hey, Olivia?"

"Yeah?"

"Thanks for hanging out with me last night. I wasn't going to admit it, but I was pretty bummed out when I found out you'd be going to your parents."

"Oh, I knew."

Brock gave a sheepish grin. "I guess I wasn't exactly subtle about the fact. But I didn't say anything because I knew that you had to go. I knew you had to see if you could sort things out with them. But selfish as it is, I'm glad I got to see you. You gave me the best Thanksgiving I've had in a really long time."

Olivia felt a lump in her throat. "Really?"

He smiled at her. "I mean, don't get too sentimental over it. I've had some pretty boring, lonely, terrible Thanksgivings over the years. But this one was good. And that was because of you."

Olivia raised a smile. "Wow, you do know how to make a girl feel good."

"Charming, isn't it? And do you know what else is charming? I'm not even going to charge you for all the beer you stole from me."

"You offered it to me!"

"I offered you *a* beer. You just chose to drink the rest."

"Well, let's call it even for all the times you've polished off my dinner," Olivia replied. She'd almost forgotten that she had a headache. She liked these moments with Brock. When she didn't have to take life too seriously; when he reminded her that there was always a reason to smile. She sat down beside him on the sofa and his face softened as he reached to pat her hand.

"But, hey. Do you need to talk about what happened yesterday? I got the sense that it must have been rough."

Olivia sighed, rubbing at her head. "I don't know yet. I'm still processing it all. Yesterday kind of kicked my butt."

"I know," Brock said softly. "We don't have to talk about it now. But my ears are open, okay?"

Olivia smiled. "Sure. Thanks."

"Anytime. And actually, I've got something for you that I think you're going to like. It's a real treat."

Olivia frowned. "You got me a gift?"

"Something better. Something you're going to love." He whipped up a pile of paper from his coffee table. "Two full, extensive autopsy reports!"

Olivia rolled her eyes. "Okay, that is kind of exciting."

She'd been waiting on the reports of Arabella and Andrew since they'd taken up the case. Of course, they knew that the cause of death had been the shot wounds to their heads, but she knew that an autopsy report could tell them a whole slew of secrets. The papers in front of her were exactly what she needed to distract her from her hangover.

"I got these emailed over Wednesday night. That was the extent of my Thanksgiving plans," Brock continued, handing over one of the reports to Olivia. It was Andrew's report. She sipped her water as she began reading.

"Did you read any of it?"

"Not really. I thought I'd wait for you."

"You're so sweet."

Brock nudged her with his foot as he lounged on his sofa, and Olivia smiled to herself as she scanned the report. Her eyes fell on something interesting, and she frowned, reading it over several times.

"Are you seeing this? Cause of death: gunshot wound to the head… or belladonna poisoning?"

"What?" Brock frowned, sitting up straight and looking over her shoulder at the report. "That can't be right. There must be a typo."

"It says it right here. Traces of belladonna found in the lining of the stomach." Olivia tried to think what she knew about belladonna, but she drew a blank. She searched the term online and scanned over the notes. "It says here that belladonna is a deadly nightshade plant. The leaves and the root have long been used in various forms of medicine, but the juice from the berries is extremely poisonous. When ingested, it can cause a slew of symptoms, including hallucinations, drowsiness, flushing, and… well, in some cases, death."

"So, the report is implying that if Andrew hadn't suffered the shot to the head, then he likely would have died anyway," Brock murmured. He sat back in his seat, looking bewildered. "This doesn't make sense. Why shoot someone in the head if they're already dying of poison? I mean, given the setup we found the victims in, it's very unlikely they somehow poisoned themselves before being shot, right?"

"Maybe they were trying to get high," Olivia shrugged. "But it's kind of unconventional, eating poisonous berries… I mean, where would they even get them from?"

"Exactly. So why would someone force their victim to ingest poison if they planned to shoot them anyway?"

Olivia chewed her lip. "Maybe they were using it as a form of torture. A shot to the head is a quick, clean death. It doesn't exactly make the victim suffer. So, they use the poison first, then shoot them… but then what's the point if they were going to die anyway? A form of misdirection, maybe?"

Brock let out a long breath, running a hand through his hair. "Well, if that was the plan, then it sure as hell worked. We've spent this whole time thinking the killer was sloppy, planting the wrong gun, tying and untying Andrew, not lining the shots up correctly… But maybe this is exactly what the killer wanted. I guess they thought a few red herrings would buy them some time."

Olivia still couldn't comprehend what she was reading. If the killer really was thinking that far ahead, then they were way behind. They'd thought they were on the right path, but this seemed to suggest otherwise.

Brock looked down at the report of Arabella's autopsy. "Same results here. Belladonna poisoning," he mused. "This was deliberate."

"Okay. Let's think about what this means then. This can't have been an impulsive, reckless decision. We're likely dealing with a sadist, someone who likes to see people suffer. It seems like they might be smarter than we anticipated too. I don't think this was just someone who decided to pick up some berries and a gun, was it? They planned this meticulously, down to the last detail. And it seems like whoever did this had some knowledge of plants—they must have, to know the properties of belladonna. So, they force-fed Andrew the plants, which they got from… where? I doubt this is the sort of plant you can just grab from your backyard."

"Your guess is as good as mine," Brock muses. "This whole thing just got much more complex."

Olivia scanned the report again, trying to see if her eyes were playing tricks on her. She swallowed.

"You don't think—no, never mind…"

"No, it's okay, say what's on your mind."

Olivia paused. "Belladonna. Do you think it's a reference to Arabella? *Bella*donna, *Ara*bella… like a signature, almost. A sneaky way of the killer saying, *hey, I really thought this one through.*

I'm going to kill her with her namesake, and you're not even going to see it until later."

Brock's eyes widened. "You might be right. If so, this killer has really stepped up a notch. Now, not only are we searching in a sea of victims for our killer, but we also have to accept that maybe this person is smart enough to hide in plain sight. Maybe we already overlooked them. Who knows how long they've had this planned? Maybe this isn't even their first kill."

That thought turned Olivia's skin cold. The autopsy really had changed everything. She swallowed.

"One thing's for sure. We're really going to have to bring our A game now. The killer is already a few steps ahead. Let's make sure that they don't get any farther."

CHAPTER FIFTEEN

THE DISCOVERY OF THE POISONOUS TRACES IN THE victims' stomachs had changed everything. Olivia and Brock spent all Black Friday frantically searching for similar cases on the database. Just as well—neither had any interest in the hot deals at every retail store in the country. They wanted to know if there were any other cases where the cause of death appeared at first to be a gunshot wound, but then traces of belladonna, or some other poisonous plant, had been found.

It was unusual. Olivia knew that much. Had the autopsy report not revealed it, they never would have known. Whoever killed the Cliffords had decided to torture them, to make them suffer. Maybe they even intended to let it kill them.

But then, somewhere the guns had come into play, and that complicated things massively. Olivia rubbed at her still throbbing head, her mouth dry from drinking the night before. She couldn't think of a worse day to be hungover.

"I can't find anything where both poison and a gun were involved," Brock said. "Nothing at all. I've checked for all kinds of poison, too, not just plant-based poisons. But there's nothing. Maybe we're dealing with something brand-new here. A brand-new killer."

"If this is a revenge killing, then that might make sense anyway. If we're still looking for a victim of Arabella and Andrew's schemes, then they might still have been pushed to murder by what they did. But somehow, the poison makes me think otherwise. It's one thing to take a gun and shoot two people in the head when all it takes is a quick pulling of the trigger… But to actually make someone suffer, to actively torture them, to make them hallucinate, make them ill… that's something else entirely."

Olivia nodded. "It's pretty sadistic. The Cliffords are no angels, but even so, they would have suffered a lot before they were allowed to die. That's the thing that changes this so much. We're looking for someone with a cruel streak in them. Someone methodical enough to have come up with contingencies like this. This wasn't done in the blind fury of revenge. Maybe they've done this before."

"Especially given the expert way they misdirected us," Brock said, shaking his head. "I don't know if it was deliberate or not, but they got us good. We're practically back at the start now."

"We just have to keep pushing. Maybe we'll get lucky and find something before we go back to Richmond tomorrow."

The afternoon dragged on, and Olivia felt as though they were stuck in the mud, getting absolutely nowhere. The database kept coming up blank. Olivia sat back in her chair with a sigh, letting her tired mind rest for a few moments. She chewed her lip thoughtfully.

"Maybe we're looking at this wrong," she suggested. "We've been looking for killings with the exact same MO. But maybe that's the wrong way to go. It's already pretty rare to find someone going on a killing spree with poisonous plants. It seems like it's niche, given that you'd have to know something about plants to do it. So maybe we're not looking for someone who used a gun *and* the plants. Because if the gun was a misdirect, a way to throw us off the scent, then the killer is getting exactly what they wanted. If we're not connecting the dots back to their other crimes, then they're winning."

Brock stretched his arms up above his head, nodding and yawning. "Okay. Let's give it a shot. What do we have to lose at this point?"

They continued to search into the evening, and Olivia finally began to feel as though they might be making progress.

"This is more like it," Olivia said, reading through a report of a murder. "A killing that took place in Fredericksburg. Anthony McDonald. The victim was forced to consume water hemlock. It contains cicutoxin, which poisons anyone that consumes it. The victim was still alive when he was found but later died in the hospital following serious fits and convulsions that triggered a heart attack."

"What a horrible way to go."

"There was evidence that he might have been tied up before the killing, just like our vics. I guess the killer had to keep the victim still in order to force-feed him the water hemlock. It sounds like they wanted the same thing that our killer wanted. To make the victim suffer before they died."

"And this case is still open?"

Olivia nodded. "It's been open for nearly a month. There are definitely similarities to our case, right? Aside from the lack of firearms on the scene. And it supports the theory that we're dealing with someone who knows a lot about plants."

"I'd say it's a pretty close match. Did you find anything else?"

"There are a couple of more recent cases nearby. According to the report, the three cases are being treated as the same killer due to the unusual MO. The second case, a young woman named Kristen Peck involved white snakeroot, an herb that has trematol content. So basically, it's massively toxic. The victim was found with a swollen, red tongue and covered in her own vomit. The autopsy of her body discovered that the plant had caused her blood to become more acidic than normal and had contributed to her eventual death."

Brock wrinkled his nose. "This is *sick*. Whoever is doing this must be really messed up. Can you imagine wanting to make someone suffer like that?"

Olivia shook her head. "It certainly seems like this person went to great lengths to put on a show. There are definitely easier ways to poison someone. You could literally just pour bleach down someone's throat. But this… this was calculated. And with different plants each time. Do you think these deaths were personalized? Like, the killer knew how much they wanted each victim to suffer and gave them different doses of different plants depending on that?"

"Well, that would explain why they used a different plant each time. What was used in the third case?"

"This one is the strangest. It's like the killer was becoming more… theatrical. It says that the killer used castor beans to kill the victim."

"Wait, castor beans? The same stuff that makes castor oil?"

"Yes, but I'm pretty sure it's okay to use once it's been processed. It says that castor beans contain ricin, a powerful poison that can kill very easily. It can cause someone to have seizures, vomiting, diarrhea… It's not pleasant. A very humiliating way to kill someone, that's for sure. But that's not the part that I was most intrigued by. The killer took it to another level by wrapping the victim up in poison ivy."

Brock frowned. "Why?"

"Why does a killer kill anyone?" Olivia shrugged. "I guess to add to the pain of the victim before they died, on some level. The victim, Sandra Collison, was left with rashes all over her skin. But if I had to guess, the killer is growing more confident. Three kills in one month… they're starting to realize that they're being chased, and I think it's thrilling to them. I think that the poison ivy stunt was more performative than anything else. A way to keep the investigators on their toes."

Brock rubbed at his chin. "Okay… so say this is our killer. It does seem likely, I'll admit. But where does that leave us?"

Olivia took a deep breath. "Well, for starters, I think we need to head down and talk to the Fredericksburg PD. Maybe they will be able to shed further light on the situation, and maybe tell us some things we don't know. And then, maybe we can try to make a connection between the other cases. What was the motive, for example? We've been assuming all along that whoever did this to Arabella and Andrew was a victim of the scam, and I still think that's likely. Unless they did anything worse that we don't know about, then it makes the most sense. So, what did the other victims do, if anything, to become targeted by a killer?"

"It must be horrible to be poisoned like that," Brock mused. "I just can't see how someone would do that to a person without reason."

"I mean, this is a potential serial killer we're talking about, Brock. They don't need rhyme or reason. But I know what you're saying, and I agree. We just need to know more."

"I guess we'll just have to ask."

Brock pulled out his phone and dialed the Fredericksburg police department. It rang out on speakerphone in the apartment.

The call went through after a few moments, and a woman's voice answered the phone.

"Fredericksburg Police."

"Hi, this is Special Agent Olivia Knight," she started and read off her badge number. "I'm calling to ask about a case your department is working on. Is Detective Grayson available?"

"One moment."

"Thanks."

Olivia and Brock waited for several minutes on hold before the line came back to life. They heard the phone being passed between hands and then a gruff-sounding man cleared his throat.

"Ron Grayson speaking."

"Detective, this is Special Agents Knight and Tanner with the FBI. We're working on a case in Richmond—you might have heard about the deaths of Arabella and Andrew Clifford?"

"I think I did hear about that, yes. Does this relate to my own case?"

"We believe so. We have just been given the full autopsy report from the two victims. We have believed all along, with good reason, that the cause of death was the two gunshots to the heads of the victims. It was staged to look like a murder-suicide, but both were found with traces of belladonna in their stomachs. We believe the victims were forced to consume it in some form and that it was used to torture them. We also think that it would've killed them, but that the killer shot them both to mislead the police. Possibly to evade your notice with the other plant poison murders."

Grayson puffed out air on the other end of the line. "Yeah, that sounds like my killer. You said this took place in Richmond?"

"Yes, so not too far from your own cases. We uncovered several online scams that our victims were running, using dating sites and other forums to con people out of thousands of dollars. We believe that our killer is a victim of the scam, or maybe they knew someone affected by it. So, we were hoping that maybe you had some theories about why your killer is doing what they're doing. Do you think it might be revenge of some sort?"

"To tell you the truth, we're still digging," Grayson responded carefully. "This has been a tough nut for us to crack. We were hoping that there might be something really obvious to connect the motives of all three cases, but none of the victims knew one another, and they all led very different lifestyles."

"We've run into similar issues on our end," chimed in Brock.

Grayson gave a thoughtful nod. "Maybe the killer knows something that we don't know about these people. You said that your victims were scammers, but that's not public knowledge, I'm sure. I'm guessing that whoever this person is, they're perceptive, smart, cunning. I think they're one step ahead of the game, and they know things that other people don't. Somehow, maybe, they found out what your victims had done and made them pay for it."

"So, you think that the other victims might have done similar things? That they have deeply buried secrets that only the killer has found?"

"It's a theory. But finding out what the killer knows is no easy feat. People like to keep their secrets as secrets. If there are things the victims wouldn't want people finding, then we might have a hard time uncovering them ourselves. The question is, how did the killer manage it? Did they know the victims well, maybe? Did they find some way to worm their way inside?"

Olivia shook her head. It was an interesting theory, but it didn't help them much. It didn't give them the solid answers that they needed. It was just another gray area for them to stumble around blindly.

"Do you have any suspects at all?" Olivia asked, trying to hide the desperation from her voice. She just wanted something small, something to give her momentum to carry on. There was nothing worse than a case full of dead ends.

"Not so far. Like I said, it's been a tough nut to crack. Maybe you can help us out here, agents. We could use an expert to get to the bottom of this. Plant-wielding serial killers aren't really our specialty."

Olivia chuckled softly. "Well, I'm afraid it's not ours either. We're in the dark too. But we can certainly be of use to one another. Brock and I are heading back to Richmond tomorrow to do a deeper dive. We can stay in contact—let you know what we find."

"Appreciate that," Grayson grunted. "I can put together some documents and send them your way if you'd like to take a look at our victims. Whatever you can do to help, we'd really appreciate it."

"That would be a big help, thanks. We'll send you what we have on ours in case you can make any connections there as well."

A few minutes later, the call had ended, and Olivia sighed back into the sofa, feeling exhausted.

"Well, this isn't how I expected to spend the holidays. Chasing down some plant-obsessed psycho…"

Brock laughed. "Me neither. But hey, at least we're in this together. You want to stay here tonight? We can set off early for Richmond in the morning."

"Sure. As long as you don't let me drink any more beer. My body can't handle it."

"You've got yourself a deal." He cocked his head to the side. "Hey, you know what I've missed in Richmond?"

"Let me guess… the diner."

Brock grinned.

CHAPTER SIXTEEN

66 "I think we should visit the School of Botany in Richmond."

Olivia and Brock were well on their way back to Richmond when she made the suggestion. Brock looked over at her in interest.

"Oh, yeah?"

"I think it's a good start. I mean, think about it. If the killer knows a lot about plants, then they must have gotten their knowledge from somewhere. I mean, this is way beyond your typical interest in gardening, right? It's not exactly information you pick up at the nursery. So maybe the killer was a student there, or still is."

"Good idea. Maybe if we speak to some of the professors, they might have some insight as to who might be capable of such a thing. Or at the very least, what to look out for in terms of poisonous plants. It's worth a shot."

Brock nodded and typed in the address to the college on his GPS.

"You know, I've learned something these last few months," he said casually.

"And what's that?"

"Not to get in your way when you've got a hunch."

Olivia felt warmth rush through her. Being on the case with Brock continued to be exciting, even though they'd hit a few dead ends. She was starting to realize that life really was just better when he was around. He reminded her why she loved her job with his never-ending enthusiasm and the fun he injected into everything they did. He made everything feel like an adventure. She imagined that he could even make something mundane like grocery shopping fun, though she doubted he'd ever bought much more than beer and frozen dinners in his adult life.

That was the fun thing about him. He took her out of her comfort zone. No one would describe her as boring with her sharp mind and her intellectual thoughts, but she wasn't spontaneous the way he was, and she did things by the book for the most part.

But when she was with him, she felt herself letting go a little more. It was freeing, even if it felt a little scarier than what she was used to. And now, she was the one changing their course, sending them off on a wild goose chase on a whim. She didn't know if the School of Botany would even take them anywhere with the investigation, but it could lead to something.

It was nearing midday as they reached the college, and Olivia felt her heart rate increasing ever so slightly. She was almost glad to leave the holidays behind and get back to work. Thanksgiving had been way too intense. It was better not to think about it, or she'd drive herself crazy.

"Let's get in there," Brock said. She fell in step with him as they headed inside. As they entered the building, students were milling around on their way to classes, and several professors were making small talk in the hallways. The energy was clearly a bit dampened after the extended holiday weekend; now was the strange in-between period where final exams for the semester hadn't yet started but the curriculum was approaching its end.

Brock glanced at Olivia.

"Where do we want to start? It's kind of a sensitive topic. And we don't have anything to go on as far as which students to even ask about."

"I guess first things first," Olivia offered. "We'll ask about belladonna. We'll say we're working a case where someone ingested it and see where that leads us. Who knows, they might be more than willing to open up to us."

"Alright. Let's see who we can get to talk to us."

Olivia and Brock spent several minutes chatting with various professors who all seemed like they weren't keen to be in conversation with them. After a while, someone directed them to the office of the head of the department, and Olivia and Brock headed right there. Who better to speak to than the department expert?

They found Professor Shen sitting behind his desk, reading what looked like a student essay. There were red marks all over the paper, and a red pen that was almost depleted rested easily between his fingers. He didn't look up as they knocked and entered.

"I'm sorry. I'm not taking student questions right now," he said. When there was no response from Olivia and Brock, he finally looked up, and then raised his eyebrows. "Oh. You're not students."

"No," Olivia said with an easy smile. "But we did come here in the hopes of learning some things. Special Agents Olivia Knight and Brock Tanner with the FBI."

They badged the man in tandem, and he frowned. "I'm sorry. Is there something wrong? Did one of our students—"

"We hope not," Olivia cut in before he could complete the thought. "We were just wondering if we could steal a few minutes of your time."

Professor Shen wavered. "Well, I'm actually very busy—"

"We understand. But this is important. It could save lives, potentially."

LOVE, LIES, AND SUICIDE

Professor Shen considered her for a moment, shifting uncomfortably in his seat. Then he nudged his glasses a little farther up his nose. "Alright, then. But please, make it quick. I have lots to do."

Olivia strode forward and took a seat opposite the man. Brock joined her, and they both watched him squirm in their presence. Olivia wondered what was making him so uncomfortable.

"So, we're investigating a case at the moment," Olivia started carefully, making sure to not mention that it was a murder case, "and we found traces of belladonna in the stomach of our victim. We wondered what you could tell us about the plant."

Professor Shen blinked several times behind his glasses.

"Belladonna? Well, it's a very useful plant in many ways. It's used in some medicines. When you visit an optometrist, they may use a diluted form of it to dilate your eyes. So, it has practical applications. But it can also be deadly when misused. Even touching it can be dangerous. Many people experience irritation after touching the leaves. It is technically legal to grow in much of the country, but it's not common. It seems strange to me that you'd have a victim who had ingested it." Professor Shen swallowed. "Although, I have to admit… we did recently have some samples of that particular plant go missing from my lab."

Olivia's eyes widened. "A student stole belladonna from your lab? Do you know who it was?"

Professor Shen swallowed again, as though he was trying to rid his throat of a lump. His voice was a little choked as he spoke. "Yes, unfortunately. We have very strict rules about keeping the samples within the lab, so you can imagine that we cracked down on the person who took them. When we caught her, she was immediately dismissed from her studies here. Permanently."

"And you didn't report it to the police?"

"We did report it to campus police," Shen told them. "We stepped up security protocols and redid the full inventory of everything."

"And nothing else was taken but the belladonna?"

Shen shook his head. "That's all she took."

Olivia leaned forward in interest. This student, whoever she was, had to be of interest. She'd been caught stealing the same poisonous plant that was used to torture and harm Andrew and Arabella. She knew enough from her studies to utilize something like belladonna for hurting someone.

"We'd very much like to speak to this young woman. Would you be able to provide us with her contact details?"

Professor Shen wavered. "I'm not sure. We have a confidentiality policy..."

"Please, Professor. We don't want anyone else to get hurt. We believe that whoever poisoned our victims might also be a suspect in multiple other murders as well. This might help us find a serial killer," Olivia told him. Professor Shen's eyes widened.

"I... I hadn't quite realized the gravity of the situation," he stammered. "Let me find the details for you."

He turned to his computer and typed for a while, then looked back at them with concern in his eyes.

"I don't know if she's the one you'll be looking for," he started. "She was always a little wild, but I can't imagine her being a killer. I... I hope you're wrong."

"The information, please, Professor," Brock said. "I'm sorry, but we have to follow this lead."

With shaking hands, Professor Shen wrote down an address for Olivia and Brock. As he handed it over, he hesitated.

"Her name is Ryleigh Waters," he finally admitted. "This is the last address we had on file for her, but I don't know how accurate that will be anymore."

Olivia offered him a tight smile as she took the paper from him.

"Thank you for your help. We'll be in touch."

As Olivia and Brock left the room together, she felt once again the thrill of how close to answers they seemed to be. They rushed back to the car, and without a word, Brock logged the address into the GPS. It wasn't a far drive—only about ten minutes at most.

"It's too much of a coincidence to ignore," Brock murmured as they drove. "Stealing belladonna from the lab? And she has knowledge of plants. But what's the motive? How would she even know the Clifford family?"

"She probably followed Arabella on social media," Olivia mused, searching for Arabella's profile on her phone and then searching Ryleigh's name on her follower list. Olivia sighed. "Yep.

LOVE, LIES, AND SUICIDE

There she is. She followed Arabella's account but didn't seem to interact too much. But if she took an active interest in her life, then maybe she took it too far. Got obsessed. What about the financial records? Do you recall any transactions from that name?

"I don't think so. And if she's a student with no money, then it doesn't seem like she'd be a likely target for the scam, but everything else lines up. We know for a fact she had hold of a plant that was used to torture the Cliffords. We know she could have used her knowledge to hurt someone. We have to at least see if there's a connection."

Brock drove as fast as the limits would allow, and it wasn't long before they were pulling up in front of a set of apartments. Brock checked the address on the piece of paper.

"This is it."

"We'll have to see if we can buzz the apartment. See if someone will come down and greet us. We don't have to mention the case. We'll just see if we can get her to talk."

The pair of them left the car and headed to the main door of the apartment building. Brock nodded to the buzzer system.

"Apartment seventeen."

Olivia pressed the button without hesitation. They waited, holding their breath and waiting for someone to answer. When no one did, Olivia impatiently pushed the button again, and this time, someone answered almost right away. The person answering was breathing hard, like they'd just been for a run.

"What?" the woman snapped. "I'm busy, leave me alone!"

Olivia and Brock exchanged a glance. Olivia was almost certain that they were speaking to Ryleigh. Professor Shen had mentioned that she was a little wild. Had that been his polite way of saying that she was unstable?

"We're sorry to disturb you. we're looking for Ryleigh Waters. We need to speak to her," Olivia said. The woman fell silent for a moment before the line went dead. Olivia hesitated before pressing the buzzer again. They couldn't afford to let her slip away. The woman answered again.

"I thought I told you to get lost!"

"We really need to speak to you, Ryleigh. It's about your status as a student at the School of Botany," Olivia lied smoothly.

She hoped that might be enough to get Ryleigh to allow them into the apartment. But Ryleigh laughed cruelly, like the entire idea was ludicrous.

"That's over. There's no going back now. Now, leave me in peace."

With a crackle of static, she was gone again. Olivia cursed under her breath. They had to find a way into the building, and quickly. Impulsively, Olivia pressed one of the other buzzers and hoped for a miracle. When no one responded, she tried another. This time, someone picked up.

"Hello?"

"FBI," Olivia said quickly. "I need access to this building. We're trying to reach a potential suspect."

"Yo, are you for real?"

"Yes, I'm for real. You can come out and check if you want, but I need access to the building—fast."

The person was quiet for a moment. "Alright, what the hell. I'm buzzing you in."

Olivia felt her heart jolt in triumph. If they could just get into the building, maybe they could get Ryleigh to talk, unstable as she seemed. She heard the buzz of the door unlocking and swung it open, racing inside and toward the staircase.

Brock and Olivia ran up several flights of stairs to reach apartment seventeen, taking several wrong turns before they made it there. As soon as they reached the door, Olivia could tell something was wrong inside. She could hear the sounds of arguing from within. She couldn't make out the words through the closed door, but the woman's voice that they'd heard on the buzzer was clearly angry.

"Brock, this is it," she whispered. "What do we do?"

"Announce ourselves. Let her know that we're coming in anyway if she doesn't come out to speak with us."

"We don't have a warrant—"

"She seems manic. She might not stop to consider that. If she's got something to hide, she's going to panic anyway."

Olivia didn't like the idea of going against the rules, but she didn't see any other way of getting Ryleigh out to talk to them. And whatever was going on inside the apartment, it wasn't anything good. Before she could stop herself, she rapped hard on the door.

"Ryleigh Waters," she called out. "This is the FBI. We'd like to ask you a few questions."

The arguing inside ceased. "FBI?" she asked in a high-pitched voice. "What do you want?"

"Come out and speak with us and there won't be an issue," Brock followed up.

"I... I can't right now! Come back later!"

"Ryleigh, open the door or we'll break it down," Brock warned. Olivia's heart skipped a beat. She knew they couldn't do that, but the lie seemed to have paid off because they heard shuffling close to the door.

"You can't come in!" she cried from the other side. She opened the door just a crack and a face peered around. She was wearing heavy makeup with green glitter smeared across her eyelids. Her eyes were red and bloodshot, and Olivia could smell the familiar stench of marijuana coming from inside the apartment. She was definitely high.

"I told you, you can't come in right now!" she snapped, her voice tinged with more anxiety than anger. Brock stared her down.

"And why is that, Ryleigh?"

"I'm busy—I told you!"

He narrowed his eyes. "Busy with what?"

That was when Olivia heard the strangled cry from inside the apartment. It was muffled, but there was no denying it was there.

It sounded like someone saying, "Help!"

Olivia was immediately alert, her hand close to her gun.

"Ryleigh, open the door," Olivia said as calmly as she could. Ryleigh shook her head fiercely.

"No!"

Brock reached forward and gave the door a quick shove, forcing Ryleigh to retreat a few steps. When the door swung open, Ryleigh cried out, but it was too late. Olivia and Brock had already seen what she was up to.

In the center of the apartment, a young man was tied to a chair, a sock stuffed in his mouth to keep him quiet. He looked like he'd been there for some time, his cheeks red and stained with tear tracks. Ryleigh's unusual makeup suddenly made sense as Olivia clocked that she was dressed as the character, Poison Ivy. Olivia immediately snatched up her gun, pointing it at Ryleigh.

"What have you done to him?" Olivia asked, horrified by the scene in front of her. It was then that she saw what littered the coffee table. A bag of white powder, a few rolled-up joints, and a bag of pills. But the drugs didn't interest her as much as the handful of dark berries beside them.

Belladonna…

"He cheated on me!" Ryleigh screamed, tears streaming down her cheeks. "I wanted to make him pay!"

Olivia knew they didn't have long. She'd seen how dangerous belladonna could be. And if Ryleigh was their killer, then she was also in possession of a gun. Olivia nodded to Brock who rushed forward and restrained Ryleigh, cuffing her.

"You're being arrested on suspicion of murder and torture," Brock told her as Olivia rushed to untie the young man. His head lolled to the side and his eyes were growing vacant. She dialed 911, trying to remain calm. Had they just stopped a murder?

"You're alright," she assured the young man. "It's going to be alright."

"You don't understand!" Ryleigh screamed. "I just wanted to make him *suffer!* The way he made *me* suffer!"

In the hallway, some of the other residents were emerging to see what was going on, but Olivia and Brock ignored them.

Olivia rattled off her badge number and address as soon as the dispatcher picked up. "I need police and an ambulance," she said quickly. "We have a man here who has been forced to ingest belladonna and potentially other stimulants. And we have apprehended the woman responsible."

CHAPTER SEVENTEEN

OLIVIA AND BROCK STOOD WITH WYATT AND GRAYSON in the Richmond police station. They were all watching Ryleigh Waters sit irritably in the interrogation room through the two-way mirror. Wyatt had been apprised immediately given the belladonna connection, and Olivia had called Grayson immediately after the arrest. Waters seemed like an obvious candidate based on what she'd done, but they still needed to figure out why she did it.

"Do you think she was capable of all those murders?" Wyatt asked, peering in at the young woman. Olivia could understand why he was hesitant to believe it. Ryleigh was small in stature and slim. She looked as though she couldn't hurt a fly. And yet, she had somehow managed to tie her boyfriend to a chair and force-fed him harmful substances.

"Don't let looks deceive you," Olivia responded. "This woman is definitely going to do time for what she did to her boyfriend. We're still waiting to hear whether he will recover from what she did to him. So, yes, I think she could be capable of it. She might not look like a killer, but what does a killer look like, really? If we can get her to talk, then maybe we can connect some of the dots, shut this down for good."

Ron nodded. "Agreed. Do you mind if I come in there with you? I've been waiting a long time to face the person who might be responsible for all of this."

"Of course. Let's get in there."

"I'll wait here," Wyatt said, watching through the mirror as Olivia, Brock, and Grayson moved to enter the smaller chamber.

Ryleigh looked up as Olivia opened the door to the room. She sighed and fidgeted in her chair, as though the whole thing was just an inconvenience to her.

"There's no way Chris is going to press charges against me, so you may as well let me go," Ryleigh insisted. Olivia raised an eyebrow as she sat down.

"Well, that's not really up to him. And since he's currently recovering in hospital from what you did, I don't think you can speak for him, can you?"

Ryleigh slumped a little in her chair as the three investigators sat down. "You don't get it. I wasn't trying to poison him or anything. I just wanted him to feel a bit sick. He deserved to, after he cheated on me."

Brock sighed. "Ms. Waters, we don't care if this man cheated on you a thousand times. You still forced him to ingest some pretty dangerous substances. You could easily have killed him, and you still did it. So, now we need to know what else you're capable of."

Ryleigh stared at him blankly. "What's that supposed to mean?"

"Ryleigh... are you familiar with the names Arabella and Andrew Clifford?" Grayson asked her sternly. Her eyes widened.

"Oh. I see where this is going. Yes, I know who they are. Of course, I do. I used to follow her before I found out she's a bad person."

"What makes you say that?" Olivia asked. She'd been keeping an eye on the news related to the Clifford family tragedy. So far, nothing had been leaked about the scam they'd been running. So, did Ryleigh know something that they didn't?

"I heard someone say that they were liars. They made a big show of helping out their fans, of being nice, but it was all fake. It was just a show."

"What do you mean by that?" she asked.

"Like, they'd pretend to be so nice to their fans," Ryleigh said. "But my friend Serena is a barista and said she doesn't tip, even when they give her free coffee. Also, she was still working with this brand that was known for bad environmental practices. And people say she posts a lot of stuff for clout, but it's all fake."

Olivia felt irritation poking at her. This felt more like petty drama than motive for murder. She was still convinced that Ryleigh knew more than she was saying. Either she was the killer, or she knew something about who did it.

"Tell me, Ms. Waters, did you hear about *how* they were killed?" Brock prodded.

"They were shot, weren't they?"

Brock nodded. "They were. But not before they'd been poisoned with belladonna."

A twinge of shock crossed Ryleigh's face, but she covered it up in an instant.

"That doesn't mean anything," she replied.

"I wouldn't be so sure about that. Is it just a coincidence that they were killed around the same time you were kicked out of the School of Botany for stealing some of those same plants?" Brock pressed. "Do you see how that makes you look?"

Ryleigh rolled her eyes. She didn't seem to understand the kind of trouble she was in. "Well, obviously that's not a great look for me. I can admit that much. But everything I stole was taken back. Apart from the belladonna. You can check that with Professor Shen. He was pretty thorough in getting all his samples back. But I managed to keep a hold of the belladonna. I figured I'd need it at some point… and I was right."

Olivia was shocked at how honest Ryleigh was being. She definitely seemed a little unstable. Then she remembered the array of drugs that she'd been keeping out in the open in her apartment. Perhaps the drugs had loosened her lips a little.

"So, what you're telling us is that you didn't kill those people," Olivia said bluntly. If Ryleigh was high, she doubted she'd have the tools in her arsenal to form a proper defense against her questions. Ryleigh smiled dopily at her, blinking slowly.

"Of course not. I'm not a murderer. When I stole that belladonna, it was just for fun. I like to collect things. Especially useful things. I know that small doses can just lead to you having like, a bad trip. It wasn't ever going to be a fatal dose. So, I thought, what the hell? I'll give Chris a dose, make him suffer a little for betraying me, but I didn't wish him any harm. Not really."

"And yet, here we are," Grayson said gruffly. "You don't seem particularly concerned about your boyfriend, Ms. Waters. Are you not the least bit ashamed of what you've done?"

Ryleigh laughed. "Oh, sure I am! I know he's not going to be happy with me when I see him. But at least now, we're even."

Olivia almost sighed in despair. Ryleigh was a wild card, that was for sure. But her blunt honesty didn't seem to be getting them any closer to identifying her as the killer.

"So, you're telling us that you had nothing to do with these murders? Despite having the same poison?"

Ryleigh finally seemed to be showing some remorse in her expression. She stuck out her bottom lip into a pout. "I know it looks bad. But I can tell you have nothing on me, or you'd be able to prove a closer link. Because I didn't do it, and you know it."

"So then, where were you on the night of the nineteenth?"

Ryleigh thought for a moment. "We had a party that night."

"Any pictures from that night?" Brock pressed. "Any proof?"

"You can probably look through my phone," she admitted. Brock snatched it up off the table. "Actually, um…"

He let out a low whistle as he scrolled through the pictures. "Seems to me you've got quite a bit of paraphernalia in some of these photos," he commented. "We'll have a talk about that later. Ah, here we go."

He turned the phone around to show everyone the selfie she'd taken of her and a young man. "This you and your boyfriend?"

"Yeah."

"Taken at 8:42 p.m.," he noted.

"That's about an hour before the unauthorized entry," Olivia told him.

He scrolled through the next few. "Looks like we have a few more. I'm going to need names and details for some of these people."

"Okay," Ryleigh nodded. "Okay, I can get those. But that clearly shows that I wasn't there that night."

"What about on the night of the twenty-eighth of October?" Grayson snapped. "The third of November? The eleventh?"

Ryleigh blinked at the question. "Now I don't even know what you're asking me. What does this have to do with anything?"

"The Clifford case isn't the only one we're talking about. There have been four murders involving plant poison, Miss Waters. We have a serial killer on our hands. Maybe it's you," he said in a low, rough voice. Finally, Ryleigh's face cracked.

"A—a serial killer?" she sputtered. For the first time, it looked like the reality of the situation was setting in. "You think I'm a serial killer?"

"Well, you had the means, didn't you? You had access to all of the murder weapons," Grayson said calmly. His approach was much more offensive than Olivia and Brock were used to, but it seemed to be working. "And you have the rare kind of knowledge that allowed you to kill those people. Not many people know this kind of stuff about plants, do they? What do you have to say for yourself?"

"No!" Ryleigh cried out now, distress in her eyes. "There's no way—I'm not a killer—I swear!"

"It really would be in your interest to cooperate with us, Ms. Waters," Brock pressed.

"I am cooperating!" she insisted. Ryleigh blinked several times and sank her head into her hands. "I swear, I am cooperating."

"As touching as your newfound clarity is, we're going to need more," Grayson said sternly.

"I don't know," she mumbled.

"So, you've never heard of Anthony McDonald? Kristen Peck? Sandra Collison?"

"I have no idea who those people are," Ryleigh insisted. They waited for a long moment for her to say anything more, but she was crashing. She started rocking herself backward and forward in her chair and murmuring to herself. Her head slumped low and she lost the manic energy she'd been keeping up.

"Well, until such time as you decide to talk, we'll be ready for you," Olivia said, standing up quickly. "In the meantime, you're under arrest for aggravated assault, attempted murder, and a bunch of drug charges. Come on."

She nodded for Brock and Grayson to follow her out of the room. Both men had troubled looks on her faces, but she let out a sigh. "We're not getting anywhere with this. I agree that she's our primary suspect for now. But we still need to connect her to the victims."

"That got pretty intense in there," Wyatt noted. "Let's hope she calms down enough to make a confession soon."

"I'm not holding out for much," said Grayson irritably.

"You stay here with her. Keep pressing her if you can," Olivia said. She knew if any of them were going to get through to her, it was going to be Grayson. Besides, he had three other cases to grill her about too. "We'll go and pay the boyfriend a visit. The moment he's conscious, we can ask him about what he knows."

Grayson nodded to her. "No problem. I'm sure Ryleigh and I will find plenty to chat about."

CHAPTER EIGHTEEN

As Brock drove to the hospital, Olivia pulled up Ryleigh's social media accounts and searched for the dates in question.

"I don't see any particular posts on the nights of those other murders," she said. "But that doesn't mean much. Not everyone posts a photo every minute of every day. Most of these are just occasional selfies with her boyfriend."

"You think it could be her?" Brock asked.

"I don't know. She had belladonna in her possession, and she's clearly more than a little unstable, but what would the motive be? Certainly, she wouldn't have killed the Cliffords in such a brutal way just because they got canceled on social media. Right?"

"That would really give a new meaning to the phrase, 'cancel culture,'" Brock joked. "But I agree. Something that visceral had to be personal, not parasocial."

"And the other thing that bothers me is that I don't know how she could've gotten in the house," Olivia went on. "Did she have the code to disable the alarm system?"

"Maybe she held the victims at gunpoint and made them disable the alarm?" he offered. "That's far-fetched, but that's the only thing I can think of. She clearly had some familiarity with tying up her victims though."

"True," Olivia acknowledged. She wracked her brain to try to fit all the disparate pieces of information together. Her head was dizzy from all of the zipping around, finding new potential suspects everywhere they went. It was frustrating. The first suspect they'd cornered had the opportunity to break in, but no motive or method. The second suspect had opportunity and motive, but no method. And now they had someone in custody that did have the method, but nothing else. It was like they were trying to put together a puzzle while only seeing half the picture.

The other huge elephant in the room was the sheer mystery of what connected the cases. Why three in Fredericksburg and two in Richmond? What connected the victims? Did anything connect them at all, or were they simply chasing another dead end?

They pulled into the hospital parking lot just as something finally clicked in her brain.

"Wait a minute, Brock," she said with a heavy frown. "Chris Marsh..."

He gave her a bewildered look. "That's... the boyfriend's name, all right."

"No, that's not what I mean. Look."

She showed him Chris's profile—in particular a memorial post from only a few months before.

"Rest in peace, Mom," Brock read out. "I'm so sorry for what happened to you. I wish I could have helped you. You deserved so much better. I hope you are with Dad now."

He locked eyes with Olivia and she immediately felt her heart racing. As if they shared the same brainwave, they spoke at the same time:

"Violet Marsh."

They quickly got out of the car and stormed into the hospital. Olivia felt anxiety clawing at her chest. If Chris knew that the Cliffords were responsible for the death of his mother, in part, then what was stopping him from getting revenge? If Ryleigh was living with him, then he had access to belladonna. The motive he would have had was much stronger than Ryleigh's, and she had pretty much told them everything before she came to her senses.

"He's got a really good reason to have killed the Cliffords, that's for sure," she told Brock as they stalked down the white hallways. "But what about all of the other cases? Why would he want those people dead?"

"We're assuming we're dealing with the same people in every case," Brock pointed out. "We can't get ahead of ourselves. Maybe Chris was smart enough to attempt a copycat version of a killer already in the area. Maybe he tried to use the belladonna, but it wasn't working, so he shot them. I don't know. We'll make sure to find out."

Olivia barely kept herself together as they rode in the elevator up to the floor where his room was. It only took a few seconds, but it felt like hours had passed. She just wanted to get in there and talk to Chris. In his shoes, wouldn't many people do the same? Seek out revenge on the people who drove his mother to suicide? When they'd spoken to him on the phone, she'd heard the pain in his voice, heard the despair that she'd felt so many times in her life. She could understand why he'd do it. But that didn't mean he could get away with it.

When they eventually made it to his room, Olivia feared they would be too late. Maybe he'd succumbed to the poisons inside him, or maybe he'd woken up and was ready for them. Either way, they might never get the information they wanted out of Chris, and that would set them back a long way. They needed to catch him unawares and grill him, even after everything he'd just gone through.

When they entered his room, he was sleeping. There was a drip attached to his arm, and a nurse was tending to him. She looked up as they entered the room.

"You must be the agents that saved his life," the nurse said with a warm smile. "I think if you hadn't come when you did, he wouldn't have made it. I imagine you want to talk to him. He should come around in the next few hours. He's been given physostigmine, which should take effect and stop his stomach pains. It'll take a while before he's up and running again, but he'll be alright."

"Thank you so much," Olivia said with a smile. "Is it alright if we wait here for him to wake up? We definitely need to talk to him."

"We don't normally allow visitors to stay late, but given the circumstances, I'll make an exception. But after my shift ends, you might face some opposition from the other nurses."

"We'll cross that bridge when we get to it. Thank you."

The nurse left the room, and Olivia sighed as she sank into a chair. As she stared at the young man in the bed, he looked much younger than he had when he was tied to the chair, at the mercy of his girlfriend. It was strange to think that the man who might be the killer in their investigation was also so fragile, someone capable of both being on the receiving end of an attack but also of wielding power. It wasn't often Olivia came across a suspected killer who seemed capable of weakness. It had always seemed to her like the people she chased down were untouchable. But the young man in front of her seemed like an exception to the rules in her head. Because if he really was a killer, he definitely didn't look like one at that moment.

Then again, hadn't she just reminded Wyatt not to underestimate a person? She kept her jaw set as she kept an eye on Chris's sleeping body. He was classically handsome with floppy hair and a pair of glasses set on the side of his bed. He had freckles on his cheeks that added to his youthful look. No matter how hard Olivia tried, she couldn't imagine him wielding a gun or forcing poison down someone's throat.

But that didn't mean she didn't suspect him of it.

The hours passed by in quiet tension. Grayson called to let them know that Ryleigh was sticking to her story and that they were sending out a team to search the apartment that she shared with Chris. Olivia wondered what they'd find. They'd almost certainly find evidence of drugs, but that was the least of their concerns for now. Maybe they'd actually find the gun, the murder weapon used to end Arabella and Andrew's lives. Maybe they'd find some of the other plants used to kill the other victims in the Fredericksburg cases. Olivia hoped they'd get some answers before Chris woke up that they could use against him. It was nearly midnight when he began to stir.

They'd run out of time. Now was the time to get him to talk.

She watched as Chris's eyes flickered open, and he blinked several times, adjusting to the low light in the room and the sensations he was experiencing. He groaned, looking nauseous as he tried to sit up. Olivia stood and moved to his bedside, careful not to spook him.

It was agonizing, but they had to take it slow. He was confined to a hospital bed and in no state to run. They could take as much time as they needed.

"Take it easy," she said to him. "You've had quite a day."

Chris immediately turned and vomited into a bucket beside his bed. Olivia wrinkled her nose and called for the nurse to come check on Chris. She checked on his meds and cleaned him up a little before leaving again. Chris smiled feebly at Olivia and Brock.

"Sorry about that. Hey, you're the guys who got me out back there. I guess I owe you my life. Is Ryleigh okay?"

Olivia blinked in surprise. She hadn't expected him to be concerned with his girlfriend's welfare after what she'd done to him.

"Well, she's in police custody," Brock started, folding his arms over his chest. "Being charged with, at least, attempted murder."

"Oh," he frowned. "I mean… I don't want to press charges or anything…"

Olivia squinted closely at the young man, trying to figure out what he meant by that.

"You don't have a choice," she told him. "She's getting charged whether you like it or not."

Chris looked down and sighed. "She's really not a bad person, you know. She's… she's special to me."

Brock's expression fell into pure bewilderment. "She tried to kill you, man. Because she thought you were cheating on her."

"She just has these… episodes," he explained slowly, still clearly weak from the poison. "It's never been anything this bad before. Usually, she's really great. A supportive partner. Someone I can rely on. But if she isn't taking her meds…"

That information filed itself away in Olivia's mind for her to peruse later. If Ryleigh had a history of violent episodes and hadn't been taking her meds, would she be capable of murder? It seemed to clearly be the case, given that if she and Brock had been even a few minutes later, Chris might be dead.

"What kind of meds does she take?" she asked.

Chris shook his head. "I don't know. Some sort of antipsychotic. It may have had a reaction with whatever drugs she was on. I'm always telling her not to do that…"

That information gave Olivia pause. "So, you don't do drugs?"

He shook his head. "Never. I've been trying to get Ryleigh to quit for a while, but sometimes she relapses."

Brock looked over at Olivia and took a deep breath. She prepared herself to ask the question that had been burning bright in her mind ever since they'd got here. They'd lulled Chris into a false sense of security, and now was the time to see how he reacted when the chips were down.

"We have something else to ask you," she started. "I'd like to know where you were on the night of the nineteenth?"

Chris's face screwed up in confusion. "Why?"

"Can you just answer the question, please?" Brock prodded him. They already knew the answer, of course: he'd been at the party as they'd seen on social media. But that was no reason not to be thorough.

"I, um… I think that was the night of the party?" he asked. He considered it for a moment and nodded slowly. "Yeah, we had a party at our place. I'm sure the neighbors would tell you as much—it was kind of noisy. But there were plenty of people there that night who could tell you that I was there. And Ryleigh, too, but I guess you'd rather have a more reliable source. Is there any chance I can get her on the phone? I want to let her know I'm not mad at her."

Brock rolled his eyes. "Jesus, kid. You really got it bad, you know that?"

Chris shrugged weakly. "Can't help who I love."

"You and I have very different definitions of love, buddy."

"Why are you asking about the party, anyway?"

Olivia gave a tight smile. "Chris, you might remember a while back, before Thanksgiving. You got a call from the FBI about your mother…"

She saw the light of realization dawn behind his eyes in real time. "Wait, that was you?" he sputtered.

"It was," Brock confirmed.

Chris looked down at the bed, a mixture of heavy emotions playing on his face as the statement settled in. "So, this is about… the scam, isn't it? And what happened to my mom?"

Olivia nodded. "We have found the persons responsible for stealing your mother's money."

"Who is it?" he asked, gripping the hospital sheets tightly.

"We're working on getting the money back to its rightful owners—"

"I don't care about the money," Chris interrupted. "Who did this to my mom?"

Olivia gave a sigh. "Does the name Andrew Clifford mean anything to you?"

Chris considered it for a moment and slowly shook his head. Anger was bubbling under his surface, and Olivia didn't blame him. But she didn't get the sense that he knew the full picture.

"Isn't that… that famous guy who just got killed?" he asked. "Wait, do you think I did this?"

"Motive seems pretty clear to me," Brock told him. "You wanted revenge against the people who took everything from you."

He shook his head. "No. I swear, I didn't do that. I—it was my mother's last request."

Chris swallowed and a tear trickled from his eye, but he did his best to hide it, gently closing his eyelids to cover the pain in his gaze.

"All she wanted was for me to live a good life. She wanted me to be happy. To not let myself fall into grief the way she had. In her note, she told me not to go after the person who did this to her. She told me to be happy for her because she was going back to Dad. She was such a good woman… of course, she fell for it. Of course, she went all in. At the end of the day, it was her kindness that killed her. And I loved her for it, even though it was painful."

"I'm sorry for your loss, Chris," said Brock.

Chris shook his head slowly. "I struggled with that, you know. I wanted those people to suffer. I wanted to find them and make them pay. But I didn't. You know why? Because my mom never would have wanted them to suffer. She told me seeking out revenge would just break my own heart again and again. It wouldn't bring her back."

Despite herself, Olivia thought of her own mother. She was lucky that her mom wasn't gone forever; she was just devoted to the case. But how long would holding on to that bitterness serve her? How long could she endure this wall of separation?

"So, what did you do?" she asked.

"I've been trying to live my life. Ryleigh's helping me through it. She's been really great to me."

"Except for, you know, trying to murder you," Brock cut in.

"She's just going through a lot. Same as me. I just want to know she's okay. And while I'm at it, maybe I can convince her that I never cheated on her. That's what started this whole mess off in the first place."

Olivia narrowed her eyes at him. "You're an interesting couple. How did you meet?"

Chris shrugged. "I went to this volunteer event planting trees last spring. We got partnered up, and we just hit it off."

"So, you know a lot about plants, then?" she asked.

"A little. Mostly from her. I'm really more into hiking and camping. The environment's important to me, but I wouldn't say I'm an expert."

"So, you didn't have her steal those plants for the purpose of your revenge then?" Brock asked sharply, trying to catch Chris off guard. "You didn't intend to torture Andrew Clifford for what he did to your family?"

Chris shook his head insistently. "I didn't even know she had stolen those samples until she got kicked out of school. I was under the impression that she had been forced to return everything she stole. I guess I should have checked. That might have saved me a trip to the hospital, right?"

LOVE, LIES, AND SUICIDE

Olivia sighed quietly. Another person who seemed to have all the answers. Another person who had an alibi, and a solid one. Sure, they'd check it out, but if an entire party full of people knew where he'd been that night, then it seemed likely he wasn't lying. So where did that leave them? With a set of tangled threads, none of them appearing to lead anywhere.

"Can I rest now?" Chris asked. "I'm feeling kind of rough."

Olivia and Brock exchanged a look. There wasn't much else they could do without more investigation. They took down a few details about the guests at the party before they left, leaving them with some leads to chase the following day. But Olivia was growing more and more concerned that they were about to run into another dead end.

And when they did, they'd be right back at the beginning.

CHAPTER NINETEEN

UNSURPRISINGLY, GIVEN THAT THEY'D ALREADY checked it out through social media, the party proved to be a solid alibi. It felt like they'd made some progress: Ryleigh Waters was still in custody. Chris Marsh was still in the hospital. But they had no further leads on who killed Arabella and Andrew Clifford.

And now they sat at a Mexican restaurant in Richmond, completely at a loss for where to go next.

"I just don't understand. We have met so many people who had reasons to kill them—so many people who could have easily done it," Brock mused as he picked at his plate of beans and rice. "But they all have rock-solid alibis. We searched every nook and cranny of their apartment, and nothing. Computers and phones came up clean. There was no evidence of more poisonous plants being kept in the apartment. So, it's another dead end. How are we ever going to catch these guys when they seem lost in a sea of other possible killers?"

Olivia shrugged. "We just have to keep pushing on. I know what you're feeling. I always hate this part—where all the best leads we have seem to have fizzled into nothing, and we're left feeling clueless. But we always get there in the end. We just need to keep going."

But even as she was saying it, she was feeling exhausted. It had been a rough week. Ever since Thanksgiving, it felt like the world was against her. Her mother kept trying to contact her, trying to work things out between them. Tom hadn't messaged her again, but the knowledge that she'd have to speak to him eventually was stressful in itself. And then there was the case, which just seemed more and more impossible as time went on.

But at least there was Brock. Reliable, safe Brock. They were in this thing together, and that made Olivia feel a little better, even if there wasn't much else to celebrate.

Brock pushed aside the seemingly endless tray of tortilla chips, which they'd barely made a dent in. "This isn't going how I thought it would," Brock admitted. "I was convinced this was just a murder-suicide. But now it seems like this is going to take a lot longer to figure out."

Olivia said nothing. She didn't need to when the answer was so obvious to them. She too pushed the rest of her food away. "Let's get out of here. We can go back to the motel and review what we know. Maybe there's something we've missed that links the four sets of victims."

Brock grabbed his jacket and slid out of the booth. "Like what though? I'm pretty sure Ron has covered every possible base over the past month. It's no wonder we're getting nowhere if we're looking for the same person. They're clearly a slippery customer."

"I know. And Ron seems pretty capable. I don't imagine he lets much get past him. But I know there's a link somewhere. There has to be. When we spoke to him that first time, he talked about digging up dirt… like how did the killer know about the scam unless they were a victim of it? The killer is smart, to say the least. But if they dug up dirt on the victims, then we can too."

The cold wind hit them as they were leaving the diner. Olivia had forgotten her coat when they left for the diner, and she shivered a little. A moment later, she felt the weight of Brock's jacket being draped around her shoulders. She smiled up at him. The warmth of his jacket flooded right through to her heart.

"Such a gentleman."

"And don't you forget it," Brock cracked with an easy smile. "Sorry for being so negative about this whole case. I'm just a little burned out. We've put so much energy into finding the culprit, and it doesn't feel like it's paying off." He paused. "You know, it's been a long time since I've felt like this."

"Unconfident? Confused?"

He rolled his eyes and pressed on. "Seriously, Olivia. I've told you before how I lost my love for the job a little, but since working with you, I've remembered how to care about it again. And I guess I'm taking it kind of personally that it's not going well. At least when I don't put in one hundred percent, I can blame my own laziness. Now I just feel a little incompetent."

"You're far from that," Olivia insisted. "This job is no walk in the park. No one is expecting us to solve these cases overnight. It might feel like we're far from the finish line, but we'll make it. We always do."

They reached Brock's car and Olivia heard her phone ringing in her pocket. She fetched it and checked the caller ID.

"Wyatt," she told Brock before answering the call. "Hey, Wyatt. What's up?"

"Need you to meet me at a house on Meadowgreen. Just got a call that a woman dropped dead in her home. She seemed to have suffered from some kind of seizure. She had foam coming out of her mouth when she was found."

"We're on our way. Do you think it has to do with our cases?"

"I remembered something that Grayson told me about one of the victims in his cases. He was found in a similar state. Had been poisoned with water hemlock. I'm wondering if the case might be the same here."

Olivia felt a flutter in her stomach. "You think this is our killer?"

"It's a theory, for sure. But I wanted to give you a heads up. It's worth checking out."

"Thanks."

After the call ended, Olivia filled Brock in on what Wyatt had told her. He frowned as Olivia was talking, taking the whole thing in.

"Interesting. I guess we'll find out when we get there. If this was the killer, then surely this will open things up a little for us? Maybe we'll get a new lead tonight."

Olivia hoped he was right. They really needed a win. Besides, if the killer was still finding new targets, they needed to stop them before anyone else was killed. If this was part of their trail, they couldn't afford to miss a thing.

The police were already on the scene when they arrived. Olivia and Brock made their way inside and found Wyatt standing beside the victim's body, his face crumpled in concern. Olivia and Brock pulled on gloves solemnly, trying not to look too much at the victim. Her eyes were still bulging and wide open. Her lips were frothy and her body seemed to be jutted out at odd angles. Presumably, her death had been violent following the convulsions she'd suffered.

In her hand were the shattered remains of a glass filled with a thick, green smoothie. Some of it was splattered all over the kitchen tiles. She clearly hadn't drunk very much before she fell to the ground.

A thin trickle of blood spilled out from behind her head, mixing in with the shards of glass and the green-brown smoothie. Olivia shuddered at the sight. The narrative seemed clear: whatever was in the smoothie had poisoned her, and she'd fallen, hit her head on the ground, and bled out. At least, that was Olivia's first impression of the situation.

Olivia circled the body carefully, checking every inch of the woman's body for clues. Wyatt stood a little further back, his lips pressed into a tight line.

"Mallory Benson," he told them grimly. "Thirty-eight years old."

"She lived alone?" Brock asked.

Wyatt shook his head. "There's a husband too. Cameron. But he isn't home," he informed them. "Seems that the next-door neighbor heard Mallory cry out and fall down and came over to check up on her."

"And where is the husband now?" Olivia asked.

"Already got a team out looking for him. Neighbor mentioned that there has been a violent past between Mallory and her husband, but if he was home at the time of her death, the neighbor never saw him."

Olivia knew that the husband was always the prime suspect—and for good reason. But something about this didn't seem right. If this truly was connected to the other victims, how did it relate to the Cliffords at all?

"What do you think?" Wyatt asked. Olivia shook her head.

"There's no telling for sure if she was poisoned until we do the autopsy. It's definitely possible that someone could have put something in that glass, given that she was drinking it when she collapsed. But she also could have just suffered a seizure. We're going to need to look into this deeper." Olivia paused as she spotted something. "But maybe there is evidence that someone was here after all..."

Olivia bent down beside the body and took a closer look. There was bruising at the base of her neck, as though someone had roughly grabbed her. Olivia stood back up, shaking her head.

"Looks like someone tried to attack her," she said solemnly. "We can't be sure of anything yet, Wyatt, but I think you're onto something. Something feels very wrong here."

∽

Olivia managed to fast-track everything from there. The autopsy of the body was quickly pushed through, and from there began the analysis of the victim's blood and the skin underneath her nails. They took the blender that had made the victim's smoothie in for analysis, too, to determine whether there was poison in the drink she'd had. Meanwhile, Wyatt checked in with his team for the whereabouts of the husband.

"He's not at work. He's not in the neighborhood. Far as we can tell, his car's not in city limits," he groused.

"It does seem coincidental, doesn't it? That an abusive husband suddenly disappears off the grid when his wife is at home, dying with bruises on her neck," Olivia said tightly. "The sooner we find him, the better."

The wait for results was tense. Olivia was desperate for answers. If Mallory really had died from poisoning, then it couldn't possibly have been Ryleigh Waters, who was still in custody. That meant it was someone they hadn't even considered yet. Perhaps it was the violent husband, but perhaps not. Olivia rubbed at her temple. The stress of it all was once again a lot to handle, but she pushed on with her work. She wanted to know what they were dealing with.

And then came the call that confirmed every one of her suspicions. First off, the cause of death was cyanide poisoning. The smoothie contained ground-up apple seeds—large amounts of them too. It was likely that the dosage had been enough to kill Mallory within a few minutes of consuming it, but not before she had suffered intense nausea, shortness of breath, and a seizure, which caused her to fall heavily to the ground and crack her skull. The crime scene unit had already taken the smoothie ingredients for evidence as well. Mixed into the can of whey protein on the counter were finely ground pieces of hundreds—possibly thousands—of apple seeds: a dose lethal enough to kill a person several times over, or at the very least, poison them slowly for weeks. This meant that her death was certainly not an accident, and that whoever killed her intended for her to suffer greatly before her death.

Secondly, the skin under the victim's nails suggested that she'd had an altercation with the killer. Perhaps she'd scratched the person after realizing what they were doing to her, or she had tried to grab them to stop them from leaving her. There was a hair under one broken nail, too, like it had been ripped straight from the killer's head. The preliminary analysis of it suggested that the killer was white, male, dark-haired. That didn't open things up much, but it was a start.

"Finally, we might be getting somewhere," Brock said as Olivia finished up the call. "So, we're looking for a white man with short, dark hair. I wonder where the hell we might find one of those?"

Olivia rolled her eyes at his sarcasm, but she knew he was right. It was still going to be a huge challenge to identify the killer based on so little.

"And where the hell is the husband, I wonder?" Olivia mused out loud.

She got her answer long after the sun had set while she and Brock were checking over the autopsy report. Mallory's husband, Cameron, had been in police custody in Fredericksburg for several hours.

"On what charge?" Olivia asked over the phone when Grayson called. He sighed.

"Drunk driving. He's in deep trouble even if he had nothing to do with what happened to his wife. He crashed into another car. He's fine, but the people in the other car? Not so much. So, we've got him locked down for now. I imagine Wyatt's going to want words with him, but I don't think he knows about his wife yet. He's still a bit out of it."

"We'll drive over and speak with him," Olivia said wearily. She was running on empty, but she was ready for answers. She and Brock drove there as the clock ticked past midnight, ready to try again with their latest potential killer. The amount of death that had surrounded them as of late was alarming. But if Cameron was their guy, then they could finish it up right then and there.

Cameron looked a little worse for wear when they arrived at his holding cell in the Fredericksburg police station. He slumped his way over to the glass window separating him from Brock and Olivia, his smile a little lopsided.

"Whatever it is you think I did, I didn't do it," he announced, slurring his words a little. Brock folded his big arms over his chest.

"Is that so? Well, then I guess we'll just let you go."

"That would be great."

"I don't think so, buddy. Maybe you should sit down. I think we need to talk about your wife."

"My wife?" Cameron scoffed. "Why would we talk about that stick in the mud? I thought you brought me in for driving too fast or something."

Olivia pressed her lips together. "Sir, when you left the house last night, what was your reason for heading out?"

Cameron shrugged. "Had some dumb argument with my wife. So, I went to hit the bars."

"After you hit her, presumably?" Brock pressed. "We saw the bruises on her neck, Cameron."

Cameron shook his head sluggishly. "I didn't hit her. I might have grabbed her a little, but it was a heated moment. What, did she put you up to this? Did she spin you some lies to make me look like a villain?"

Olivia watched him carefully. It really seemed like he had no clue what was going on. She stared him down.

"She didn't tell us anything, Mr. Benson. She's dead."

Cameron stared at her blankly, unblinking. "No, she isn't," he blurted. "When I left the house, she was swearing at me like a sailor. She can't do that if she's dead, can she now?"

"I'm sorry, but we received a call last night while you were out driving," Brock said stiffly. "Your wife passed away."

Cameron's face slowly, but surely, crumpled. Olivia could see from his face that it was a complete shock to him. And all at once, she knew she wasn't looking at the person responsible for killing her. He might have hurt her, sure. She had no doubt that he'd given her the bruises on her neck. But now, as the man heard that she was gone for good, he was completely floored. He hadn't been expecting it. And the more Olivia thought about it, she didn't see how it would be possible for him to kill her. He'd left the house to drink and had never come back. He'd been in police custody for most of that time. So, in what world would he have had time to kill her? In what world had he returned to the house and made up that smoothie himself, adding the deadly poison to the concoction to end her life, then left before the neighbor came over?

None of it made sense. How was the killer doing it? How were they accessing these people's homes, finding new ways to slip poison into their systems? And the biggest question was still *why* were they doing it?

"Mallory ... oh God, my Mallory..." Cameron sobbed. Olivia watched him, the cogs in her brain turning as she considered him. She kept coming back to the idea of dark secrets, of the things they didn't know about the victims and their lives. Who would want Mallory Benson dead? What was she hiding? Something dark like Arabella and Andrew? Something terrible that they couldn't even comprehend?

Or did the killer get the target wrong?

Olivia could see the kind of man Cameron was. Big and violent and capable of throwing his weight around to get what he wanted. The things he could do behind closed doors were unthinkable. He had violent tendencies; they knew that much already.

So, what if the killer knew that and wanted him dead?

What if the killer had uncovered that dark secret and was ready to use it against him?

The more she looked, the more she noticed small subtleties in his demeanor. Even outside the drunkenness, he was pale and clammy, and lesions were starting to flare up under his sleeves.

"Cameron," Olivia said quietly. "Do you use your blender often?"

Cameron snuffled, staring up at Olivia in shock. "What?"

"Your blender. You know, the kitchen gadget."

"Um. I don't know what you mean," he stammered, clearly bewildered by the question.

"Your blender in your kitchen. You ever make protein smoothies?"

He sputtered in disbelief. "I—well—yeah, I guess. I make them for my workouts. But why the hell are you asking me about this? What's wrong with you? My wife is dead!"

"But it was meant to be you," Olivia murmured under her breath. She turned to Brock. "I think whoever poisoned the smoothie meant it to be for him. But it had to be someone with access to the house. Someone who could make it inside, go to the trouble of grinding up all those apple seeds, without seeming out of place. That's the key here. That's how the killer has been getting around without leaving much trace. Whoever they are, all of the victims trusted them enough to allow them inside their homes. But it wasn't a friend. Not someone they all knew, because we would've found them by now." Olivia tapped her lip with her fingers, bouncing on the balls of her feet. She turned back to Cameron.

"Do you hire staff for your house?"

"What? Why are you asking me this?"

"Just answer the question!" she exploded.

Cameron flailed for an answer. "I mean, we have a cleaner! And someone who comes to do laundry for us. Why are you asking me these questions? I want my lawyer!"

But Olivia had got what she needed. She grabbed Brock's arm and hurried him away. "We need to see if these people hired the same staff. I think maybe that's how we find our killer."

CHAPTER TWENTY

Brock and Olivia stopped off at the motel for a power nap and a cup of coffee, hoping that when they woke up, they'd be able to investigate the lead they'd uncovered; but Olivia's short slumber was interrupted by a call from Wyatt. She answered the call with her eyes still closed.

"Mhmm?"

"Sorry, I know you must be trying to get some rest. But we've just found out that there was a break-in at the Clifford residence. The alarm system went off, and we got there in time to apprehend three people. They were discovered with a car full of things stolen from the house."

LOVE, LIES, AND SUICIDE

Olivia rubbed at her eyes, trying to process the latest news. Everything was suddenly moving at lightning speed, and she'd barely had a chance to catch her breath.

"Do we have the identities of the robbers?" she mumbled, trying to will her eyes to open properly.

"My guess would be they're scam victims trying to claim back some of what was stolen from them," Wyatt said.

"That makes sense. But how did they find the house? And how did they discover that the Cliffords were behind the whole thing?"

"Your guess is as good as mine," Wyatt replied. "But if I was the killer right now, I'd be doing anything to throw people off the scent. Maybe they provided intel privately to some of the scam victims to distract us from the main event."

Olivia definitely believed that was possible. She didn't think it was likely that a bunch of people breaking into the house so recklessly was related to the killer directly. It seemed like a ridiculous thing for someone to attempt, though she could understand why the scam victims might want to do so. If they were involved in the murder, why would they go back to the crime scene? If they'd wanted material goods, they would have taken them when they'd killed Arabella and Andrew in the middle of the night.

She thought again of the alarm from the very night of the murder. It had recorded an unauthorized entry, but the intruder had had the code to disable it before police had been called. These robbers had not been so careful, meaning they were dupes. Wyatt was right. If the killer thought that would distract them from attempting to track them down, they were dead wrong.

"Thanks for letting me know."

"No problem. I've got a few officers interviewing the suspects. I'm hoping they might admit why they did what they did."

"Did the blood test come back on Cameron?"

"It did," he confirmed. "Cyanide poisoning. It must have been building up for weeks. We're transferring him to the hospital in custody for treatment."

After Olivia ended the call, she tried to doze back off, but her mind was feeling sharper by the second. She knew they had to be close to answers. If the killer was starting to get scared, then at least they had some sense. It was bold of them to kill someone so brazenly when they must know the FBI was close on their tail. But Mallory's death had given them the first solid evidence that they'd had since the first crime scene. If there was anything on Mallory's body that might help them, they'd have it in their clutches soon.

And if the killer was trying to play games with them, then Olivia wasn't having any of it. She'd been played before, but she was learning every single time. She'd brought down tougher people than this botanist she was chasing. Soon enough, she would have them locked away, just like every other killer who had dared to mess with her.

Olivia left Brock to sleep for a little longer and grabbed herself a coffee. As the caffeine worked its way through her body, she considered how the news of the break-in would affect the case. They'd done their best to keep details of the deaths of Arabella and Andrew on lockdown. Speculation and amateur sleuthing had been running wild, of course, but nobody knew the truth of what had happened. Olivia had a feeling that was soon about to end.

The people caught breaking into the house, in theory, had nothing left to lose. If they wanted, they could come out with all of the Clifford family's dirty laundry, turn the public on them, and put the killer in the public's favor. They might see it as a public service, someone taking care of the con artists that had ruined so many lives.

"Like some goddamn vigilante," Olivia murmured to herself. It was starting to seem more and more likely to her that the killer envisioned themselves as some kind of hero. Attacking the Cliffords was one thing, and then the apparent accidental death of Mallory Benson was another. If the killer intended to attack an abusive man, to end his reign of terror over his household, then didn't it make sense that the killer wasn't necessarily taking things personally? Perhaps they weren't vengeful in terms of their own life but on a wider scale. Taking on other people's problems and trying to solve them with a killing spree.

It was sick, and yet Olivia could almost understand how the killer might consider this a moral crusade. They were wiping out the scum of the earth, using their skills for good. But the more Olivia thought about it, the more repulsive she found it. It reminded her of the society of Apep and The Messenger's desperation to morally cleanse the world. She knew how a simple ideology with good intentions could easily get out of hand. Was that what had happened to the botanist? Had they set out to make things right but made the world a worse place in the process?

"Olivia?"

Olivia turned to see that Brock had woken up. He looked a little worse for wear after the sleepless nights, but after a huge yawn, he stood up.

"I'm ready when you are. We can dive right back in," he said. She offered him a smile.

"Okay. Would you believe me if I told you that while you were asleep, even more stuff went down?"

Brock rubbed at his eyes. "At this point, nothing would surprise me. Why don't you fill me in while we do some investigation?"

As they settled down to trawl through the contacts lists of the victims, Olivia told Brock about the call she'd had with Wyatt earlier. He shook his head in disbelief.

"So, you're telling me that these thieves thought they could just rob the house and take back what they were owed? Way to shoot yourself in the foot. Because now, they're not likely to get a single dollar."

"You can't blame them for wanting to take matters into their own hands, I suppose," Olivia said leniently. "But yeah, I don't think this is going to work out for them in the long run."

"Definitely not. But it's interesting. I wonder how this is going to change the public perception of this case. All this time, social media's been lighting up, searching for a cold-blooded killer, wanting to blame someone for the demise of their precious celebrities. But maybe things won't be so clear-cut when the thieves tell the world who Arabella and Andrew really were."

"I thought exactly the same. Once social media gets wind of this, there's going to be one hell of a storm, I think. Everyone loves a hero-to-villain story… and the Clifford family perfectly fits the bill, don't they?"

Brock shook his head in disbelief. "I still can't understand how people got so obsessed with these people. They're just glorified pretty people who have no talent. But I guess that's the way of the world now. Hell, I've got a pretty face, but I had to go out and find a job when I was sixteen. All these slackers wind me up."

"Don't flatter yourself," she told him as she reached over and tossed him a breakfast bar. "It'll get to your head."

"You wound me, Knight," he winced with a chuckle.

Olivia smiled quietly to herself as she worked through the contacts lists of the victims. She didn't have time for Brock's flirting today. She had to find a common connection between all of the victims so far. Her theory had been that since the killer must have had access to all of the victim's homes, perhaps they all hired the same cleaner or house staff. All of the victims had money, so she wasn't shocked to find that each of them had a cleaner on their contacts list. However, none of the names or numbers matched up.

"This is so frustrating. Not one of these cleaners works for the same agency. None of them have the same number or the same name. I guess maybe I was wrong about them hiring the same people," Olivia sighed. "Another dead end."

"I can't even find much in the way of records online either," Brock chimed in. "I'm assuming most of this is under the table. Cash only."

"Perfectly untraceable. Just our luck."

Brock gave her a small smile. "It was a good theory. But hey, maybe today is the day our luck changes. Once this case hits the news again, which it's going to after the thieves start talking, we'll maybe get some leads."

"You're right. And I'm not being defeatist about this. Not this time," Olivia said firmly. She'd doubted herself enough times in the past, and she didn't want to do it again. "Maybe we should head over and see Wyatt—see what he's managed to get out of the thieves."

"Good plan. Let's head out."

Still reeling from the dead end, Olivia was quiet on the drive over to the police station. She hoped that whatever Wyatt had learned might be of use to them.

But when they reached the station, things were not as Olivia had expected them to be. Outside the station, a whole bunch of reporters crowded around Wyatt as he tried his best to fend them off. Olivia and Brock exchanged a look before rushing out of the car and toward him. He was clamoring to talk over all of the reporter's questions, but he was fighting a losing battle. Olivia threw herself into the frenzy.

"Alright, everyone, back off!" she said in her sternest voice. Some of the reporters moved back a little, though others tried to surge forward in their place. Brock stood steadfast beside her, glaring out at the reporters.

"Stand back!" Brock shouted. "Have some respect!"

Olivia heard Wyatt sigh in relief behind her. She turned to check on him.

"You alright?"

He nodded, wiping his brow. He was sweating even though it was freezing cold outside. "I think so," he murmured. "I came out for a cigarette break and found all these reporters here. One of the thieves used their phone call to persuade a friend to leak what they know, I guess. So, the secret's out."

Olivia had known it was coming, but it was still a shock to see all of those people gathered there causing chaos because of the case.

"Do you want me to send them away?" Olivia asked him. Wyatt shook his head.

"No. I'm hoping to make a public appeal for information now that the cat's out of the bag. Maybe you can help me out. Add anything that you think I've missed."

Olivia nodded and then stepped out of the detective's way to allow him to speak to the reporters. They gobbled him up eagerly with their flashing cameras, and Wyatt winced a little, unused to the limelight.

"You may have heard some rumors regarding Arabella and Andrew Clifford, the individuals who were murdered in their home several weeks ago," Wyatt said carefully, wetting his lips with his tongue. "We can confirm that the rumors are true. The two of them were running an elaborate scam for at least several years via dating websites, forums, and social media, conning people out of their money. We understand that a lot of people have likely been affected by this over the years, and we sympathize entirely with those who suffered at their hands. But we are in the middle of a murder investigation here. We have to find the person who sought out revenge on these people. Only then can we begin to get some support to the people who lost money to their schemes. That's why we implore you, if you have any information at all about the death of this couple, please come forward and talk to us."

Wyatt paused to clear his throat. "We are also investigating a string of other killings that we believe relate to this case. The murders of three, possibly four, other people seem to tie in with this case. I would be happy to give a full statement about each of these cases in order for us to finally get through to the public that this is serious. If anyone has any information, they need to contact us now. It might even save lives."

Olivia added, "We will be providing a hotline for the public to call if they have anything they'd like to talk to us about. No detail is too small. If you think you know something, then it's vital that you don't hold back. That one small detail might be the difference between us finding this killer or not."

"Thank you for listening. I'll take some further questions now," Wyatt said with a curt nod to the reporters. As they all began to clamor again, Olivia and Brock left Wyatt to it, heading inside the police station to reconvene. Brock puffed out air.

"Well, that was something."

"It was necessary," Olivia said. "I don't like the media much, but if they can help us reach witnesses, people with information, then so be it."

She looked down at Arabella's profile on her phone. Already, thousands of shocked reactions and comments were rolling in.

"Let's see how this goes."

CHAPTER TWENTY-ONE

OLIVIA'S HEART SEEMED TO BE PERMANENTLY ON overdrive as she and Brock examined the other victims in the poisoning cases. She had been disappointed when the lead about the house staff hadn't panned out, but she was determined not to let that ruin her momentum.

She kept coming back to the idea that all of them had some secret that the killer had known about, a reason to want them dead. She was also still sure that Mallory's death had been an accident and that the poison had been intended for her abusive husband. Maybe that was also a reason that the killer had not struck again since. They were in hiding, considering their approach more deeply. At this point, Olivia welcomed it if it bought them more time.

But finding out more about the victims was proving difficult. Family interviews with the various victims had proved bunk over the last few days. She had managed to get Grayson to sign over the phones and laptops of the victims to see if she could find anything incriminating against any of them, but so far, she had turned up nothing.

"Why does it feel like all of these people are squeaky clean?" Olivia asked Brock, reaching for her cup of coffee and taking a long sip. "I'm looking through text threads, emails, private messages on social media, and there's just nothing. There are no secret affairs going on in their lives, no drugs, no shady deals, no nothing. I just want to know why the killer chose these people. Surely it wasn't just random?"

"I don't think random seems like the killer's style. Not when the killings are so drawn out, so brutal. It makes it seem like the whole thing was super personal," Brock agreed. "I just think they had knowledge that we don't have. Yet. We're going to have to look deeper."

Olivia nodded and kept pushing on. She was no stranger to trawling through computers, looking to dig up dirt on people. But often when she was looking for dirt, she found it pretty quickly. Ordinary people usually didn't know how to bury their secrets deep enough. They thought that a quick wipe of their browser history and a few deleted texts would save them, but Olivia knew it was much more complicated than that.

Still, the deeper she looked, the less she found. The three victims who had come before Arabella and Andrew seemed almost like a dead end. Olivia began to feel frustration building inside her, threatening to burst out.

"If we can just crack this, then I think we'll blow the case wide open," Olivia muttered to herself. "But I just don't see anything here. What was the motive? Why these people? Who did they anger?"

"Hey, wait. I think I might have found something about the first victim. Look at this message request."

Olivia moved over to Brock to see what he was talking about. In the inbox of Anthony McDonald, there was a single screenshot that had been sent to him by an anonymous user.

LOVE, LIES, AND SUICIDE

"Remind me about Anthony again?"

"He was the middle school teacher. Late forties, unmarried. And this screenshot might explain why…"

Olivia clicked on the image to zoom in on it.

The screenshot showed a message thread on a public forum. The subject being discussed made Olivia's skin turn cold.

"Student-teacher relationships?" she murmured.

Brock nodded stonily and gave her a look. "Could this be motive?"

Olivia took a deep breath and scanned the screenshot again. "Definitely. But this doesn't actually mention Anthony directly. It's about some case in California. But why send this to him? Did they know about him having some secret affair with an underage student?"

"It's entirely possible. I don't think Anthony ever saw this message though. It was left unread in his hidden inbox. I guess he wasn't big on using social media and overlooked it. Maybe if he had seen it, he might have known what was coming for him. But then again, what could he have done about it? Gone to the police?"

Olivia let out a caustic chuckle. "Not a chance. If he did have relations with an underage student, then that makes him a rapist by law. He'd do serious jail time for this, no matter how the student felt about it. Even if he did see this screenshot, even if he took it as a threat from whomever sent it, there's little he could've done about it."

Brock nodded. "Well, if it is true, then it sure explains a lot. It's a pretty dark secret to keep under wraps, and it certainly gives a vigilante killer a reason to target him. But how did the killer know about it? That seems like something that would be hard to keep a secret, but if it ever got out, it would have ruined Anthony's life a long time ago. So, what? Was the killer a witness somehow to what they claim went down?"

"From what we know so far, this killer certainly seems to have ways of uncovering the truth," Olivia said solemnly.

"What about Kristen Peck?" Brock asked. "She was barely twenty years old. What could she possibly have done?"

"I have no idea," Olivia said. "We've got almost the opposite problem with her. I'm having to comb through thousands and thousands of social media posts and messages here and can't really find much of anything. Whatever it was she did, I can't find it here. I've even got records from high school and college, but by all accounts, she was a popular student with no behavior issues. Squeaky clean record."

Brock grunted. "Wonderful."

"Hold on..." she said, scrolling back up. "What if it follows the same pattern? A message not about something she literally did, but an oblique reference. Something similar to what she may have done but not directly about her..."

She leaned forward and squinted, combing through the comments. "Look here," she announced. "Someone commented on a few of her pictures with the same one each time: hashtag tongue."

"Tongue?" he frowned.

"She was found with her tongue swollen. Maybe something to do with words? Did she say something hurtful to somebody?"

"It's all we have to go on," Brock nodded. "But what about Sandra Collison? She didn't have social media."

"I'm going to see if there's anything else Grayson can send us," she said.

"Good idea."

She placed the call and asked specifically if there was anything relating to the victims they might have overlooked.

"We're looking for messages, warnings, sent to Sandra Collison—something that could have been sent to the killer almost as a taunt. Like it was something similar to what they did, but not what they did."

Grayson was silent for a moment as he pawed through the evidence locker. "I think I've got something."

"What did you find?" Brock asked eagerly. There was some rustling on the other end of the line.

"In our initial investigation, we found an envelope open on the coffee table," he explained. "At first I thought it was something she'd kept. There are a bunch of newspaper clippings in here. All about eating disorders, weight loss, diet pills, that sort of thing."

"Why would they send newspaper clippings?" Brock frowned.

Grayson sighed. "A while back, Collison's twelve-year-old daughter Delaney died. It got some attention around town. She had a heart attack caused by an overdose of diet pills."

"That's awful," Olivia said softly. She couldn't imagine what that young girl had been through. "Young girls have so much pressure on them these days."

"They do. I've been thinking this whole time that she kept these articles, but do you think someone sent them to her? It wasn't a keepsake but a warning?"

"But why would he taunt her?" asked Brock.

"Hold on, Brock," Olivia said, pressing her fingers against both temples. Then something clicked in her head. She thought of the screenshot in Anthony's inbox and the comment on Kristen's page. Why would someone send Sandra a letter filled with those articles? Unless...

"...she played some part in her daughter's death," Olivia finished her thought out loud.

"My thoughts exactly," Grayson said gravely. "Those diet pills aren't the kind of thing that a young girl can just pick up at the store. They're prescription, and they're not meant for young people. We never found out how she got her hands on those pills. Collison didn't even have a prescription for them. At the time, she said her daughter must have gotten them from a school friend, but our killer might suspect she provided them to her directly. And there's the motive."

Olivia shook her head. "It should make sense. I mean, the facts are in front of us. But at the same time, I still can't understand it. Was she ever accused? Was she a suspect?"

"That's what stumps me," Grayson replied. "I wasn't on this case back when it happened, but I do recall it. We spent time at the school ramping up our anti-drug programs. But nobody ever figured out who gave her the drugs. Which is what makes me think that this is a conclusion that the killer just drew up themselves."

"But again, the question is why?" Olivia pressed. "Did the killer have some personal connection to Sandra and her family? Or did they just create a story in their head to fit their reasons for killing?"

"Either possibility could be right," Brock mused. "The more we learn about this killer, the more it seems like they like what they do. The performative killings, the drama of it all, and then the whole vigilante vibe… it suggests that the person doing this would manage to find dirt on anyone they decided they wanted dead. It wouldn't even have to be something big, or anything completely true. It's like they're searching for a good enough reason to end someone's life. And I guess with all of the victims, they made sure there was something at least semi-solid, but maybe when they run out of people to target, the killings will become more and more erratic."

Olivia shuddered. She didn't want to think about any more murders. Back when she thought the killer had only struck once, she could almost understand why they did what they did. Arabella and Andrew had done plenty to rub people the wrong way, and anyone who knew their secrets could see that their eventual death wasn't that surprising.

But now, things were getting way out of hand. Did the killer even know for sure that Sandra Collison had a part to play in the death of her daughter? Or was the killer assuming they were right because they had a superiority complex?

"Whatever is going on, we have to consider that the killer might strike again," Grayson said. "It seems like we might have found a pattern now. This person wants people not to just die but to suffer—to make them feel pain for their sins."

"Killers these days… all of them trying to make out like they're doing the world a favor," Brock muttered, rolling his eyes. "We need to put a stop to this before anyone else gets hurt."

"Agreed. I'm going to see what else I can find while I get these clippings down to the lab. Who knows? Maybe the killer got sloppy and we can get some fingerprints?"

"Okay. Keep us in the loop."

As the call ended, Olivia let out a long sigh. "Well, looks like we're close to connecting the dots. We just need to find some dirt on the last victim, and then we've got ourselves a pattern."

But that was easier said than done. Even as Brock and Olivia decided to join forces and focus on the same victim together, they couldn't find anything of significance. It seemed that some secrets just stayed buried deeper than others.

As they took a coffee break together, Olivia turned over the same thought in her head. It had been haunting her for a while, and it wouldn't let go of her. Brock watched her, noticing her quietness.

"Got that look in your eye again," he observed.

"Exhaustion?"

"Case madness."

"And what, pray tell, is that?"

"When you get so engrossed in a case that you let your coffee go cold." He gestured to her cup, which, sure enough, had cooled considerably. "The Olivia Knight I know would never let it go to waste."

Olivia gave a wry smile. "You're really one to talk. Don't act like I can't see those bags under your eyes."

"Guilty as charged. But what's on your mind?"

She sighed and took a sip of the cold coffee. "I keep thinking about the case with The Messenger. That whole time, he was desperate for one thing, right? He wanted to push humanity to some new era. He thought he was doing the world a favor. And I just keep thinking… isn't that the same thing that The Botanist wants? Or seems to want? Helping the world by making bloody sacrifices?"

Brock raised an eyebrow. "The Botanist? Given 'em a name, huh?"

Olivia shrugged. "I guess I have."

Brock frowned. "Well, maybe. There are plenty of killers who have a hero complex. They think they're doing good by the citizens of the world. It's not that unusual."

"Maybe not. But I can't help thinking… we never caught everyone involved once that case was supposed to be done and dusted. We know that the network for the cult was bigger than we ever imagined. We know there's more of them out there, lying low. What if The Botanist is just an extension of their ideologies? I know they're not leaving behind cryptic messages and weird symbols, but it just feels like they want the same things. And I don't want to ignore that possibility, just in case it could be relevant."

Brock nodded slowly. "I guess I can understand that."

Olivia took a shaky breath. "The thing is, Brock, the more I think about it, the more it worries me. Because if killers like these just keep coming up out of the woodwork, then we're going to have a real problem on our hands—more than we're going to be able to handle. People aren't going to feel safe, and it's only going to get more and more extreme. I know we deal with killers all the time, but when killers start to group together, start wanting the same things… that's a kind of terrifying thing. How are we supposed to keep people safe?"

Brock's face was creased as he listened to Olivia's troubles. He shook his head slowly. "You really carry all that worry around all the time? Damn, Olivia. It's no wonder you're always so stressed."

Olivia choked out a short laugh, but she relaxed a little as she felt Brock reach out to cover her hand with his. Across the table their eyes met, and she felt the fight leaving her body. It always did when she knew Brock was right there, fighting at her side. He smiled at her.

"Honestly? Part of me was thinking the same thing," he admitted.

"Really?"

"I don't know about so specific, but yeah," he shrugged. "Although for me, I was almost thinking more like the Grim Reaper. I know we dealt a big blow to his organization, but big international syndicates like that don't just disappear overnight. I was remembering Jake Walker. He was forced to use his chemistry skills to help the Reaper's operation. Now, I don't know much about chemistry—or botany—but I feel like there might have been someone in that organization who could have done something like this. Maybe they're still at work."

Olivia nodded. She hadn't considered that angle, but it was a reasonable worry. She let out a sigh. "I don't know. Maybe I'm just overthinking this whole thing."

"You? Overthinking things? Well, I never!" Brock cracked.

She stuck her tongue out at him.

"I don't know, I just keep feeling like we've done a great job of scratching the surfaces of things, but there are whole shadows out there waiting to strike. On us. For revenge."

LOVE, LIES, AND SUICIDE

Brock nodded slowly. "Well then, let them come."

A real laugh sputtered out of Olivia so quickly that it shocked her.

"What?"

He gave her his trademark grin. "I'm serious. Let 'em come. The cult, the Reaper, whoever. Yeah, there are still people out there that we haven't chased down. Dangerous people—people who will try anything to shift the power balance back to them. But I'm not worried about that. You know why? Because when the time comes, you and I are going to kick their butts."

The two of them let out a much-needed laugh. It felt good to laugh with Brock. It always did. He smiled back at her.

He was right. The big picture was scary in their job, but she didn't need to think about that right now. She had to take it one step at a time. All the shadows and unknowns still worried her. They wouldn't stop worrying her until they finally, definitively, put a stop to all of it. But worrying about it wasn't about to catch The Botanist for her. She had to regroup, refocus, and put all of her energies in the right place.

"The other thing about these deaths is that they're all so personal," she stated. Brock perked up. It was like the two of them could simply start a conversation halfway through and still be on the same page. "I'm just convinced there's some sort of revenge angle here. There's got to be."

"Well, if anyone's going to find it, it'll be us."

They finished up their coffees and got back into their work. They didn't hear from Grayson again, and other than a few updates from Wyatt about the thieves they'd apprehended, the night was quiet. Eventually, it became clear that the best thing they could do for the case was rest. Both Olivia and Brock managed a few hours of sleep before getting up and getting back to work.

As the sun was beginning to rise, Olivia woke up with a brand-new idea poking in her mind. She pulled up a search to confirm her idea, but the ball of momentum had clearly started rolling in her gut now. She felt the connections putting themselves together in her mind already.

"You know, I've been thinking," she announced to Brock as they got ready for the morning. "It's not just the belladonna we're after, right? Ryleigh stole that, but Professor Shen confirmed that's all that was taken. But some of these cases had water hemlock. White snakeroot. Castor beans."

"Or apple seeds," Brock pointed out. "What are you getting at?"

"Every case has had a different type of poison," Olivia explained. "A lot of these plants don't naturally grow in this environment, and surely not in the middle of November. The killer would need some sort of space to store and grow them."

"That could be anyone with a backyard though, couldn't it?" Brock offered. "I don't see how this narrows it down."

"You think our killer would risk those plants being caught in their own backyard?" she said. "They would want somewhere plausibly deniable. Somewhere public."

"Like a community garden?" he asked.

"Like a community greenhouse," she clarified.

"Is that a thing?"

"It is," Olivia confirmed. "And interestingly enough for us, look who I found as the director of the local community greenhouse organization."

She turned her phone to Brock to see the picture of the woman smiling from outside a greenhouse.

"Sarah Campbell Romero."

CHAPTER TWENTY-TWO

THE COMMUNITY GREENHOUSE WAS OFF TO THE SIDE IN A small park. It was much taller and more extensive than Olivia had been expecting. The pictures on the park website implied that the facility was a small operation, but the tall glass panes towered over Olivia's head as they approached the entrance.

"Let's go over it again," Brock said. "I want to make sure we have it all straight." Olivia nodded without taking her eyes off the prize. They were so close. She could feel it.

"So, Sarah, here, definitely has the means, right?" Brock began. "She knows all about plants. You saw her house and how meticulously she took care of them. I don't doubt she knows exactly how to poison someone."

"She must have gotten the security codes from her husband somehow as well," Olivia said. "That was how she disabled the alarm."

"And we have regular monthly donations from her account—under the name Sarah Campbell—to Andrew Clifford's account. She thought she was donating to the Green Gardens Initiative. But it was really just to his pockets."

"Do you think that's motive for murder though?" Olivia asked. "I mean, a hundred bucks every month or so isn't nearly as much in the scheme of things."

Brock shrugged. "I mean, that stuff adds up. She's been a regular donator for a couple of years now. Maybe she feels personally betrayed not only because her money has been stolen but also because what she thought was a good, noble cause has just been enriching the pockets of a couple of thieves."

They lowered their voices as they stepped into the entranceway of the greenhouse. The fresh scent of foliage and damp air immediately wafted into Olivia's nostrils. She breathed deep, relishing the pleasant air. Even in the midst of a murder investigation, she was grateful for a chance to smell the flowers.

All around them were various plots marked off with letters and numbers featuring all sorts of flowers, vegetables, and herbs: roses, tomatoes, carrots, onions, even a few sunflowers raggedly hanging on to the end of their lives. One corner was taken up by an absolutely massive bird of paradise and was surrounded by several large buckets containing pineapples with buds just beginning to poke out from the tops of their leaves. Hummingbirds flitted this way and that to various hanging feeders, clearly grateful for a respite from the November cold. Even at this early hour, about a half dozen people were shuffling around in their plots, watering or trimming or tilling their soil.

In the center of the greenhouse was a tall fountain surrounded by a concrete courtyard. Water spilled over the edges of the structure, splashing down into the pool below with the sound of a waterfall. A couple of small birds perched on the edge of the pool, flitting back and forth and happily chirping. Most importantly, though, it was tall enough to even hide Brock's large frame from the field of view of their suspect.

Sarah Romero, née Campbell, was seated on one of the benches lining the courtyard. Her outfit was smeared in mud as if she'd been working the soil, and a pair of gloves lay beside her on the bench, but now she was staring intently at her laptop screen and typing.

"You ready?" Olivia whispered.

"As I'll ever be."

They nodded. Their task this morning was not to make an arrest just yet. After all, it had been a hunch—a good one, Olivia thought, but still a hunch. They just needed one last piece of proof to make the final arrest.

Olivia and Brock both pulled up a plant identification app on their phones and slowly began a sweep of the greenhouse. It was a slow process: they had photos of the specific plants they were looking for and were trying to match the ones in the greenhouse to the photos. Unfortunately for them, they seemed to be running into the same plants over and over.

"So many onions," Brock groused. "People eat that many onions?"

"You have got to start eating more vegetables, Tanner."

"Hey, I like onions. If they're battered and deep-fried in ring form."

They stalked up and down the rows slowly. The place, for some reason, made Olivia feel very uneasy. Perhaps it was the possibilities of what might be hidden underneath each tall branch of leaves. Somewhere in the building, the killer might be storing their murder weapons.

They made their way to a deep corner of the greenhouse, behind the bird of paradise and far away from the entrance. She passed a tall flowering bush with small white flowers and paused. She looked at it again and frowned.

"Hold on," she told Brock. "This is..."

"It looks like water hemlock," he completed her thought, pointing at the photo on his phone.

Olivia's heart was in overdrive now. She quickly pulled up a search to find the attributes of the plant, and immediately felt her heart sink as quickly as it rose. "Flowers look right," she said. "But it's too tall. Hemlock only grows up to five feet, and this is bigger than you. Plus, the stem is different. I think we're looking at an elderberry shrub."

Brock rubbed the bridge of his nose with his fingers. "The search continues, then."

Olivia looked back to the shrub, down at her phone, and at the shrub again. She shrugged and continued on behind him. "Yeah, must be. I don't know how we're going to—*ow!*"

She backed away from where she'd just walked and stumbled to the ground. A much smaller plant had been a little closer to her ankle than she'd intended, and she'd brushed against it. Already, the burning, itching sensation was spreading like wildfire up her right ankle.

Brock whirled around, his face drawn with fear. "Are you okay?"

"Careful," she winced, pointing to the small sprout with jagged leaves she'd tripped over. She exhaled deeply. "Wow, that stings."

Brock quickly looked it up on the app. "That's a stinging nettle."

"Is it deadly?"

"Thankfully, no," he said. Both of them exhaled a heavy sigh of relief. "Looks like it causes a rash similar to poison ivy, but the symptoms typically don't last more than twenty-four hours."

Olivia was still working on controlling her breathing and getting herself under control. A spike of terror had shot through her when she'd first touched the nettle. For a moment, she thought she'd be the latest victim of The Botanist's attacks—and completely unwittingly so.

She took a few calming breaths and motioned for Brock to help her to her feet. "Okay. Okay. I think I can walk."

Fortunately, once the shock wore off, the worst of Olivia's symptoms became simply an incessant itching on her ankle.

"You sure you're okay?" Brock asked as he skirted around the path of the nettle.

"Not much we can do right now. I'll get some itch cream on the way back to the motel," she said. "I don't want to give up our momentum here."

"Actually, it looks like we may not have to," Brock said. He had come to a stop just a few feet ahead of her was looking straight down at Lot 74C.

LOVE, LIES, AND SUICIDE

"Oh, my God," Olivia whispered as she saw what he was staring at. She had stared at the photos of poisonous plants so often that she didn't even need to consult her phone to know exactly what they were.

Wolfsbane. Deadly nightshade. Rosary peas. White baneberry. Belladonna.

All of them deadly.

"Seems to me Ms. Campbell has some explaining to do," Brock said.

∼

They stalked their way back out the way they'd come. Most of the other gardeners were gone now, but Sarah remained, still typing away at her keyboard. She finally looked up at the sound of the two of them coming through the brush. Recognition, confusion, and concern passed through her face in a matter of seconds.

"Sarah Campbell Romero?" Brock asked.

"Can—can I help you, agents?" she asked.

"You can, actually," said Olivia. "Do you mind telling us about your donations to the Green Gardens Initiative?"

Sarah frowned. "Sure," she said. "I have a monthly donation to them. I like their newsletter. I was actually trying to contact them this morning to see if we could do an event here at the greenhouse."

"No response?"

Sarah gave a cautious nod, her eyes darting back and forth between Olivia and Brock. "How did you know this? And I'm—I'm sorry—does this have anything to do with that man impersonating my husband? Why would the FBI be involved?"

Brock proceeded forward as if she hadn't asked the question. "Right now, we're focused on that donation," he said. "Tell me, how long have you been donating to them? At least a couple years, right?"

Sarah nodded. "I really believe in what they do. I've even put together a few fundraisers for them. Last fall we raised nearly twenty thousand dollars to help provide fresh produce for families that can't afford it."

"Did you ever have any contact with the director of this organization?" he asked.

"You mean Alan?" she asked. "Just through email. I never got to meet him in person."

Olivia gave Brock a pointed look. There it was: motive, means, and opportunity.

"Ms. Campbell," she started. "Were you aware that the Green Gardens Initiative is a fraudulent organization?"

Sarah practically jumped in shock. "What?"

Olivia watched her body language closely, looking for any hint of guilt underneath the seemingly innocent eyes. So far, her innocence seemed just as sincere as Sergio's. But it couldn't be a coincidence that this investigation had started with her husband sending threats and now the murder weapons being found in her care. Could it?

Olivia nodded. "This organization was completely fraudulent. The man you know as Alan is actually Andrew Clifford, who was recently found murdered alongside his wife."

"That's the case from the news… oh, God, that's the case you thought Sergio was…"

"Where were you on the night of November nineteenth?" she asked.

Sarah's eyes went wide at the revelation. "I was, um… I was…" She started hyperventilating and shaking with terror. Her mouth flopped open and closed, but she couldn't say anything.

"Sarah Campbell, I'm placing you under arrest for the murders of Andrew and Arabella Clifford," Brock said. He reached forward before she could react and cuffed her quickly as he read out her rights.

"I—I—I don't know what you're talking about," Sarah protested. "I'm innocent!"

"Then why are you growing the murder weapons in your greenhouse?"

That stopped her in her tracks. "What do you mean?"

With Sarah Campbell in cuffs in front of them, Brock and Olivia marched her back through to the back corner they'd come from. Olivia pressed on through the itchy rash on her ankle, determined to put an end to this madness once and for all. She was sure this was the answer to all the questions that had been plaguing her in this case. She didn't yet know what motive Campbell would have to murder the first three victims, but she knew they'd uncover something. As soon as they left here, they'd go back and interview Sergio as well—perhaps the two had been working as a team, a sort of sick Bonnie and Clyde situation.

Something seemed off as they approached Lot 74C. There was something different in her field of vision, something she couldn't quite place. She stopped at the elderberry shrub they'd seen before, giving it a long look and wracking her brain. Something was wrong here.

Brock was still pressing forward and pointing out the belladonna, wolfsbane, and other deadly plants growing in the lot when the lightbulb went on in her head.

"Brock," she called, trying not to let alarm seep into her voice. "Can you come meet me at that elderberry shrub we saw earlier?"

Brock turned back, Sarah still in tow, and frowned. "What's going on?"

"Something's not right here. There's something about this plant that's bothering me."

Brock looked it over for a long moment. "The flowers are gone. Or mostly trimmed, anyway."

Olivia turned to him, her anxiety ratcheting up like a live wire. "Somebody came behind us and trimmed this shrub." She took a step forward to get a closer look and reached her hand out—

"Don't touch that!" screeched Sarah. Olivia froze.

"Why not?"

"That's not elderberry," she said. "Look. You can tell because of the leaf shape. That's a giant hogweed. Oh, my God, I have a giant hogweed in my greenhouse…"

She almost looked more upset at this revelation than she did at being placed under arrest for murder.

"What's a giant hogweed?" Brock pressed.

"It's one of the most dangerous plants. It's phototoxic. Even just touching the stem or the flowers can cause a horrible reaction when exposed to light. Blisters, scarring, extreme pain. Even a light touch into the eyes can cause permanent blindness if not treated within twenty minutes or so."

Olivia snatched her hand away from it and took a couple steps back. She had no desire to even accidentally touch it. But who had come behind them and trimmed the flowers?

Who had taken the poison from right under their noses?

She turned around and scanned the greenhouse closely—and then she saw movement in the shadows.

"Hey!" she shouted, and a dark, hooded figure in a ski mask took off.

Olivia waited only long enough to untangle herself from the weeds and potentially poisonous plants and chase after him, but it was a losing battle. The irritation in her ankle was still flaring up, and she was having a hard time moving her legs fast enough to keep up with him.

Brock wasn't far behind, but he had to push Sarah along as well, which slowed him considerably. "Olivia, wait!"

"There's no time!"

The figure ducked and weaved in and out of the shadows behind the trees, and Olivia stayed right on his heels. She felt like an explorer cutting her way through the jungle as she barreled through the heavy, dense foliage.

She stumbled back out into the courtyard to find it empty. Olivia whipped her head left and right. She strained her eyes into the shadows to try to see him, strained her ears to hear his footsteps, but all was silent. She made her way toward the front of the greenhouse now. If he'd escaped, certainly she'd have heard him running off, right? He wouldn't have been able to get away without their notice.

"Do you see him?" called Brock as he made his way toward her, frantically pushing past foliage as he tried to get to the courtyard.

She opened her mouth to respond, but it was too late. She caught a flash of movement to her left side so suddenly that her heart jolted in her chest, and she turned just in time to see a baseball bat swinging at her. She didn't have time to scream or move out of the way. The bat connected with her cheek, and as sharp pain jolted through her face, she felt herself topple to the ground, her body dropping with a thud.

"Brock!" she choked out, the shock of the impact throwing her entire body out of whack. She grappled for the gun on her belt, but she was so dizzy that she couldn't seem to make the rest of her body work properly. The swing of the bat was immediately followed by the sharp sensation of leaves being rubbed on her face. The mere touch stung and burned an order of magnitude hotter than the stinging nettle she'd tripped over earlier.

Olivia squeezed her eyes and mouth shut tightly to protect herself. She clawed at her face to brush the leaves away and tried to get off the ground, but her assailant wasn't done. The bat came down again with a sickening crack over her head, and flashes of white shot past Olivia's vision. She crumpled to the ground in a heap.

"FBI! Put your hands up!" she heard Brock shouting hazily. His footsteps thundered toward them, but the man had already fled the greenhouse.

Olivia managed to get herself up on her knees, but the dizziness sent her sideways once again. She felt so nauseous that she couldn't focus on anything else. The pain was bad, but the dizziness was worse. Her vision was blurry and she couldn't see straight. She heard the ringing of shots fired—one, two, three— but it was all far away, somewhere distant.

She didn't know how long it was before she heard footsteps approaching and felt gentle hands on her shoulders. Her eyes fluttered open, and she could see a very blurry version of Brock.

"Did you get him?" she asked slowly. He shook his head, and it looked as though there were two of him in front of her.

"I had to make sure you were okay."

"I'm fine," she insisted despite the throbbing in her head. "You should go after him…"

"He's gone, Olivia. And you're in a bad way. You got poisoned with that hogweed. I need to get you to a hospital now."

A twinge of irritation shot through her as he pulled her up to her feet and carried her out to the car. That had been their chance to catch the killer in the act, to corner him and put him away right then.

And Brock had chosen to let him get away.

Brock rushed her out to the car and strapped her into the front seat, then sped off in the direction of the hospital. It was then that Olivia slipped away for a few moments, the dizziness sending her into darkness. When she opened her eyes again, they were at the hospital, and Brock was guiding someone with a wheelchair to come and collect Olivia. She slipped away again for a while, and when she woke again, she was in a hospital bed.

She seemed to be feeling much better this time when her eyes opened. She couldn't feel the pain so much in her cheek, and some of the dizziness seemed to have gone away. She glanced to her left and saw Brock sitting at her bedside, reading something from a file. His face was fixed in a frown, and he looked as though he'd been that way for a while. She smiled a little, ignoring the pain throbbing in her entire head.

"Hey…"

Brock immediately looked up and moved to her bedside. "Hey… are you doing okay? You had me worried for a moment there."

"I feel okay. It doesn't hurt so much anymore."

"You were very lucky."

"My head is on fire."

"That would be the concussion," he said. "Lucky for us, they were able to wash off the hogweed sap before it took hold. They said there should be no lasting damage. You can see, right?"

"I think so." She squinted. "Yeah, I can see."

"Just be glad you can't see your face though," Brock cracked. "You've got a pretty impressive bruise and a few days' worth of dizziness to face up to. The whole side of your face is purple."

"It feels purple," Olivia mumbled, slowly starting to feel the numbness increase. She hazily looked around the room. "Do they at least have me on the good stuff?"

"Only the finest," he replied.

A nurse bustled into the room to check her out and update the chart, but all the while, Olivia was bursting with frustration. The woman's words seemed to fade into the background as she watched Brock hovering anxiously in the corner. She was mad at him—furious, actually, when she could get her swirling thoughts to cooperate.

After being thoroughly checked out and a fresh IV placed, the nurse left the room, leaving the two of them in silence.

"Brock..."

He held up a hand. "I know. I know, and I'm sorry."

"What if someone else is killed because you let him get away?"

"That's a risk we'll have to take then, Olivia."

She groaned in equal measures of pain and frustration. After so long spent spinning their wheels, they'd come so close, and now it had been snatched away from them at the last moment.

"You could have chased after him."

"No," he replied firmly, emotion brimming in his eyes. "I couldn't leave you behind."

Olivia sat there in the bed for a long moment. Could she really be mad at him for coming to her aid? If he'd been any later, she could have been killed or seriously blinded. If he'd gone after her assailant, there was no guarantee that he'd get the man in custody or—given their luck—that he was even the killer after all.

But he was a lead. He was a concrete *something*, and they were rapidly running out of somethings in this case. Even if apprehending him didn't put an end to all this madness, it would have at least put some final pieces of the puzzle in place. They'd been so close.

Brock's face was deep with a mixture of emotions that Olivia easily recognized: worry, regret, fear, and determination. She wanted her anger with him to burn bright enough to solve this case once and for all, but she couldn't muster up the energy. How could she be mad?

He'd let him get away. But he'd saved her. Wasn't that worth something?

For better or worse, they were a team.

Olivia finally tore her gaze away from him and looked back down at the blanket covering her on the bed.

"What happened to Sarah?"

"I had the police come down and take her in while I drove down here. I'm not sure how long they can keep her though. I don't think she's our killer. She says she's never seen that plot of plants before."

"So now what?" she asked sullenly.

The silence stretched long between them before Brock broke out into his trademark grin. "So now, we follow up on the information I did get from her."

"You found out who the plot belongs to?" Olivia asked, her eyes widening. "Who?"

Brock's eyes seemed to be sparkling with mischief. "Ryleigh Waters."

CHAPTER TWENTY-THREE

"Ryleigh..." Olivia said out loud. The name rang out in her head like a siren. "But our killer can't be Ryleigh. She's still in custody. And so that means it has to be someone with access to her plot. Someone she shares everything with..."

Olivia and Brock caught one another's eyes. Brock nodded to her.

"I've had time to consider this while you've been out of it. Chris Marsh had a solid alibi that night of the party, but we both know that his friends dabble in drugs. Even the ones who don't certainly drink. So, if he disappeared for an hour in the night, who would really notice? You know how hazy parties can be. I wouldn't be surprised if everyone there that night had gaps in their memories that they would never admit because they were taking illegal substances. And look here," he pointed at his phone and showed her all the pictures of that night.

"We see this selfie with Ryleigh at 8:42 p.m., but then he's in no other pictures for the next two hours. And when he shows back up around 10:36 p.m., he's got a little spatter of something on his sleeve that he didn't before. Does that look like blood to you?"

Olivia squinted, her head still throbbing. "It does."

"I think Chris planned that night carefully; he used the party to cover his tracks, knowing no one would suspect him in the least."

Olivia considered that for a moment. "I guess that could make sense. But what about Ryleigh poisoning him? What was that all about?"

"I think she was telling the truth. I think she thought he was sneaking out to see another woman. But another explanation for him disappearing multiple times in the night?" Brock's face darkened. "You know what I'm getting at."

Olivia took a deep breath. "Alright. Let's say all of that is true. We know Chris had reasons to want revenge on the Cliffords. But what about the rest of the killings? And how did he do it?"

"I thought about that too. I think maybe we were too quick to dismiss the idea of the cleaners. You were on the right path, but we stopped looking because we couldn't find any common links. But then I started thinking… Who's to say that the killer isn't using that network to access people's houses, and he's doing it under a false name to cover his back? So, I checked in with all of the families and showed them a picture of Chris. All of them recognized him. He was working for the Bensons under the name Evan Fox. The cleaner on Arabella's phone was under the name Peter Wright. And then the other families said he seemed familiar, even though none of them hired him directly. Josephine King said she'd definitely seen him before. My guess is that he got himself hired by the Cliffords so he could get close and get revenge for what they did to his mother. This is our guy, Olivia. He had knowledge. He had motive, means, and opportunity. I feel like we keep saying that, but this time it feels right."

"He was in the hospital when Mallory Benson was killed, though."

"But not before he put those apple seeds in the protein powder," Brock countered. "Cameron Benson also had evidence of long-term cyanide poisoning. I don't know how long he'd been doing it, but it seemed like it was over a long period. Even if Chris was in the hospital when Mallory died, he could have planted that stuff weeks ago."

Olivia shook her head in disbelief. "I didn't think it was going to come to this. We have to find him. Pin him for this and get him off the streets for good before he kills someone else."

"That's the problem. We already sent the police to his house, but he's gone. He must have known from the moment we showed up at the rental unit that we were hot on his tail… and now we have no idea where he might have gone."

Olivia chewed her lip and then stopped when pain shot through the damaged part of her face. "Where would he go? We know already that he doesn't have any family left now that his mother is gone. And if he knows we're chasing him, then maybe he'll just get the hell away. It'll be like finding a needle in a haystack."

"I thought that too. But he was at the greenhouse. He was getting that poison for somebody, presumably, right? And he clearly knows we're onto him; I think he knows we'll catch up to him now. He's going to strike again. We may have slowed him down for the time being, but he's got no intention of stopping. And this time, it'll certainly be personal."

Olivia's head was thumping. "The question is, who does he want dead more than anyone? If we were in his shoes, who would he want to kill? Maybe us? We're the ones trying to end his reign of terror."

Brock chuckled. "Why is it we always find ourselves the ideal targets for these guys?"

Olivia sighed. "Probably because we're always sticking our noses in places and interrupting their plans."

"Well, it's worked out so far, hasn't it?" he replied cheekily, but Olivia leveled him with a look.

"So how do we find him?"

"He'll know that you've been in the hospital after what he did to you and that I've barely left your side. Getting either of us in a position where he might be able to poison us would be damn near impossible."

"Good point," Olivia nodded. "I wonder if he's past the point of being patient enough to poison someone, especially now that we've found his stash of poisonous plants. He might escalate to using his gun."

Brock tapped his fingers on his chin. "So. If we were him… he's out in the world alone, no one to turn to… his mother is dead, his girlfriend is in custody… he wants to hit someone hard—end their life as one final hurrah before we take him down. Who would you pick?"

Olivia shook her head. "He clearly has a thing for taking down people who he believes have done wrong to the world. Assuming he's responsible for all of Grayson's cases too, he took down the teacher who had the affair with a student, and then the woman who gave her daughter diet pills. So, who else does he think has done wrong in the world?"

Brock and Olivia both fell quiet for a moment, considering what the answer to their own question might be. There were endless possibilities in the world, but they didn't know Chris's mind well enough to decide who he would narrow it down to.

And then a thought struck Olivia. She was drawn once again back to her case with The Messenger. He'd drawn her out to the waterfall to kill her. He hated her for interfering, for trying to stop his reign of terror. The pattern was so familiar to Olivia that it seemed like there was only one possible target in their killer's mind this time.

"Wyatt," she breathed. Her eyes met Brock's, her heart flailing in panic. "Wyatt spoke to the press, put out a manhunt on social media. He's the one who drew attention to the case. I think if Chris knows he can't have either of us, then Wyatt is the next best thing. And if he goes for Wyatt, if this really is his final hurrah, then all he has to do is find him. There won't be any messing around his time. He'll just shoot him dead. Brock, we need to do something."

Brock pulled out his phone. "I'll call him now, try and warn him…"

He tried Wyatt's number and Olivia held her breath, waiting for Wyatt to respond.

No one picked up the phone.

"He's not answering," Brock said quietly, tucking his phone away again. "I need to go. I'll call the police on the way, get some backup. I'll go and see if he's okay."

Olivia began to sit up in bed. "I'm coming too."

"What? No, Olivia, you can't. You are in absolutely no state to come. You should be resting."

"I'm perfectly fine," Olivia insisted, though she was still a little dizzy. "If Wyatt's in danger, then I want to be there. I want to help protect him. And I want to take Chris down for good, after everything he's put us through. Let's go. Let's end this."

Olivia swung her feet out of bed and found that she was dressed in a hospital gown—at least this one had a back that closed all the way. Her gun was neatly laid atop her clothes, but there was no time to change. She grabbed her gun and left the rest. Her shoes were beside the bed, so she slipped them on with no socks, charging for the door. Brock was helpless to stop her and followed her out into the sterile hallway. She used the wall to help her balance as they stumbled toward the exit. She wasn't in her best state, but she wasn't going to lie in bed and wait while someone was in danger. She couldn't handle it if Wyatt died because they hadn't reached him in time. She was determined that Chris wasn't going to get his final kill.

They made it out to Brock's car, and he began to drive fast. While he was driving, Olivia called the police for backup. With a squad on their way to Wyatt's address, too, Olivia knew they were doing the most they possibly could to make sure Wyatt made it out alive.

But would it be enough?

Olivia's heart was hammering in her chest so hard that it hurt. She felt sick and dizzy, but she kept her eyes on the road ahead and told herself that she only had to make her body obey her for a few minutes. Long enough to take Chris down, to make sure he never hurt anyone ever again. After so many weeks of investigation, Olivia could barely believe it was him behind it all. But the more she thought about it, the more it made sense. Behind that kind, innocent smile, there was a very cunning young man, taking lives so easily that it scared her a little.

But no more. They were going to catch him this time. Olivia would make sure of it.

They were closing in on Wyatt's home address. Brock gripped the steering wheel hard, his breathing a little ragged.

"When we get there, stay back, okay? You're in no state to be out there. You're still in a hospital gown, for God's sake."

She looked down and smiled a bit sheepishly. "I guess I could have taken the thirty seconds to put clothes on, huh?"

"Olivia…"

"I'm fine. Besides, you need me. If the police haven't arrived by the time we get there, then it's just you and me against him. You can't afford to go in there alone."

Brock cursed under his breath. "Come on, Olivia, don't fight me on this one. I bet you couldn't shoot straight now even if you wanted to. I don't want you to get hurt. This isn't me being overprotective. This is you being stubborn."

Olivia clenched her jaw. She knew he was right. She wasn't at one hundred percent, and that could hinder them when they got there. But she had never been one to stand back and let someone else do her work for her. This case was as much hers as it was Brock's, and the thought of not being there for the end of it all didn't sit right with her.

Still, she had to consider her own safety, and Wyatt's. Any mistakes she made would put him in danger. That was the last thing she wanted. She sighed irritably, more at herself than at anyone else.

"Okay. I'll cover the front door. But if I see an opening to take him down, I'm going to take it. I don't want him getting away. This feels like it's our last shot."

"Agreed," Brock murmured. "We can't afford for this to go wrong. Wyatt's life is on the line."

Brock swerved onto Wyatt's street where neat rows of houses lined up. It was quiet. Too quiet. Olivia could hear her heartbeat in her ears. Had they gotten it wrong somehow?

But no. As they pulled up outside the right house, she saw the jagged broken glass of one of the front windows. Someone had

LOVE, LIES, AND SUICIDE

smashed their way inside. In the house next door, Olivia saw a frightened woman standing in the window, talking frantically on the phone. She was obviously calling the police, but Olivia knew that they only had minutes to save Wyatt—if he wasn't already dead.

"Go. I'll wait out here," Olivia insisted, readying her gun. She ducked out of the car and positioned herself behind it, ready to strike if needed. Brock didn't hesitate before running toward the house, gun drawn, and diving in through the broken window.

Olivia felt like she couldn't breathe as she waited for something to happen. She crept forward to the front of the fence, trying to get herself some cover while also getting closer. The night was far too quiet. She felt sick. She didn't like Brock being in there alone. Sure, it might be two on one against Chris, but if Brock got shot, Olivia would never be able to forgive herself.

That was when she heard the cry from inside the house. Olivia's heart jolted at the exact same time that a gunshot ripped through the night. A scream caught in her throat before she could release it. Who was shooting? Had anyone been hit?

Olivia didn't realize she'd surged forward until she was standing by the broken window, just out of sight of anyone that might return there. She gripped her gun with sweaty hands. She didn't want to consider the possibility that either of her friends might be dead, shot through the chest by a man who didn't deserve to see outside of a prison cell ever again. She kept herself as steady as she could for someone who was waiting to see if her friends were alive. She might be their last line of defense.

She might be the only person who could take Chris down.

She heard another yell from inside the house and the sound of footsteps thundering down the staircase. One, two, three more shots echoed out into the night as the footsteps darted toward the front of the house. Olivia prepared her gun. Either it was Brock chasing down the killer—or running for his life.

She readied herself for anything. The sound of police sirens approached from the distance, but they were too late. It was now or never. Either she was going to take their killer down, or it was over, and he'd get away.

She was ready.

She heard someone breathlessly scrambling up onto the kitchen counter just inside the window. Olivia knew it had to be Chris trying to make his escape. Little did he know what was waiting for him outside. Olivia might be alone, she might be dizzy and disoriented, but it wouldn't stop her from securing the target.

As Chris's nimble body flew through the window, Olivia pounced on him like a big cat, crashing into his side and knocking the wind out of him. She heard the moment all of the air left his lungs and felt the impact of her body against his ribs. It hurt, but she ignored it. She'd already proved that she could take a few bruises.

He writhed and wriggled, trying to get out from underneath her, but Olivia landed a heavy blow against his face, stunning him just quickly enough for her to secure her footing and pin him down.

"How's that feel?" she snarled.

Quickly, she pressed her gun against Chris's temple, managing to get in a position where her knee was digging into the small of his back. He was breathing hard, his face pressed against the gravel of the driveway. He looked at her through the side of his eyes, panting and smiling.

"I should have known," he muttered into the ground. "You couldn't just leave it alone, could you?"

"Not when you made this personal," Olivia snarled. "You're under arrest for the murders of Arabella and Andrew Clifford. And pretty soon, we'll get you for the rest too."

Olivia watched as Chris closed his eyes in resignation. "You'll never understand. You people never do."

Olivia ignored him. She wasn't interested in hearing his excuses. All she wanted to know was if her friends were okay. She twisted her head around, trying to see if anyone was coming out of the house, but there was no one there.

The police arrived moments later. Olivia allowed them to handle Chris, cuffing him and dragging him over to the car. Olivia ran toward the house desperately. She couldn't understand why neither of them had come outside. She had to go in and see for herself.

LOVE, LIES, AND SUICIDE

She clambered in through the window, her dizziness almost making her fall down, but she staggered toward the stairs and scaled them as fast as she could. She needed answers. She needed everything to be okay.

Olivia's heart stopped as she turned into the main bedroom. There was someone slumped on the floor. Olivia covered her mouth in shock.

"He'll need a hospital, but he's going to be okay," Brock said as he leaned over Wyatt, pressing an old T-shirt against the officer's arm. It was stained red with blood. With his other hand, he was deftly untying the ropes that had bound Wyatt to a chair. "Chris was force-feeding him foxglove. When I came in, he shot him in the arm. Is the ambulance coming?"

Olivia nodded. It was then that she noticed a trickle of blood coming from Brock's forehead. He shrugged it off. "I'm okay. I chased him down the stairs but tripped and fell. And I heard you take him down." He smiled up at her. "I shouldn't have doubted you, yet again. You always know exactly how to save the day."

Olivia finally allowed herself to smile, the tension leaving her shoulders. It was over. They had their guy. He wasn't going to be able to hurt anyone else now. Olivia sank to her knees and reached for Wyatt's good hand, squeezing it gently. His face was pale, and he was breathing hard, but he managed a smile for her.

"Thank you. For coming to find me. I—I really thought he was going to kill me," Wyatt wheezed. He was sweating, his forehead damp and dark circles forming under his arms. Olivia offered him a smile as the medics burst into the house, ready to take him to the hospital.

"We wouldn't have let that happen. It's going to be okay now. It's done."

And as she said those words aloud, she truly began to believe them. She closed her eyes for a moment. Another case done and dusted.

Now all that was left was to talk to their killer.

Face to face.

CHAPTER TWENTY-FOUR

It was the following day when Olivia and Brock arrived at the Richmond police department to speak to Chris Marsh in person. They had spent the previous night at the hospital ensuring that Wyatt was okay and getting Olivia checked out once more.

But first thing that morning, Olivia and Brock were determined to speak to Chris. It had been a long time coming, after all. After the wild goose chase he'd led them on, Olivia wanted answers. She wanted to know why he'd done all of those things.

She had started the case with some sympathy for their killer. It had seemed all along that their killer was out for revenge after something terrible that had happened to him. But now that Olivia had become aware of the other killings, she couldn't understand why Chris had started the spree to begin with. She wanted to understand the complicated young man in their custody. She wanted to know what drove him to murder so many people, why he did it the way he did, and when he planned, if ever, to stop.

He was waiting for them when they arrived. He looked tired, like he hadn't slept much the night before, but Olivia was past feeling sorry for him. She sat down opposite him, her face somber.

"Feel like talking to us today?" she asked him. He shrugged.

"Sure. What do I have to lose?"

Olivia hadn't quite expected that. But she had suspected that when he went to hunt down Wyatt, he was ready to be caught. Maybe that's why he was feeling loose-lipped. Was it relieving to him, she wondered, to finally have been caught? Was he hoping that they'd catch up with him all along, give him a chance to rest?

Or was this still a part of his scheme?

Brock cleared his throat as he took his seat too. "Thanks a lot for taking a shot at me last night, by the way. Much appreciated."

Chris sighed, closing his eyes. "I didn't want to. Not really. It was just an act of desperation. Nothing personal. Are you okay?"

Olivia frowned at Chris. "Don't you worry about me," she said harshly. "You tried to blind me with giant hogweed."

Chris shook his head. "I told you, you people never understand. You don't know what it's like to be in my shoes. To have this... *need* to keep doing this. I was just trying to put the world to rights. You don't have to believe me. But that's my story, and I'm sticking to it."

"I see. And what is it that you think you achieved by killing all those people?" Brock asked tersely. Chris lowered his gaze to his handcuffed hands.

"Justice."

Olivia cocked her head to the side. "Justice... okay then. We suspected, once we connected you to the other killings, that you might be acting like a vigilante. Is that what this whole thing was? We found those newspaper clippings, the screenshots from the anonymous account to the victims... we presume that was you?"

Chris nodded. "I wanted them to know that I knew their darkest secrets. I wanted to rattle them a little, I guess. The thing about being poisoned is... no one sees it coming. It's too sneaky.

No one thinks that someone is going to slip something in their morning coffee. Or their protein smoothie. They feel safe in their homes, feel invincible from that kind of thing. I didn't want them to live their lives not knowing that someone was out to get them. I wanted them to fear someone following them, using their secrets to chase them down… and that was never going to work if I wanted to poison them. Not without some encouragement. So, I had them believing that someone had it out for them—that at any given moment, someone might round the corner and shoot them dead. I wanted them to know I was coming for them."

Olivia stared at Chris for a long time. "So, you wanted your victims to be scared. Why? Why these people? You said you knew their secrets. Why did that make you feel responsible for killing them? The teacher, Anthony McDonald. You accused him of having an affair with a student—"

"No," Chris cut her off. "That's not what that was."

Olivia raised her eyebrow. "Alright, then. Enlighten me."

Chris glared back at her, a darkness in his gaze. "I knew I wanted him dead for a very long time. Since I was a child. He didn't have an affair, Agent Knight. That's not what it's called when a teacher takes advantage of a child. That's called rape. Especially when the child in question in no way consented to what happened to them."

His eyes softened a little as pain flooded his gaze. "That child was me. The screenshots I sent him… they weren't about him, but they could have been. A teacher taking advantage of a student. Destroying the lives of the people they're supposed to protect. He kept what he did to me a well-hidden secret. He must have, because he still worked at the school where he attacked me up until the day he died. He probably did it to countless other students—ones who never came forward, just like me. He got to keep living his life while we were all tainted by the pain he put us through."

Chris set his jaw, looking more angry now than upset. "So, I decided I wanted to put an end to it. But first, I wanted him to feel terror. The kind of terror I felt when he was abusing me. He made a decision that changed my life forever, so I thought I'd do the same to him. Effectively, he ended the life I wanted to live. So,

LOVE, LIES, AND SUICIDE

I ended the life he was living. I poisoned him. I made him suffer, made him beg for his life. And I thought that I would regret that after a time, but I didn't. I never will."

Olivia's blood ran cold. How could she ever tell Chris that what he'd done was unjustified? He'd had his fate sealed for him when he was just a child. He lost his father before he even had a chance to meet him. His childhood had been tainted by what his teacher, a man he was supposed to be able to trust, had done to him. His mother had taken her life after having her heart broken and life destroyed by a cruel scammer. Olivia felt her stomach twist painfully. Some of the empathy she'd felt for their killer was slowly beginning to resurface.

"I'm sorry that happened to you," Olivia said quietly. "But you killed a man in cold blood. You must be able to see that it's ... it's wrong."

Chris raised his eyes to meet hers. "More wrong than what he did?"

Olivia was stumped. She tried to speak, but she couldn't. How was she supposed to compare pedophilia and a revenge killing on the man who had committed such a perverse attack?

"That's not what's in question," Brock said in her place. "You still killed someone. You knew all along you were breaking the law. Why didn't you just go to the police?"

Chris shook his head slowly. "I was twelve years old. I didn't know what I was supposed to do. And then the years passed me by, escaped from me. Before I knew it, I was a young man, not a boy. And then what was I supposed to do? Report something that happened years ago with no evidence? Yeah, what a great way to re-ruin my life. I didn't want that for myself."

But killing a man felt right? Olivia wondered to herself. *Poisoning a man, making him suffer so horribly?*

But didn't she understand that on some level? Hadn't she wished pain upon the people who had killed her sister? The ones who had savagely ripped her life out of the world? How could she claim not to understand Chris's motives when they seemed to make so much sense?

"But he wasn't the only person you killed," Brock pointed out, his voice cold. Olivia snapped herself back to reality. Because he was right—he'd killed other people too. If it had come down to it, he even would have killed Brock in order to escape. Olivia was looking at Chris as though he was a tortured soul, not a cold-blooded murderer. She wished she could give herself a shake.

"Tell me about Kristen Peck," she said.

Chris sighed. "When I was in high school, I devoted my time to studying because I didn't have any friends. No one wanted to hang around with the surly kid whose best friend died when they were still kids. And no one knew the rest of what had happened to me, but that didn't matter because I could never talk about it anyway. Roll up my sleeves."

The request came so suddenly that it made Olivia blink. She gave a quick look to Brock, who nodded, and then reached out and rolled up the sleeves of Chris's T-shirt to expose his shoulder. Being that close to him for the first time made her notice the faded scars and marks all over his arms.

"They used to put out cigarettes on me," Chris said lowly. "Kick me around. Torment me just because I was already going through so much pain. They would hunt me down and attack me all the time."

"I don't understand," Olivia frowned. "We looked through her school records and didn't find any reports of bullying or fighting."

"Kristen herself would never be so stupid as to do it directly," Chris replied. "She just ordered the boys to do it—had them wrapped around her finger. Every time she so much as looked in my direction, she'd tell the boys to come beat me up or break my fingers. And then she'd laugh and laugh and laugh about it. She'd use her tongue to inflict such pain on me. So, I made her tongue swell up until she couldn't breathe anymore."

His anger was shaking him now, as if he were still experiencing all the pain and torment all over again. Olivia allowed him to take a deep breath before continuing his story.

"Just a year before I was attacked by my teacher, I lost a friend. She was the only friend I had in the world, actually. Just thinking of her now, remembering how she was… it hurts. She meant so much to me. But her mother couldn't love her the way she was. Because in her mother's mind, there was nothing worse than the fact that she had a fat daughter."

LOVE, LIES, AND SUICIDE

"Sandra Collison," Olivia whispered.

Chris nodded and sucked in air between his teeth, his anger seeming to resurface. "That woman... I hated her guts. Every time I used to go to Delaney's house, her mother would serve us a plate of leaves. She'd hound her about calories and sugar. She never let her so much as look at sweets. She'd tell Delaney that she should be more like me—take up sports, eat less. Every conversation we had centered around her weight. And it was killing her slowly. She would cry every night. She started taking diet pills, trying to please her mom. Her mother even encouraged it. She helped Delaney order them over the internet and told her how proud she was that she was trying to lose weight..."

Chris grimaced in disgust. Olivia could see why. She knew where the story was headed, and she couldn't even stand the thought of it. She imagined Chris as a young boy, standing at the funeral of his only friend, wearing black and mourning someone who had her entire life ahead of her. Chris shook his head, almost like he was trying to shake off the memories too.

"She died. I have no idea if she did it on purpose or by accident, but she took too many pills. And maybe her mother didn't force them down her throat, but she was sure as hell the reason Delaney started taking them in the first place. All she wanted was to make her mom happy. And right before our eyes, a human being was just wasting away..."

Olivia's throat was tight as she listened. Chris had paused, his eyes filled with tears. He looked away, almost unable to speak out loud.

"I was already losing faith in the human race by the time I left school," Chris went on quietly. "I had lost everything that mattered to me. Except for my mom. She was the only good thing I had left in my life. I'd lost so much. The world kept finding ways to kick me in the teeth, and I just kept building my hate up and up and up. There was nowhere for me to direct my anger. It just stayed inside me. And I'd see the people who ruined me all the time. I passed my teacher every day in the hallway. He'd give me this sick kind of smile that no one else ever noticed. I'd see Kristen constantly watching, waiting to sic her bullies on me. And I'd see my best friend's mother at the grocery store, going on with her life as though she wasn't responsible for the death of her own child."

Olivia and Brock remained quiet. There was nothing they could say as the story grew darker and more out of control. Chris was shaking his head again, his eyes pained. Olivia could see how hard it was for him, locked in with his own thoughts. He'd lived through so much that others wouldn't survive.

But he'd had to kill to get through it.

"I've been wronged a lot of times in my life," Chris whispered. "And I guess that's why I was drawn to Ryleigh when we met. She was a loner, too, and I could see why. She was always unstable, but I didn't mind. I thought that I only had room for pain and chaos in my life. Our relationship was never easy, and there were plenty of times when she hurt me… but that felt normal to me. It felt right to be treated like dirt. And despite all of her flaws, I loved her. I still do. You know, I really wasn't lying when I said she'd supported me so much after all I've been through. She's really special to me. I wouldn't have been able to do any of this without her."

"You mean she encouraged you to kill?" Brock asked. Chris shook his head gently.

"No. Ryleigh is many things, but a killer isn't one of them. I know that given what you've seen of her capabilities, you might not agree, but she has a good heart. But she did start talking about what she'd do in my shoes if someone had taken her mother away from her. She said she'd want those people to suffer the way I had. And I started to agree with her. I'd go to work every day dreaming up the ways that I could get payback for all the people who wronged me. And lucky for me, I had a partner who could tell me all about what plants could do."

"She taught you how to poison people?"

"She taught me what to avoid when we would go camping—what plants would be dangerous to eat. All I had to do was apply that same principle," he shrugged. "Plants. You never think about them so much as dangerous. But they are. Practically every living creature eats plants, but sometimes, plants fight back. You may be killing and eating them, but even as you do, they'll take you down too. I've really come to admire that about plants. In some ways, they're kind of like me: just waiting to take their revenge."

He said everything so plainly, so calmly, it was like they were back at the hospital right after they had saved him from Ryleigh's torture. But now Olivia could see the light behind his eyes. It didn't even glint with malice, but with pure rationality. He knew he was dead to rights. He knew he was going to prison for the rest of his life. But he didn't care anymore.

"Then came my mother's suicide. I had been worried about her since the moment she began speaking to Alan online. I didn't trust him. After everything I've been through, I've become a pretty good judge of character. I always know when someone is trouble. And I was right, because within weeks, she had killed herself. And the pain of it... it devastated me. She was one of the few things I had left. And I began to understand... some people are just not destined to be happy. Some people aren't made to have good lives. And I'm among those people."

Chris shifted in his seat, meeting Olivia's eye. "I know what you must think of me. But I've been numb for so long. I thought maybe this was the cure. I thought revenge would help. And you may not believe me, but my intent was never actually to kill anyone. I figured I could torture the people who had been on the wrong side of me and then just walk away. It wouldn't even matter if they knew it was me because they knew their silence was the only thing keeping them safe." Chris closed his eyes once again. "But when I confronted Mr. McDonald, it went wrong. I made the dosage too high. He died because of my poisons. I never meant for it to happen. Even after what he did to me, I never wanted to see dead bodies in front of me, knowing I'd caused it. I'd been through enough already. But after it happened, I felt so much relief that I couldn't stop."

Olivia wrapped her arms around herself, feeling suddenly cold. It was always chilling, hearing a killer admit that they loved what they did. She was glad when he didn't look her way again.

"So, you decided you were all in," Brock stated.

Chris shrugged. "Sometimes, life pushes you in one direction or another. I think that I was always meant to live this way. It wasn't something I took joy in, but it eased the pain. And I know in my heart that I did a good thing. I rid the world of some very, very bad people. I know my mother never wanted me to hunt down the person who took everything from her, but she didn't understand the way of the world. She couldn't see the bigger picture. People like the Cliffords... they're like leeches, sucking the life out of people. They never stop. So, I killed them both for the good of everyone else. It was an act of service, in a way. My little way of bringing justice."

What he said made a twisted sort of sense. The people he'd gone after had caused so much pain and had completely escaped culpability for it. It was the fault of the police that all of the victims had been allowed to continue living as if they weren't responsible for the horrible things they'd done. Olivia understood his desire for justice, even if she disagreed with his methods.

This wasn't justice. This was revenge.

"So, you posed as a cleaner to get into their homes and poison them?" Olivia asked. The final piece was slotting into place—no wonder he'd had the code to disable the alarm. He'd been freely given it by the homeowners.

"Since the beginning, I'd found that the easiest way to get into people's homes was to apply to work for them. You wouldn't believe how many rich people are desperate to find a young, white boy that they can trust to clean their houses. They felt at ease around me. They invited me in as a part of their lives. And then, when they least expected it, I showed them why they should be afraid of me. I considered letting them live—that had always been the plan originally. But I looked at them, and I knew it would satisfy me more to finish the job. I thought it would take some of the heat off me too. I knew the police were closing in. But I never expected that the FBI would get on my case. And now, here we are."

"And the death of Mallory Benson? You worked for her, didn't you? Did you intend to poison her?" Olivia asked. Chris bowed his head.

"Never. I wouldn't ever have wanted to hurt her. You see, I didn't know what kind of a house I was walking into when she hired me. This was a legit job. I had to earn money somehow, so I worked freelance under different names, ensuring I never gave my true identity away, just in case. But Mallory... sweet Mallory. She was just a lonely housewife. She confided in me. She told me about her husband, the things he did to her… and I knew I couldn't just let it slide. She was like me. We'd shared similar experiences. I felt like it was fate that our paths had crossed, and I decided to help her."

"You thought killing her husband would help?"

The corners of Chris's lips twitched. "It always worked for me. Solved a lot of my issues, so yes, I guess I thought it was a good idea."

Brock grunted in disagreement but nudged him to continue.

"She used to make him these smoothies every single day. She made them special for him. Never touched them herself—or so I thought. So, I started adding cyanide to his protein. I knew it'd take a long time. I knew he'd suffer for what he did. I just didn't know that she would also drink his smoothies. That's where I messed up. Maybe it was to spite him somehow, but I regret that I ended her life. My only regret, really. And now, thanks to you, the world will finally know what these people were truly like. The horrible things they did. And they won't forget."

I certainly won't, Olivia thought to herself. She was relieved that it was over, that Chris would be going to prison for the rest of his life… and yet it all felt bittersweet. It only went to show how the cycle of violence seemed to be unstoppable. He had been hurt, so he chose to hurt others. And he could freely and openly admit to it. His only hint of guilt was that he'd made a mistake with Mallory. Even if he hadn't intended to kill the others, he certainly didn't mind that they were dead by his hand.

It made Olivia feel glad that she'd never taken a darker path. She understood Chris. She knew where he was coming from…

But she'd never be like him.

Later, when they left Chris and the case behind them, Brock put a gentle hand on Olivia's shoulder.

"You doing okay? That was a lot, that thing back there."

She nodded slowly. "I'm okay. I just… I feel sorry for him."

Brock sighed. "I know. Me, too, in a way. Although let's not let Wyatt hear us saying that. At least it's over now. He said he wanted justice, and I guess we got it."

Olivia thought of everything Chris had said. All those people dead. All those people who brought darkness into the world. Was the world lighter without them? She had no idea.

All she knew was that she and Brock had done a good thing. That was what mattered.

CHAPTER TWENTY-FIVE

AFTER ONE LAST NIGHT IN THEIR MOTEL, SLEEPING AWAY all of the stresses that the case had brought them, Olivia and Brock packed up and headed out to his car. It would take them a couple hours to get home, but neither of them seemed to mind. With another case under their belt and a chance to let go a little, they were both in good spirits as they hit the road.

"Well, I don't know about you, but what I really need now is a nice, cold beer," Brock said. Olivia raised an eyebrow.

"At nine o'clock in the morning?"

"Hey, it's five o'clock somewhere."

Olivia laughed, tilting her head back and letting her shoulders relax for the first time in weeks. It was over. They had their guy, and it was over. The case had been a tough one to crack, but now that they'd done it, she felt an overwhelming sense of pride.

And she knew she wouldn't have been able to do it without Brock at her side. Not just because he was her cheerleader and she was his. Not just because it was better working with him than on her own. No, it was something to do with the two of them together. It only worked when it was him. It had to be him.

Olivia glanced over to the driver's side and realized just how much she appreciated Brock. He carried her through their cases with a smile. He was the light in the darkness of her life. Even though the past few months had been crazy, impossible, hard to handle… he made all of that better.

She felt a connection to him that her other friends just couldn't provide. She loved her friends, and yet Brock had made up for their absence since he came into her life. She had been alone when she arrived in Belle Grove, and she had thought she'd have to stay that way. But he'd shown her that even though she was running away when she retreated to Belle Grove, she didn't have to run anymore when he was around.

For the first hour, as they were driving, Brock turned up the radio until the music was blasting out the speakers at full volume. He sang along to every song and only kept one hand on the wheel. He was the picture of ease, and it made Olivia feel at ease too. She hadn't been used to that kind of feeling before him. There had always been something to disturb her peace. When she was trying to hide from the world inside a good book, or she was keeping her distance from troubling things, trouble seemed to find her anyway. Not a day went by when she wasn't worried about family drama, cases at work, or where her life was headed. That was no way to live, and she knew it.

Maybe that's what made her feel so drawn to Brock. He was so different from her, but she found that she didn't mind. He made her a better version of herself, and she liked to think she had the same effect on him. When they were around one another, everything just seemed to make sense.

Olivia considered for the first time what it would be like to tell Brock those things. To finally admit out loud to him that he was someone special in her life. She tended to be an open book when it came to Brock, always so at ease that her deepest secrets just slipped out of her mouth.

But she'd never really stopped to tell him what he meant to her. Not even after the times when they had fought over silly things, things that threatened to keep them apart. Not even when Brock had been angry with her for not telling him about Tom. Thinking back now, she couldn't make sense of why she'd kept it a secret from him, because why did it matter? So, she'd been engaged once. It hadn't worked out. Now she was here, in the moment with Brock, and he meant more to her than anyone ever had before.

She should have been honest with him from the start. She should have told him that it didn't matter how many exes walked back into her life. They were exes for a reason, and she wasn't interested in resurrecting those relationships from the dead. She wanted to focus on her future, on what might happen next.

And she wanted to fit Brock into those plans.

She took a deep breath, steadying her racing heart as the music continued to blare from the speakers. She could tell him right then and there that he'd been on her mind. But was she ready for that? There were so many other things waiting for her back in Belle Grove that she had to face up to. She had to think about how she was going to deal with Tom being back in town. She had to consider that a new case could come up at any time and disturb the peace she was feeling in the car with Brock. And then there was the whole fallout from Thanksgiving to deal with—a situation that Olivia wasn't sure could be fixed.

The truth about Olivia was that her life was complicated. It always had been, and it always would be. That was the product of growing up on her mother's lies, even if she'd only just come to realize that. It was also the product of the turbulent times she'd faced in the last few years. And it was the product of never truly knowing her place in the world. The ground beneath her feet was always too unstable for her to get her footing. Could she really take on a relationship in that emotional climate?

And that was assuming she was even right about Brock's feelings for her. She had taken his dislike of Tom to mean that he wanted her, but perhaps he was just being overprotective as a friend. She'd never know for sure unless she asked him.

But as she glanced over at Brock again, watching him sing at the top of his lungs, a smile spread across her face, and she felt her heart warm. How many people did she feel comfortable being around in this way? She was sure that Brock felt the same way, given the way he acted around her. Wasn't that a form of love? The comfort of one another's presence, the quiet joy they brought to one another's lives? Wasn't that the kind of thing that people searched for when they looked for someone to spend their time with?

Olivia's cheeks flushed at the thought. She didn't know how to navigate romance anymore. It had been so long since she was with someone, and she wasn't sure she'd ever let herself fall for someone fully. But every time she glanced in Brock's direction and felt the flutter of butterflies in her stomach, she was reminded that it was possible. Maybe for the first time, she was really ready to let go—to give in to the feeling and let herself fall.

Brock's head turned slightly, and he caught Olivia watching him. Horrified, she looked away quickly, then she heard Brock chuckle as he turned down the music.

"What, do I have something on my face?" he cracked. She couldn't see his face, but she could tell he was grinning. His smile was one of the first things she'd noticed about him all those months ago when they met for the first time. At first, his laid-back nature and his teasing attitude had driven her crazy. But now, it was one of the things she liked so much about him. It made her ease up a little, at least. And given how tightly wound she'd become in recent years, it certainly wasn't a bad thing.

"Yeah, there's a bunch of arrogance and smarm all over it."

"Damn, I must have missed a spot when I washed my face this morning."

He let his smile fall a bit—not in a bad way—but so he could parse his lips curiously. "What's on your mind?"

Olivia felt the breath leave her lungs so suddenly that she felt a little dizzy. He was giving her an opportunity to say what she was really thinking and feeling. Was she brave enough to take that opportunity?

LOVE, LIES, AND SUICIDE

She cleared her throat, trying to buy herself some time to figure out what she wanted to say. Brock surprised her by watching the road ahead patiently, a warm smile playing on his mouth. Could she do it? Could she actually admit what was on her mind? If things went wrong, then what would it mean for their friendship? Their work partnership? And she'd still have to spend the entire car journey back to Belle Grove stuck in a car with the person who didn't return her feelings.

Olivia swallowed.

"I'm just... I'm just..."

She hesitated. Then she let out a sigh.

"I'm just thinking about how great a friend you are," Olivia said after a while.

Brock puffed out his chest. "Oh yeah? Tell me more. Make me feel good about myself."

Olivia let out a shaky laugh. She was annoyed at herself for chickening out, but she told herself there was no rush. She had all the time in the world to test the waters, to make sure she wasn't making a big mistake.

"Well... I guess I was just reminding myself that the past few weeks would have been impossible without you. Because it's not just about the work. It's the emotional support. I always know I can count on you. I don't take that lightly."

Brock wasn't laughing anymore, but his smile remained. He glanced over at Olivia with warmth in his gaze.

"I feel the same about you."

"I know. But the difference is, you don't *need* me. That's what I always think, anyway. The stuff that I go through would be impossible without your support. Everything with my family blowing up the way it did, you gave me a place to call home for Thanksgiving. I don't think I've ever had a friend like that before. Not quite the same, at least. You just make everything bearable when I'm on the verge of tearing my hair out."

Brock chuckled softly. "Well, that's quite a compliment. And I'm glad you feel that way because I consider you family too. I don't really have people in my life like that either. Not since I lost my parents, at least. So, you might think that I don't need you or whatever, but I'm telling you right now that you've got it wrong. I need you, and I want you in my life, Olivia. Don't ever forget that."

Olivia's cheeks turned bright red, and her heart flooded with warmth. Brock wasn't big on talking about his feelings to her. He always claimed that he saved his emotions for his therapist. So, hearing him talk like that was a big deal. Such a big deal, in fact, that Olivia almost found the courage to be honest. To actually tell him what she'd wanted to say at the start.

But she kept quiet. The moment passed. Brock turned up the radio again a little, but he didn't sing along this time. It seemed their conversation had put him in a contemplative mood, because he had a serious look in his eyes as he watched the road.

"What are you going to do? About your family, I mean?"

Olivia let out a long sigh. "Truthfully? I don't know. I asked my mom to do one thing for me—not to go back to the case that tore our family apart. The case that almost got her killed. But she's just so damn… stubborn."

Brock smiled sadly. "Like mother, like daughter. You know what I thought when we were going to catch Chris at Wyatt's place? When you kept saying you wanted to be a part of it, even though you were in no state to be fighting anyone… I thought about how similar you are to her."

Olivia made a face, but he shrugged. "I'm serious! And I know you've said that you're alike before, but I just wonder… what would *you* do in her shoes? That's not me making an assumption. I actually want to know the answer to that question."

Olivia thought it over for a minute. The problem was, Brock was right. She was a lot like her mother. She liked to see things through. She'd felt that way during her own cases, no matter what was thrown at her. She'd come face to face with death once before, back when The Messenger had her where he wanted her. She'd put herself in that position without any thought about anyone else. She'd done it to save someone else, sure, but she hadn't thought about what would happen if she died. She hadn't thought about how devastated her family would be or how it would tear Brock apart. And still, she'd known in her heart it was the right thing to do.

"The problem is... this is my mom I'm talking about. In her shoes, I might do the same thing as she would. I might think to myself that I'm the one person in the world able to solve the problem put in front of me. But I can't think like a mother because I'm not one. I can think like a daughter, and I know that my parents would be devastated to lose me if I put myself in the firing line. And I think if one of them asked me to stop, to leave all of this life behind—"

Olivia paused. She'd been about to say that she'd do it. She was about to say that she would be willing to sacrifice the career she loved to make her family happy.

But was that the truth?

Olivia sighed, shaking her head to herself. "You know what? I don't know what I'd do. Maybe I actually have to be put in that position to know how I'd react. But I think if I had a daughter... if I hadn't seen her for years, and I came home to see how devastated she was, I don't think I'd ever be able to consider putting her through that again. That's the thing I can't understand with her. How did she see all the damage she'd done and then just decide that she was willing to do it all over again? She broke me, Brock. I think she must realize that. But at the end of the day, the job always comes first for her. It always has, even if I didn't know it before. All those times she was just gone—not a part of my life because she had things to do for work—that's what stings. I know I'll never matter as much to her as all of that. That's what I struggle to move past. So, I don't know what I'll do about her—about us. I guess I need more time to think it over."

Brock nodded in understanding. "I can't blame you. Telling you that she was taking the case back on during Thanksgiving dinner? After she promised you she wouldn't? That's a lot. There's no denying that. But give your emotions some time to settle. Maybe she'll see sense. Or maybe you'll decide to take her as she is. She's by no means perfect. Far from it, in fact. She's made mistakes, and she keeps repeating them. But you only ever get one mom. If she disappeared again, and you hadn't even talked to her... I know that would hurt you, Olivia. I don't want to see you hurt that way."

Olivia nodded. As usual, Brock's advice was sound. She was angry, and it felt like she'd never stop being angry. But she also couldn't bear the thought of never speaking to her mom again. She closed her eyes for a moment, resting her head against the cold glass of the window. Why did all of the decisions in her life have to be so damn complicated?

Olivia didn't realize that she'd dozed off until she moved a while later and her neck felt stiff. She opened her eyes and saw the familiar trees of sleepy little Belle Grove. She smiled tiredly. The familiarity of the place was exactly what she needed after such a grueling case. She was already thinking of sleeping in her own bed, of eating dinner at the diner with Brock over a few beers, of reading in her chair before she went to sleep at night. Another killer brought to justice. That was enough to keep her smiling for a while.

"So. Dinner at the diner later? I bet you've missed the burgers, haven't you?" Olivia asked with an easy smile. But she watched as Brock wavered, looking a little uncomfortable. Olivia frowned. "Are you okay? Something on your mind?"

Brock shook his head and forced a quick smile. "No, nothing like that. I was just thinking… maybe we could eat somewhere else tonight."

Olivia did a double take. "Oh, my God. Now who's the evil robot from the future?"

Brock chuckled, but Olivia could tell his heart wasn't really in it. He looked nervous, a look that was unfamiliar on him and didn't suit him one bit. He cleared his throat.

"Nah, it's just that… you know. We're hitting the diner, like, every other night sometimes, right? I was thinking something like Italian. We could hit up Sapori Toscano."

Olivia raised an eyebrow. "Isn't that place really upscale?"

"It is," he nodded. "It would be nice though, wouldn't it? We could dress up all fancy. I'll even put on a clean shirt."

Olivia took a few moments to process what was happening. Was Brock asking her out to *dinner*? Like, a dinner date? She felt her lungs flail a little. She hadn't been prepared for that.

LOVE, LIES, AND SUICIDE

They were close to her house now, and Olivia could feel the silence hanging heavily between them. Why wasn't she saying anything? What was wrong with her?

"It's just an idea," Brock said breezily, but his face told a different story. She could see from the look in his eyes that it mattered to him how she responded. And it was important to her too.

So why couldn't she say a single word?

"Hey... there's someone waiting on your porch," Brock said quickly, like he was changing the subject. But when Olivia looked up, she saw that Brock was right. And when she saw who it was, she felt her heart drop to her stomach. As if things weren't complicated enough already.

It was Tom.

CHAPTER TWENTY-SIX

"**W**HAT ON EARTH IS HE DOING HERE?" Olivia murmured to herself. Brock killed the engine, and the pair of them sat in silence for a minute, both of them staring at Tom. Olivia couldn't understand why he was there, waiting on her doorstep. Hadn't the fact that she hadn't responded to his messages made it clear to him that she wasn't ready to talk?

"I guess he's here to finish what you guys started," Brock said quietly. Olivia's head snapped to look at him. She was surprised by the change in his tone. Was this his jealousy resurfacing? Hadn't she been clear about where she stood with Tom, even if she hadn't been clear about where she stood with Brock?

"What's that supposed to mean?"

LOVE, LIES, AND SUICIDE

Brock shrugged. "He clearly thinks there's something to salvage here. Kind of a romantic gesture, isn't it? Showing up on someone's doorstep out of the blue. I'm surprised he hasn't come with flowers and a boombox."

Olivia shook her head at him. The mood had certainly soured in the car. Tom had spotted them both and was watching them in return, making the whole thing even more uncomfortable. Olivia drew in a deep breath.

"Look, Brock… We had a history, but that's behind us now. I haven't even spoken to him since we saw one another at the diner. That was weeks ago now. What do you want me to do? Get a restraining order? Stop him from visiting the place where I live?"

"I never said I wanted you to do anything," Brock said mildly. "And I never presumed what you might want from Tom. I'm just telling you that he, very clearly, still has feelings for you. And now he's come here because he wants to make that clear to you. I'm just stating the obvious."

Olivia sat back in her seat, feeling irritable—not with Brock, or with Tom, but with the situation. She wanted to tell Brock that she would love to go to dinner with him, but she also wanted to hear what Tom had to say to her. Clearly, their paths were going to have to cross at some point, and she wanted it over and done with. If he did still have feelings for her, then she'd have to tell him where to go. She'd moved on.

She was so certain she'd moved on.

But seeing him did stir butterflies in her stomach. Nerves, perhaps? He was approaching the car and Olivia held her breath. She turned to Brock.

"I'm going to roll the window down, okay? Please, just give me a moment."

Brock put his hands up in the air like he was surrendering, his eyebrows raised. Olivia let the window down, and Tom peered in, staring at her face in shock.

"Olivia… are you alright? That's a nasty bruise you've got there," Tom said, his forehead creased. She nodded.

"I'm fine."

"You don't look fine," Tom said. He reached out his fingers as though he was going to touch her face, but his fingers hovered just above her skin. Olivia held her breath, saying nothing. Tom shook his head. "How did you manage that?"

"Perk of the job," she said lightly. "I took a baseball bat and some highly poisonous giant hogweed to the face."

"Jesus, Olivia. Hell of a combination. You're lucky you don't have a fractured cheekbone. Are you in pain?"

"It's okay, Tom, really. You don't need to give me a medical examination," Olivia replied, forcing out a laugh. "What are you doing here?"

Tom shoved his hands in his pockets awkwardly. He took a quick glance at Brock, but he was pretending like he wasn't in the car at all. Tom shrugged after a moment.

"Well, I tried messaging you, and I never heard back. So, I've been coming to the house every day to see if I could catch you. I knew you were out of town for a case, but I wasn't sure when you'd be back."

"Well, I'm here now," Olivia said. She hated that Brock was sitting there, listening to every word like a fly on the wall. She wanted to get out of there, to rewind five minutes to before Tom showed up and rocked the boat. Tom was clearly uncomfortable too. It was written all over his face. But it was his own fault for showing up out of the blue and expecting Olivia to be waiting there for him. She had a life, just like he had his. So, what could he possibly need from her?

"Well, if you've got the time, I was wondering if you'd like to catch up? We could go somewhere for dinner. Maybe that little Italian place in town?" Tom said.

Olivia winced. That was the worst place he could have suggested after Brock's proposition. She cleared her throat.

"Well, actually, Brock and I were just making dinner plans together," Olivia said quickly, hoping that might solve her issues. If only she'd accepted his invitation right away like she wanted to, it would have saved her the awkwardness.

"Oh," Tom said, but Brock cut in before he could say anything else.

"Nah, we weren't," Brock said. Olivia stared at him, wondering what was wrong with him.

"Yes, we were."

LOVE, LIES, AND SUICIDE

"Well, okay, we were. But they can wait. You guys clearly have a lot of catching up to do," Brock said. Olivia examined his face for signs that he was angry or bitter, but Brock just smiled tightly at her. "It's fine. We'll go for dinner another night."

Olivia wavered. She didn't want to put her plans with Brock on hold. She had been waiting for weeks to have a night with just the two of them. He'd finally just asked her out on a date, and now it was like they'd taken a step back. She didn't want that for them. She didn't want to go to dinner with Tom over him.

But she knew she had to talk things over with Tom. Living in the same town as her ex was never going to be comfortable. The sooner they reached the same level, the sooner they could live peacefully alongside one another. She just wished that he'd shown up on any other day. She drew in a deep breath.

"Brock..."

"It's okay," he said gently again. Olivia swallowed.

"Let me call you tomorrow, okay? We'll rearrange."

"Sure," Brock nodded, but it felt like he was already moving back into his shell. Olivia got out of the car hesitantly and watched as Brock drove away from her, back to his place. She wanted to call out to him, to tell him to come back, but there was no going back.

Only forward.

Olivia turned to look at Tom. He ran a hand through his hair nervously.

"Sorry. I never intended to ruin your plans. I just... well, I couldn't wait to see you."

Olivia managed a smile. "It's okay. I... I'm sorry I didn't respond to your messages. I've had... I've had a crazy few weeks."

"I can see that," Tom said. Olivia didn't know if he was referring to her bruised face or the obvious tension between her and Brock in the car. Had Tom noticed it the last time they'd seen one another? The way that she and Brock connected, even when they weren't saying a word? Did Tom see the electricity that hung in the air between Brock and Olivia, the kind of electricity that she'd never had with him?

"So... you wanted to grab dinner?" Olivia asked, checking her watch. It was only midday, but she suddenly felt very tired. There was so much going on at once that she could barely process it.

"Well, I guess if you're free now then we could do lunch? I'm guessing you don't have other plans if you've just finished up a case... and I don't have my practice up and running yet. What do you think?"

Olivia nodded slowly. "That would be good. Do you mind if I step inside and freshen up?"

"Of course not. Can I come in and see your place? It's kind of cold out here."

"Of course."

The pair of them walked up to her house in uncomfortable silence. Olivia made sure that Tom was comfortable before rushing upstairs and jumping in the shower. She took longer than she should, knowing she had a guest downstairs, but she felt numb. Had she missed her chance with Brock? Was it worth it? She had no idea anymore. Nothing felt quite right.

But she tried to ignore all of that. She had to deal with one thing at a time. She headed to her bedroom to pick something to wear. She felt guilty as she considered a nice dress, thinking of Brock's comment about dressing nicely in the car, and opted for a pair of jeans instead. She put on a sleek black top, wanting to look like she had at least made some effort for the man she had once loved. And even though there were other places she'd rather be, she did still feel a little flutter as she went down to greet him.

Tom stood up as she entered, adjusting his coat as he looked at her. He smiled at her.

"You look lovely."

Olivia's fingers moved to the bruise on her cheekbone. "Apart from the fact I look like I'm turning into a blueberry, right?"

Tom chuckled. "It's not that bad. But I'm realizing now that maybe asking you out for food was a little cruel. Doesn't it hurt when you eat?"

"A little, but nothing would stop me from eating a three-course meal right now."

Tom smiled at her fondly. "Some things never change, then." He nodded toward the door. "Shall we?"

Tom admitted as they left the house that he'd walked to her place, so they decided to leave Olivia's car and walk to the restaurant. As they walked, Olivia engaged in polite small talk with him, asking about his move back to Belle Grove, telling him a little about the case she'd been working on, and talking about how much she liked her little cabin in the woods. But in the back of her mind, Olivia was thinking about Brock. She prayed that they wouldn't cross paths in the town center. She didn't want to see the disappointment on his face or feel the pang in her heart at the sight of him. It was too much when they'd been so close to finally getting what they wanted.

She just had to get through lunch. Then she could deal with the rest.

As she suspected, Sapori Toscano restaurant was mostly empty when Olivia and Tom walked in. She ordered herself a glass of wine right off the bat and made small talk about the menu. She was doing what she'd been doing a lot lately—avoiding what they really needed to talk about. But once the menus were gone and they both had a glass of wine in their hand, Tom smiled at Olivia, and she knew she was about to face the music.

"So," Tom said with a smile. "This is a bit weird—having dinner with my ex-fiancée."

Olivia smiled back, her cheeks turning a little red. "I know. But it was so long ago now, even if it doesn't feel like it. I guess life just keeps coming at us, doesn't it? Everything moves so fast."

"Do you think so?" Tom asked. "I feel like life has slowed down since we've been apart, Olivia. I think life gets that way when you're doing the same thing, day in and day out. And then when you don't even have someone to share that with, it makes the days long."

Olivia sipped her wine and said nothing. Was he implying that he wished he could go back?

"Sorry," Tom said with a quick laugh. "I don't want you to feel like I'm doing this to try and win you over or something. That's not what this is about. But I missed you. I never wanted to admit that to myself. I thought I'd be fine alone. And I was, I guess. But it wasn't as good as being with you."

Olivia shrugged uncomfortably. "Well, to be honest, it hasn't been the same for me. It's not something that's been on my mind that much. Not because I didn't care, or that there's someone else in particular… but my life hasn't really had space for romance in a long time. Things have kind of blown up in my life lately."

Tom nodded solemnly. "I know that now. All that stuff with your mom, and of course the aftermath of what happened to Veronica… I should have been there for you, Olivia. You shouldn't have had to go through that alone."

Olivia kept her eyes on the table. "It's alright. I'm healing. Slowly, but I am."

"And how was your Thanksgiving? I assume you got to spend it with your family for the first time in a while?"

Olivia pressed her lips together. There was so much that he'd missed in the time he'd been away. She didn't feel like talking about it either. It wasn't the same talking to him as it was to Brock—with Brock she could really let her guard down. Even when she'd been with Tom, she reserved her feelings a lot more.

"I don't want to talk about Thanksgiving."

Tom nodded. "Oh, okay. That's fine."

There was a short silence between them, and Tom cleared his throat. "Look… I know this is a little uncomfortable. Our history complicates things. I know you've moved on now, and you have your own life here, but when I think back to the way things ended between us, I hate how easily I let you go. You're one of a kind, Olivia. I was stupid not to realize that at the time. And now, I don't know… maybe you have other stuff going on. But if it's okay with you, I'd like to explore the possibility of being in your life again. Whether that's as a friend to you, or… well, you know. I don't need you to be open to anything more than being acquaintances if that's what you want. But I'd be an idiot if I came back here to live in the same town as the one woman I've ever loved and didn't even try to communicate with her."

Olivia felt a small smile tugging at her mouth. She was starting to remember how charming Tom could be. That was what had always drawn her to him in the first place. He always knew exactly what to say. She wasn't sure where their dinner talk was headed, or how she might respond to what he was saying, but she felt a wave of nostalgia rush over her. He was right. Some things just never changed.

LOVE, LIES, AND SUICIDE

"I think I'd like to try the friends thing first," Olivia said, her eyes meeting Tom's for the first time since they sat down. "If that's okay with you."

He hesitated for a moment before smiling at her properly, raising his glass to her. "Cheers to being friends."

Olivia raised her own glass in return. "Cheers."

As the dinner went on, Olivia felt some of the knots in her stomach unraveling. Sitting with Tom and talking was beginning to feel more and more natural. After all, when they were together, they'd talk for hours and hours. It wasn't like they were short of things to catch up on either. Olivia was actually beginning to enjoy herself. After her disastrous Thanksgiving dinner with her family, it was nice to have a reunion that she knew wouldn't end in tears.

Tom was a complete gentleman the entire time. He was pleasant and funny and charming, and as they left the restaurant together, he offered to walk her back home. Olivia accepted the offer gladly. She still had Brock on her mind, but she slipped her arm easily through Tom's as she walked, feeling a little tipsy as she went. She hadn't realized just how long they'd been in the restaurant for, but the sky was darkening above them, giving way to the wintery night. As they got closer to her house, Olivia smiled at Tom warmly.

"Thank you for lunch. It was nice to catch up."

"It was my pleasure," Tom insisted. "And I'd like to do it again sometime, if you'll allow it?"

"Only if you're paying," Olivia joked easily. Tom laughed.

"Oh, well, I wouldn't have it any other way. But hey, in all seriousness. I want to make it clear that there's absolutely no pressure on you to hang out with me. And there's no pressure to make this anything more than two friends just getting together and talking. But I think you know where I stand, in terms of my feelings."

Olivia felt the ease of the conversation drift away, just as she was beginning to get used to it. She had been hoping to avoid the subject of feelings for a while. But the way Tom was looking at her, she knew that he wasn't looking for a friendship. He wanted to pick up where they had left off before. Olivia cleared her throat as they arrived at the bottom of her driveway.

"Look, Tom, I..."

A gust of wind tugged through her hair, and at the house, she heard something bang. She turned to see that the door of her house was wide open, thrown back by the wind. Olivia's jaw dropped in horror. She began to run toward the house. She knew she'd locked the door when she left. She always double-checked it. And yet, there it was wide open...

And when she got to the house, she saw that everything had been turned upside down. Her heart was racing hard in her chest. She checked the door and saw that the lock had been busted off.

Her heart plummeted to her stomach. Someone had actively broken into her home. And then they had rummaged through her things, looking for something. What had they wanted? Why were they there?

She turned in a slow circle, taking in the scene before her eyes. She knew one thing for sure. She had nothing worth stealing, nothing of monetary value. So, if someone had come looking for that, they'd be disappointed.

But if they had done it to scare her, then they'd gotten exactly what they wanted.

A chill ran over her skin. She knew that she, of all people, had plenty of adversaries willing to hurt her. It came with her job. She'd made more enemies than she could count over the years. So, if this was an act of hatred, then who had she upset? Who was coming after her?

And more importantly... how had they found her?

AUTHOR'S NOTE

Thank you for reading *Love, Lies, and Suicide*, book 4 in the Olivia Knight FBI Series.

Our intention is to give you thrilling adventures and an entertaining escape with each and every book. However, we need your help to continue writing this new series. Being indie writers is tough. We don't have a large budget, huge following, or any of the cutting edge marketing techniques. So, all we kindly ask is that if you're enjoying the books in the Olivia Knight series, please take a moment of your time and leave us a review and maybe recommend the book to a fellow book lover or two. This way we can continue to write all day and night and bring you more books in the Olivia Knight series.

We cannot wait to share with you the upcoming thrilling adventures of Olivia and Brock!

Your writer friends,
Elle Gray & K.S. Gray

P.S. Feel free to reach out at egray@ellegraybooks.com with any feedbacks, suggestions, typos or errors you find so that we can take care of it!

ALSO BY
ELLE GRAY | K.S. GRAY

Olivia Knight FBI Mystery Thrillers
Book One - New Girl in Town
Book Two - The Murders on Beacon Hill
Book Three - The Woman Behind the Door
Book Four - Love, Lies, and Suicide

ALSO BY
ELLE GRAY

Blake Wilder FBI Mystery Thrillers

Book One - The 7 She Saw
Book Two - A Perfect Wife
Book Three - Her Perfect Crime
Book Four - The Chosen Girls
Book Five - The Secret She Kept
Book Six - The Lost Girls
Book Seven - The Lost Sister
Book Eight - The Missing Woman
Book Nine - Night at the Asylum
Book Ten - A Time to Die

A Pax Arrington Mystery

Free Prequel - Deadly Pursuit
Book One - I See You
Book Two - Her Last Call
Book Three - Woman In The Water
Book Four - A Wife's Secret

Printed in Great Britain
by Amazon